CONSERVATION OF LUCK

Conservation of Luck

By Lesley L. Smith

Quarky Media

Boulder Colorado

Conservation of Luck

Published by Quarky Media, PO Box 3332, Boulder, CO 80307

ISBN: 978-0-9973131-5-4 (ebook)
ISBN: 978-0-9973131-4-7 (print)

CONSERVATION OF LUCK

Chapter One

I gave Wei my most intimidating beady-eyed stare. Poker just calls for a beady-eyed stare, doesn't it? It was working, too, because there were only three of us left in the game.

We were all sitting around a table in the family room of Wei's apartment. It had all the bachelor accouterments, complete with a side-of-the-road couch, an empty-beer-can pyramid, and the latest cutting-edge flat-screen TV and gaming system.

"Give me a minute, Ella." He glanced down at his cards and gulped. Wei was a wiry little guy, a grad student in computer engineering, aka a nerd. He did not do well under pressure. Was that a drop of sweat rolling down his cheek?

Ha. I smiled ever so slightly.

The window air conditioner chugga-chugged in the background.

I didn't need to look down at my cards. Full house, kings over fives.

"Come on, Wei!" Malik, Wei's roommate, said. "Bet or get off the pot, dude." Malik was an engineering physics grad student, so also a nerd.

I flashed a real smile at him. He was pretty hot for a nerd with a football player's physique. I was figuring we might hook up later. After I won, of course.

Wei and I were the only ones left with money; this hand was winner-take-all. We had an informal game once a week. Lately, the guys had been bitching about me winning too much. What can I say? I rock. And as a physics grad student myself, I needed the money--so, what was I gonna do? Go easy on them? I don't think so.

Wei glanced at the time on his phone and said, "You can

give me a minute. This is the last hand."

"Yeah, this is the last hand. Get on with it, already." Malik grinned at me. He must be thinking the same thing I was, namely, impending possible hookup. I grinned back. I was very hot for a nerd.

Pounding on the front door interrupted us. "Ella," a woman's voice said. "I know you're in there! Open this door!" I knew that voice.

Wei breathed a sigh of relief and carefully placed the cards face down on the table. "I better go get that. It sounds super important." His tone of voice said it didn't sound super important. His tone of voice said he was avoiding losing a lot of money.

"It's not," I said. "Come back and finish the hand." I knew who it was, my best friend Crystal. She was in grad school for nursing and worked as a nurse's aide. Technically, I had asked her, begged her, to give me a ride to work tonight. I needed to get back to work at the lab.

He ignored me and answered the door. "Crystal? What's the emergency? Do you need Ella for something? I bet you do. Something important."

Crystal ignored him and stalked into the room, right over to me. "There you are!" She was short, with dark blonde hair and a cute upturned nose. When she'd been younger, she reminded me of an elf, but starting when we were about seventeen, she'd been steadily gaining weight. Now, she reminded me more of a soccer mom. She said that we covered all the bases between the two of us- her small and blonde and me tall and dark.

"Can't this wait?" I said. "I'm about to win over two hundred dollars."

"No!" she said. "It can't wait. You made me swear, swear, to make sure you made it to the lab tonight by ten o'clock at the latest." She grabbed my cards out of my hand and threw them on the floor. Some of them landed face down, luckily. "You made me swear. Tomorrow is your master's defense. May 31, 2030. You said it was your deadline!"

Ugh. She was right. That pressure on my chest wasn't the excitement of winning; it was dread about not being in the lab. I did need to finish my project. I only had like twenty-four hours to finish, or I was screwed.

I looked down at the cards on the carpet. But I was about to win. Three kings. And two fives. There was no way Wei could beat that.

Crystal grabbed my arm and pulled me towards the door. "Come on."

I resisted.

"Sounds like you better go, Ella," Wei said. "Gosh, too bad."

"No," Malik said. "If she leaves, she forfeits. That's not fair."

Crystal grabbed for something in her purse. "Don't make me tase you."

I stared at her. "Seriously?"

"You're the one who gave me the taser," she said.

Technically, that was also true. Well, damn. She pulled on me again.

I let her lead me through the room, out the door, and into the hall. Outside, the heat hit us like a ball-peen hammer.

"Bye, Ella. Good luck tomorrow," Malik was saying when Wei slammed the door after us.

The cards and the money were calling to me, 'Ella, come back!'

But I made myself take a step away from the door. And then a second step.

Once we started walking down the hall, I felt a little better. I did need to finish my project tonight. If I didn't finish it, I would flunk out of grad school. That would be almost three years down the drain. There was that chest pressure again.

Crystal's mouth pressed into a thin line as we exited the apartment building and tramped across the parking lot. "You have a problem, Ella," she said as she unlocked her car.

Why had I blown off work when I needed to do it so badly?

"Did you investigate Gamblers Anonymous as I told you to?" she said as we pulled out.

"I love you, Crystal." We'd been friends since we were little kids. She was like a sister to me. "But you're wrong. I don't need Gamblers Anonymous. I'm not addicted to gambling." Frankly, I didn't think anyone could be addicted to gambling. The idea didn't even make any sense. It wasn't like it was a drug; it was nothing like coke or meth.

"So, it's normal that a twenty-five-year-old woman doesn't

have money for a car or rent." She drove us towards my lab on campus.

"I have a lot of debt from student loans. Lots of people do," I said. "And Mom needs me. She'd be lost without me." I still lived with my mom; it had just been the two of us from the beginning.

Crystal flashed me a look that said she didn't believe me.

My stomach rumbled. My dinner had consisted of chips at Wei and Malik's place. We approached the campus. "You can drop me here," I said, pointing at the convenience store on the corner. "I want to get a snack."

She pulled into a parking place.

I opened the door and hopped out.

"You are going into the lab now, right?" she asked.

"Yes. Thank you," I said. "Have I told you lately how awesome you are?"

"No." She may have thawed a degree or two.

"Well, you're very awesome," I said. "I owe you one." I'd have to put on my thinking cap to come up with an appropriate thank you. But later, after I'd successfully earned my master's degree.

"Yeah, I am, and yeah, you do." She put the car in gear. "And stay away from those scratch tickets!" she called back as she drove away.

It was do-or-die time, and so far, it looked like I might die. I sighed, examining my supposed quantum computer on the lab table.

The lab of my advisor, Professor Smithson, was a fifty-foot by thirty-foot high-ceilinged room filled with bolted-down old-school black lab tables. Over the last few years, I'd piled a few of them pretty high with electronic components and computers and such.

Maybe I had bitten off more than I could chew. There were a few other q-computers in the world, but they'd been created by large groups of experts.

Professor Smithson had warned me the project might be too big for a student. He said most master's students got teaching jobs at the university rather than doing research, but I'd convinced him I could do it. I thought I could do it. I'd bet I could do it.

The machine should be working.

Why wasn't the damn thing working?

My cell rang. It was Mom. I stepped over and stood in front of one of the windows. "Unless you know why my qubits aren't working, I don't have time to talk to you right now," I said.

"I just called to see how things are going, Ella," she said. "I'm guessing not good."

She meant well, but she didn't understand the pressure I was under. "No."

"So, will you be home at all tonight?"

"I'm not sure."

"What did you do for dinner?" she asked. "Should I leave something out for you?"

"No," I said. "I'll just grab something out of the vending machine here if I need it." I'd already eaten a questionable convenience store burrito and gotten a thirty-two-ounce cup of soda on my way into the lab. The soda sat here on my desk, next to my purse. It should last me all night if necessary.

"Okay, honey. I'm sure you'll figure it out."

"Thanks." Usually, I would share her confidence. But I was getting uncomfortably close to the wire--even for me.

"You're a brilliant young woman. I don't know where you get it from; you're nothing like me."

How many times had we had this conversation? She was a nurturing artist, and my mysterious MIA dad was supposedly the good-with-numbers one. She was brilliant in her own way. But I was sick of telling her that."Thanks, but Mom, I'm busy."

Of course, I didn't know my dad, so everything about him was a mystery. Mom said she updated him periodically about me, and yet I never heard anything from him, and we certainly never got any child support from him. Or birthday presents. Or Christmas presents. Or anything. So, basically, what I knew about him was he was an asshole.

"Okay," she said. "Good luck, not that you need it--"

"Thanks. Bye." I hung up and put my phone back in my purse. Geez. It was hot in here. You wouldn't think it would be almost a hundred degrees at 10:00 p.m., but there it was: Hello, global warming.

LESLEY L. SMITH

I took a drink and then opened the window over my desk and strode over to my equipment.

A breeze wafted across the room as I stared at my computer. It should be working. I'd used a scanning tunneling microscope to selectively remove hydrogen atoms on the surface of the silicon. Then, I'd added the doping gas. I peered at the small machine through the microscope. The acceptor atoms were at high density in several layers. Bottom line: it was still silicon, and it was superconducting.

I straightened and powered up the current again. This time on the monitoring computer, I noticed a blip of something that disappeared almost immediately. Ah ha. The info on the qubits was decaying too rapidly. My continuous measurements weren't correcting for this as they should. I knew what the problem was: something was wrong with the readout resonator.

I got to work.

After I didn't know how many hours, I fired everything up again and held my breath.

The monitoring computer registered eight qubits operating with no information decay. I jumped up. My lab stool clattered to the ground as it fell over. "Yes! It's working! It's working!"

I jumped up and down a little more. "Oh, yeah. Yay for me. I'm gonna graduate. Yeah, yeah. Hurray for me! I rock!" After a few minutes of this, I felt a little sheepish. I righted my stool and sat down again.

"Okay, easy, does it." I sent it a question: '1 + 1 = ?' Of course, q-computers were built for complicated calculations, but they could do arithmetic too.

The quantum superpositions collapsed, and I got back '2.'

"Yes!" I screamed and threw my fist into the air. "Yes, yes, yes! It works. It works. Master's degree, here I come!"

Then, I heard a sound from the doorway.

When I turned to look that way, an older man wearing a security uniform was pointing a gun at me. "Freeze." I couldn't take my eyes off the gun. It looked ginormous.

I froze. "Uh, hi. Why are you pointing a gun at me?"

"What are you doing here?" he said. "Are you an intruder? Are you here to steal something from the lab?" The gun, still pointing at me, shook. I felt my pulse ratchet up.

"Please calm down. I'm Ella Hote. I'm not an intruder. This is my lab. I'm a graduate student."

"Yeah, right." A bead of sweat rolled down his face. "What are you, like, eighteen years old? This isn't your lab." His color didn't look so good. His skin was sort of gray.

Still frozen, I said, "I'm twenty-four. And a half. But, are you all right, buddy?" He looked like he might collapse any second. "Do you want to sit down? Maybe you should sit down."

"You're just trying to get the jump on me." He waved the gun around, and I felt sweat break out on my face. "If this is your lab," he said, "show me your ID."

"Yes, sir. I'd be happy to do that. Whatever you want." I paused. "Can I un-freeze?"

"Yeah. But slowly."

Slowly un-freeze? A hysterical giggle almost escaped. "My ID is over there on my desk." I very slowly walked over to my desk, opened my purse and took out my wallet. I opened my wallet.

I heard a very loud pop, like a big firecracker going off as something zinged by my head. The window behind me shattered.

By instinct, I crouched down. My heart hammered in my chest. This guy was going to kill me. How could he kill me when I just got my quantum computer to work? How could he kill me when I was about to get my master's degree?

The glass stopped falling. I looked over at the guard.

He seemed confused. "Sorry," he said. His gun was still pointed my way. "I don't feel so good." He was having trouble catching his breath.

What was wrong with him? Clearly, something. "Are you sure you don't want to sit down?"

"ID!" he said.

Unfortunately, now, I had no idea where my wallet was. It wasn't in my purse. It wasn't on my desk. I looked around on the floor. Nope. "I can't find my wallet." I glanced out the broken window. Three stories down, I saw my purple wallet and assorted cards and IDs lying on the ground behind the bushes. "Uh, I think it's outside." Had I somehow thrown them out the window?

"That's it. I'm calling the cops." His shaky gun was still pointed at me.

I couldn't be arrested. I'd miss my master's defense. I pulled my phone out of my purse and checked the time. Oh, no. My defense was scheduled for 10:00 a.m.--a mere four hours away. "Let me call Professor Smithson. It's his lab. He'll verify I work for him."

Right as I was about to dial his number, I heard a loud thunk. Scared another bullet might be coming, I jerked down and dropped my phone. Splash. It went right into my soda. "Shit."

In the meantime, the security guard had dropped the gun and slumped against the doorway. "My arm hurts." He clutched his left arm against his chest.

I ran to him. "Do you have a cell?"

He nodded and fumbled at his shirt pocket.

I grabbed his cell and dialed 911.

At somewhere around 9:00 a.m., I arrived home in a taxi. Of course, I didn't have my wallet. I prayed Mom was still home. Since she was almost always late for work, the odds were in my favor. "Just a moment, sir," I said to the cabbie. "I have to get your money from inside."

I ran up the stairs in front of our duplex and unlocked the front door. "Mom? Are you still home?" Our place was small and old, filled with furniture that was small and old--but it was ours.

"There you are, Ella," she said. "I was worried." Her concerned expression contrasted with her cheerful hand-made rainbow-colored teddy-bear scrubs. Even in her scrubs, Mom was beautiful with glossy dark hair, animated eyes, and luscious curves. She was proud of her appearance except for the fact that most people thought she was Mexican rather than Native American. People said I took after her.

"I'm sorry I worried you. I'll tell you what happened later. Can you pay the taxi driver?" I was already headed to the bathroom. I should have just enough time to shower, put on my suit and dash back to school in time for my defense.

"I don't think I have any cash," she said.

"I'm begging you, Mom," I called back to her. "I don't care what you use: credit card, beer, sexual favors; please just take care of him."

I reached the bathroom, turned on the shower, and started

stripping.

I came back out of the house about fifteen minutes later. Mom stood in front, still talking to the swarthy taxi driver. He looked like he'd just arrived from Iran or Turkey, all brown skin and black whiskers, with plenty of wavy black hair.

She giggled and tossed her hair. Correction, still flirting with the taxi driver. Her flirting abilities were legendary. Who do you think I learned from? I grinned, seeing her in her element.

"This is great," I said to the driver. "Can I get a ride to campus?"

The taxi driver inclined his head at Mom and said, "I already have a fare."

Mom smiled. "He offered to take me to the hospital. Such a nice man."

"I'm sure he is a nice man," I said. "But aren't you late for work, Mom?"

"Mom?" the driver said, smiling broadly. "Impossible. You must be her sister. You couldn't be old enough to be her mother." The cabbie clearly had flirting skills of his own.

Mom smiled some more and looked into his eyes.

I got into the taxi. "Can we please go? Please." I was already starting to sweat into my fresh clothes. It was going to be another scorcher.

The driver shrugged. "Whatever the lady desires." He stared at Mom.

"The lady desires to go." She gestured for me to move over and scooted into the back seat next to me.

As we drove away, she asked, "Why didn't you come home last night?"

In the rear-view mirror, I could see the driver's eyebrows rise as he looked at me.

"Unfortunately, the security guard on duty last night in the building had a heart attack."

Mom raised her hand to her mouth. "Oh, no."

"I had to call an ambulance and rode with him to the hospital. And then I called his wife and waited until she got there. I guess he's going to be okay." I yawned. My lost sleep hadn't been for nothing.

"It sounds like he was very lucky you were there," Mom said. "Quick treatment makes a huge difference with heart attacks. We see it all the time in the ER."

"Do you usually work so late?" the driver asked me.

"No, not usually," I said, mind whirling. It was lucky for the guard that I was there. Probably any other night, he would have collapsed and not been discovered for hours. Probably any other night, he would have died. It was a sobering and sad thought.

When I came out of my reverie, traffic had crawled to a stop. What time was it? I didn't have my phone to check. Ugh. I needed to get a new phone. "What time is it?"

Mom glanced at her watch. "Nine forty-five. You're cutting it close, Ella."

"I see that." I craned my neck. No traffic was moving. We were already across the street from campus, a couple of blocks from my building.

I opened the door and stood on the pavement. Traffic was at an absolute standstill. I leaned down and said into the taxi, "I'm gonna hoof it."

"Okay," Mom said as I closed the door. "Good luck!"

I started speedwalking toward campus.

Behind me, I could faintly hear the taxi driver ask, "Good luck with what?"

Moving quickly but trying not to sweat too much on my suit, I passed several parked cars. And then I passed several crunched cars.

Moaning, bleeding people lay on the pavement. It was horrible. "Oh, God."

As I approached, an older woman whispered, "Help me, please." She was bleeding from her head, and her leg twisted unnaturally underneath her.

"I will. My mom's a nurse. She's just back there. I'll go get her." I turned and started running.

I helped Mom triage. We enlisted some other commuters to apply pressure to bleeding wounds and keep the less-wounded but scared people company until the ambulances arrived. Thank goodness none of the injuries were life-threatening.

And then I ran to my defense.

CONSERVATION OF LUCK

I got there, panting, at 10:40 a.m. The room was surprisingly empty. Oh no. Professor Smithson and a couple of graduate students were there, but that was it. Professor Smithson looked just like you'd imagine the perfect grandfather to look. He always wore dapper suits, and his full head of wavy pure-white hair was always perfectly groomed. I half expected him to take a pocket watch out of his vest and examine it. "Did I miss it?" I asked him. "Did you flunk me?"

Professor Smithson frowned. "No. Everyone's late for some reason." He looked closer at me. "Are you all right? Is that blood?"

I glanced down at my wrinkled bloody suit. "I'm okay. It's not my blood." I collapsed in a chair and tried to catch my breath. "There was a pretty bad car accident in front of campus."

"That's unfortunate," he said.

I nodded and sucked air into my lungs. "Especially for the people who were hurt."

When I finally got my breathing under control, I stood up. "So, what's happening? Are we going to start? Can we without the rest of my committee?"

"I think we're going to have to wait for them," Professor Smithson said.

"I'm going to take a few minutes to go freshen up, then." I shuddered to think what I must look like.

As I walked past him, he touched my arm. "Ella, did you get it to work?" The look of concern in his eyes was how I always imagined a dad would look at his daughter. Of course, Professor Smithson was old enough to be my grandfather, but still.

I nodded, throat suddenly full. "Yes. I got it to work." I smiled.

He smiled. "That's wonderful! I knew you could do it, Ella!" His praise was amazing. It washed over me like a warm wave. I'd never felt so good. Was this what it was like to have a proud father? My eyes felt full.

I tried to fix the moment in my memory forever. He was proud of me.

We stood there for a few moments, smiling, until one of my other professors entered the room.

"Sorry!" Professor Perez said. "Are you waiting for me?

There was a terrible traffic accident."

The moment was gone. "I'll be right back."

"No, Juan," Professor Smithson said. "Everyone else is late, too. We haven't started yet."

"Good." He rubbed his hands together. "I'm eager to put Ella through her paces."

I wasn't sure I could handle many more paces. So far, this whole day had been very challenging. I tried not to let my nerves take over as I raced down the hall to the restroom.

Chapter Two

When I looked in the bathroom mirror, I was sorry I had. My hair was plastered to my head with sweat, and my mascara was runny. "Damn."

I shrugged out of my jacket. My blouse was sopping with sweat. Damn. I took off my shirt, finagled it to hang in front of the hand dryer, and powered it on. I blotted my eye makeup with a paper towel. I finger-combed my hair. I rinsed the blood spots on my jacket in the sink.

"Whoa." Crystal stood in the open bathroom doorway. She'd said she'd come to my defense for moral support.

"Close the door!" All I needed was to have one of my professors see me standing around in my bra.

She stepped inside and closed the door behind her. "The dress code in grad school has really gone downhill. Are shirts optional now? Wait. Is that blood? What happened?"

The slow-draining sink held red liquid, but the water running off my jacket was now mostly clear instead of red or pink. "What didn't happen?"

"What do you mean?"

Unfortunately, now my jacket was too wet to wear. I glanced at Crystal. She was wearing a jacket. It was gray rather than black and sort of sporty, with a zipper, but beggars can't be picky. "Listen, can I borrow your jacket?"

"Why didn't you text me?" She took off her jacket and handed it to me. "Hey! Did you get your q-computer to work?"

The hand drier powered off.

"Can't text. Dropped my phone in my soda last night, right after," I paused, checking out my shirt, "right after I got the q-computer to work!" My shirt was dry-ish. Better than it had been anyway.

"Hurray for Ella!" Generally, Crystal was very enthusiastic and uncensored; that was one of the things I loved about her. "I'm a little relieved," she said. "I told you that story about the guy who flunked out at his defense because his committee didn't think he answered the questions well enough."

"Don't remind me." I was under enough pressure as it was. Even with the q-computer working, I could flunk because my thesis wasn't good enough. I could flunk the defense if I didn't answer all their questions right. It seemed like there were far too many opportunities to flunk.

I put on my shirt. I put on Crystal's jacket. "How do I look?"

"Not great..."

Someone knocked on the restroom door. "Ella?" It was Professor Smithson. "Are you all right?"

"Oh," Crystal said. "I was supposed to come to get you for your defense. They're ready."

I gave her a look that said, 'Now you tell me,' and opened the door. "Yes, sir, Professor Smithson."

"Let's go then," he said.

"Yay," I said weakly. I suddenly felt like I was walking to my execution. If I didn't pass this defense, I would be out of here after almost three years of school with nothing to show for it. I'd have no possibilities for a good job. I'd never be able to pay off my student loans from undergrad. And I didn't think Mom would kick me out if I couldn't pay my meager rent, but she had said she would.

Earlier, I'd been so worried about just getting here on time I hadn't had a chance to be worried about flunking out.

The conference room was full of professors and graduate students. My master's committee sat at a long table in front, facing the viewscreen. But I didn't recognize one of the professors. And Professor Diaz, the only woman on my committee, was missing. Where was she?

I gestured to Professor Smithson and pointed at the stranger with raised eyebrows.

Professor Smithson shook his head as he stepped to the front. "Thank you for coming to Ella's defense. Sorry for the delay. Professor Diaz had to bow out due to a family emergency."

Oh, no. I hoped it was nothing serious.

"Replacing her is Professor Chan from the Electrical Engineering Department." I stared at the stranger. He was older. Could he be Emeritus? I'd never heard of the guy, and I thought I knew most of the professors over there.

Professor Smithson cleared his throat. "Ella Hote got her B.S. here at the University of Kansas with a double major in Physics and Computer Engineering. She's been working in my quantum computing group for over two years and has been a co-author on several papers with us."

While he was talking, I moved to the podium. I'd finished my presentation several days ago and sent it to Professor Smithson. It contained the history and principles of quantum computing, how my quantum computer was supposed to (and now did) work and our preliminary results. It was loaded up and ready to go.

"Ella will give a short, thirty-minute presentation on her research. Then, we'll go up to the lab, and she'll show you the working quantum computer she built." He looked at me, and I nodded and smiled.

The audience looked impressed. I hoped the q-computer still worked. The way things had been going, who knew what would happen? But at this point, there was nothing I could do but forge ahead.

"And then we'll come back here for questions," Professor Smithson continued. "First, the public can ask questions and then we'll let the committee members ask their questions. So, hold your questions until the end. Okay?"

Folks nodded or looked bored. Everyone here had been to defenses before, so the procedure wasn't exactly a mystery. My presentation was the easy part--especially since I'd already gone over it with Professor Smithson, and he'd okayed it. The tough part of a defense didn't come until the end, when the committee members would grill me on anything and everything.

"Take it away, Ella." Professor Smithson went to the table and sat down.

I started my presentation. "The ideas behind quantum computing started way back in the 1970s and made use of the superposition principle. The superposition principle, also known as quantum superposition, is a fundamental concept of quantum mechanics that states a physical system exists in all its theoretically possible states simultaneously until it is measured. Each of these theoretically possible states has a corresponding probability..."

"So, to summarize, the key innovation was the Josephson junction embedded in a microwave on-chip resonator where the resonator design was based on a simple coplanar waveguide."

By the time my thirty minutes were up, I was very thirsty. It was also around noon, and I'd skipped breakfast, so I was hungry. I was nauseated from nerves, too, so it was an odd combination. Surprisingly, after being up all night, I wasn't tired.

The crowd was getting restless if their shifting and talking were any indication.

Professor Smithson stood up. "Let's take a short break and regroup up in the lab at 12:15 p.m."

The group dispersed like dust in a windstorm. I guessed they were hungry and thirsty like me.

I was pondering if I had time to make a quick dash to the small cafeteria in the building next door when Professor Smithson approached me. "Can you show me the q-computer?"

He was the boss. "Of course, sir."

When we entered the lab, the window was still broken, glass everywhere. "What happened in here?" he asked. The room was even hotter than it'd been last night.

"Oh, right, you didn't hear. The security guard shot at me. The bullet broke the window."

"Shot at you!" His strong emotional reaction was making me even more nervous, which I didn't think was possible.

"He thought I was an intruder. But he wasn't thinking clearly. He was having a heart attack."

"A heart attack! Is he okay?"

"Yeah. I went with him to the hospital. He's okay."

Professor Smithson just stared at me for a few moments. Finally, he said, "So you were up all night last night?" When I nodded, he added, "That was lucky for him."

"So, do you want to do this thing or what?" I pointed at the q-computer. I was hoping I'd have a chance to at least go to the drinking fountain before we resumed.

"The trouble was the info on the qubits was decaying too rapidly," I said. "I adjusted the readout resonator, and that fixed it."

"Great job, Ella," Professor Smithson said.

A piece of glass fell from the window with a loud crash. We both jumped.

He said, "Maybe it's too dangerous to have a bunch of people in here. What if someone gets injured on the broken glass?"

"What are you saying?" I asked. "We have to postpone?" That wouldn't work. I was already up against the time deadline for getting a master's at the university. You automatically flunked if you didn't have your defense within the allotted time. We'd already postponed my defense while I tried to get the q-computer to work. He knew that.

It felt like my heart was beating in my throat as I waited for his response.

"I guess we can't postpone," he finally said. "And I am impressed with what you've achieved, even though it took a little longer than we thought it would."

His positive words fired me up. I was excited to show him what I'd achieved. I quickly woke up the monitoring computer. All eight qubits were operating. "Do you have a request?"

"How about one plus one?"

I grinned. That was his favorite test. He said it was his version of 'Hello, World.' When I asked him what that meant, he said it was one of the first computer programs ever.

"I think that can be arranged," I said and sent the q-computer: '1 + 1 = ?'

The superpositions collapsed. '2.'

I couldn't help it; I grinned some more. My nausea was even subsiding. Maybe this would all work out after all. In fact, I was betting it would.

Professor Smithson grinned back at me.

Crystal entered the lab. "There you are. What's up? You guys look like the farmer that just inherited new water rights." She had a unique way with words.

Professor Smithson cleared his throat. "Ella was showing me her q-computer." His phone chirped. "Just a second."

She approached me, carrying two bottles of water covered with condensation. "Here." She handed me one. "I got an extra. It was weird. I just pressed the button on the machine, and two bottles came out."

"Awesome." I was already unscrewing the cap. I swallowed. The ice-cold liquid in my mouth was like heaven. I chugged it.

Professor Smithson hung up his phone and turned to us. "That was a colleague of mine, Dr. Tuche, in Kansas City. He has an opening in his q-computing startup, and I recommended you for the job. He says you're the leading candidate. You'll have to interview. And pass your defense, first, of course." But the way he smiled made me think I had a very, very good chance.

Crystal squealed.

"Awesome!" I said. If I hadn't been about to be the dignified Master Hote, I would've jumped up and down.

While all this was happening, the rest of the group trickled into the lab. There was some pointing and muttering about the broken window.

Once they settled, Professor Smithson said, "Go ahead, Ella."

"So, this," I pointed at the q-computer, "is my quantum computer. It works as I described downstairs in the presentation. Are there any requests for a calculation?"

Professor Smithson said, "How about one plus one?"

I turned to the monitoring computer to type in the question.

"Not so fast," someone behind me said.

I turned back around. It was Wei.

"An abacus could compute that, or my baby niece," he said. "How about something more complicated? Like 610580418 divided by 14537629?" I didn't know Wei very well, but I was starting to think he was an asshole. What did he have to complain about, anyway? He'd won over two hundred bucks off me last night. He should be kissing my feet.

If Wei was here, Malik should be here. I looked around and saw him in the back. He nodded and smiled at me. That was more like it. I smiled back at him.

A new graduate student (whose name I couldn't remember) said, "What good's a quantum computer if it only does stuff like addition and division?" Good grief. These guys were ganging up on me. I was nervous enough without hecklers.

"Hold your questions until later, please," Professor Smithson said.

"Can I answer?" I asked.

He nodded.

"The idea with a quantum computer is each qubit can have an infinite number of values, unlike traditional computer bits, which can only be zero or one," I said. "So, basically, a quantum computer is a massively parallel computer on steroids. They can be used for computations like decryption, which standard computers can't even do. They're also much faster than traditional computers. And computer scientists are working on implementing fuzzy logic which is more subjective and resembles how humans think."

The ignorant people in the room looked impressed.

"So, what were those numbers again?" I asked.

Wei said, "610580418 divided by 14537629."

I input the equation and added '= ?'

I got back '42.' "Huh. It says the answer is forty-two." Such a nice integer seemed like a weird coincidence. I glanced out at the crowd, but they didn't seem surprised.

Most people were checking the result with their phones. Somebody said, "Yep. That's right."

Glass from the broken window fell, and we all jumped.

Professor Smithson had his phone out. "I'll call maintenance. Do you want to show off the hardware?"

I was just about to suggest that. "Sure. Gather around, and you guys can take turns looking through the microscope."

They crowded around.

By one thirty, when we finished, I was exhausted. I was even too tired to be hungry anymore. I started walking out of the room.

Professor Smithson approached me as the non-committee members filed out. "Please wait outside in the hall." The committee members were having a final confab inside. "See you in a bit," he said and rejoined them.

Malik smiled as he walked by. I nodded back at him.

Crystal met me in the hall. "I'm starving," she said. "Do you want to go get something to eat?"

"I don't think I can. Professor Smithson told me to wait here."

"Well, that's either a very good sign or a very bad sign," she said.

That was my thinking as well.

"When you're available, let me take you out to lunch to celebrate or to commiserate." Her cell rang. "Just a sec."

That sounded great. Alcohol, here I come!

Professor Smithson came out of the conference room beaming. "Congratulations, Ella." He held out his hand for a shake. "They're signing the paperwork."

Crystal gave a little jump. "Awesome! Congratulations, Ella! I knew you could do it!"

I tried to look like it was no big deal, but I was so relieved I almost giggled as I shook his hand. "Thank you, sir."

Crystal said, "You should text Hannah. She's waiting to hear." Hannah was my Little Sister from the Big Brothers, Big Sisters program. We'd been together for ten years. We were like bio sisters at this point.

"I was just about to," I said. "Can I borrow your phone?"

Crystal handed it over, and I quickly texted Hannah the good news.

She texted back, 'W00t!'

I smiled.

Crystal's phone rang, and I handed it back to her.

Professor Smithson looked around like he might leave.

"Shoot," Crystal said, holding her phone to her ear.

We looked at her.

"I got called into the hospital." She frowned. "I can't take you out to lunch."

Professor Smithson said, "I wish I could take you out, Ella, but I have a class at two o'clock. Sorry."

"No problem," I said.

Professor Smithson went back inside the conference room, leaving Crystal and me alone in the hall.

"So, can you meet later and get drinks or something to help me celebrate?" I asked.

"No, damn it. I'm sorry," she said. "I have to work late. And I specifically asked for today off. I have to go. Sorry." She gave me a quick hug and then turned and started walking down the hall. "Congratulations!" she called back to me.

She was right. Congratulations to me. I was a Master. I'd accomplished my goal and finished my degree.

My life was changing for the better.

Chapter Three

None of my friends were available to help me celebrate my successful master's defense. Malik said he had a study group he couldn't get out of. None of my other poker buddies wanted to get together for some reason. I even asked Mom, but she said she was working late.

Well, there was no help for it. I decided to go out by myself. After taking a shower. And a nap.

I even remembered to go out to the front of the physics building and retrieve my wallet from under the bushes.

Five o'clock sharp found me walking into the Freestate Brewery on my own. The brewpub featured lots of unique microbrews and good bar food and was a favorite of mine and my friends. I sidled right up to the long wooden bar and sat down. The restaurant portion of the pub was all one big room, filled with wooden tables and chairs. The brewery was in the back, separated by a wall of windows so that we could watch the brewers at work.

The bartender strolled over; I appreciated the view. He was a tatted-up hot twenty-something wearing worn jeans and a tight Freestate Brewery t-shirt. Just my type. "What can I get you?" he asked.

"What do you got that's appropriate for someone who just passed her master's defense?" I smiled charmingly.

"I got a congratulations," he said, smiling back. "And we've got a very special limited-edition porter. How about that?"

"Very special?" I said. "Sounds great."

"Coming right up." He strolled to the other end of the bar. I watched his backside as he did so until I realized two other women at the end of the bar were doing the same and drooling.

Oh well.

This was fun, right? I was out on the town, celebrating. Good for me. I looked at myself in the mirror behind the bar. Master Hote. I didn't look any different.

In the mirror, I watched the rest of the patrons. Were any of them masters? Probably. And doctors, too. Lawrence was a university town, after all.

How long did it take to get a beer, anyway?

I turned and stared at bartender-man.

He was crouched down doing something to a keg. He stood up as I stared at him. He was frowning.

He saw me looking at him as he walked my way. "Sorry. We seem to be out. Or there's something wrong with the keg; I don't know." He grinned. "Can I get you something else?"

Bummer. Very special limited edition sounded good. "Do you have anything else on special?"

"We have a seasonal beer flavored with green pepper." He looked at me like anyone and everyone would be thrilled to drink green pepper beer.

"Uh, okay," I said. "I'll try it." How bad could it be? It was beer, after all.

He poured one up and placed it in front of me on a coaster. "It's not as popular as I thought it'd be."

"Huh. Imagine that." I gingerly took a sip. It tasted like beer with a faint hint of green pepper. Fortuitously, I liked beer, and I liked green pepper. "Not bad."

"Good." He nodded.

The two drooling women from down the bar called, "Oh, Zander! Down here, Zander!"

Zander, apparently, ambled their way. I watched him walk away. Who knew breweries had such nice scenery?

I sipped my vegetable beer and watched people in the mirror.

A hot guy sat down on the stool next to me and smiled (of course). It was almost like he knew I was a master.

I grinned to myself.

"Hey, sexy grin," he said and gave me his own sexy grin.

"Back at ya," I said. We chatted for quite a while until we finished those beers and another round. I was debating if sexy grin was worthy of a hookup when someone yelled, "Shit!" back from the direction of the brewery equipment.

A wave of water washed into the room.

People screamed and scrambled out of their chairs, rushing for the exit.

The bartender ran past me. "Everybody out!"

I hopped down and followed the flood of people out the front door. My feet got wet in the six inches or so of water already on the floor.

Outside on the sidewalk, it was still hot out, and everyone was talking at once. "What happened?" "What's going on?"

The bartender shrugged. "Some kind of plumbing problem back in the brewery. I guess everybody's food and drink is on the house."

At least it looked like no one had gotten hurt in the melee. Sadly, I'd lost track of sexy grin.

But I'd gotten free beers out of it. Yay, flood.

A fire truck roared up, and firemen jumped off.

The bartender went to meet them.

I looked back inside the pub through the windows. The water was still rising and now starting to flood out the front door.

So much for my night on the town. Why was I plagued with so much bad luck lately? It was weird.

There was one person I hadn't contacted yet because she wasn't old enough for grown-up celebrating.

I texted Hannah. 'Are you available to help me celebrate?'

She texted back. 'W00t! Come on over!' I interpreted that to mean yes.

When I got to Hannah's house, she answered the door on my first knock. She was tall and lanky for a girl, an athlete. She stopped and clapped, her freckled face covered in a beaming smile. "Yay, Ella! Yay, Master Hote! Come in." She swept her hand towards her family room, where I saw a homemade banner, 'Congratulations, Master Hote,' a bunch of balloons, and a cake that said, 'Congratulations' in crooked letters.

I had to blink back tears. "Wow, Hannah. This is wonderful. Thank you."

Her foster mom, Amelia, came in from the kitchen in the

back. She was also tall but very chunky and powerful. "Yeah, congratulations, Ella. Nice job." Reserved, as usual, she nodded at me.

"Thanks," I said. "I really appreciate all this, you guys."

"Are you staying for supper?" Hannah asked, bouncing on the balls of her feet.

"Homemade pizza," Amelia said.

"Sure!" You could never go wrong with pizza.

"Well, come on," Amelia said, gesturing towards the kitchen. "Everybody can do their own toppings."

Hannah's congratulations quickly turned to gossiping about her friends and teammates and complaining about her softball coach. But it was fun chatting and joking around. I enjoyed her; she reminded me of what it was like to be a teenager. All in all, it was a very nice evening. The only sour note was Hannah seemed worn out.

At least my bad luck streak seemed to be over.

The next morning I woke up at, like, 5:30 a.m.--which was a first for me. Of course, it may have had something to do with the fact that I'd gone to bed before 10:00 p.m. On a normal day, I tended to stay up late playing cards or working in the lab.

Imagine my surprise when the landline rang at 6:00 a.m. I'd forgotten about that old thing. I was already showered and in the kitchen drinking coffee, anticipating sunrise on my first day as Master Hote.

Imagine my further surprise when the caller was Professor Smithson. He'd never called me this early before. "Why didn't you answer your cell?" But before I could answer, he kept talking. "I'm sorry to call you so early, Ella. Especially after you were probably up late last night partying." His voice sounded rough, like he'd just woken up himself.

Ha. "Uh, yeah, right." Did pizza and helping Hannah with her math homework count? "Lots of partying, tons of partying. But, no, it's okay. What's up?"

"I'm glad I got you." He sighed. "I've got good news and bad news. Which would you like first?"

My mind immediately went to the horrifying idea that something had gone wrong with my degree. We'd missed the deadline after all or something equally dire. "Bad news." My heart staccattoed in my chest. Or what if the q-computer broke? Oh, no!

"I know I told you I could keep you on here at the lab for at least a couple of months while you looked for a job, but there's been a problem with the funding. I'm going to have to let you go at the end of this week."

"The end of this week?" I was getting fired? That was not good. "But my degree's okay?"

"Yes. Why wouldn't it be?"

"No reason." Geez. Losing my job was bad. But, wait, that was the bad news, right? "What was the good news?"

"My friend Dr. Tuche said he could take you on--"

My heart leaped. It was getting quite a workout these days.

"If you do okay on the interview," he continued.

That did sound good. "When's the interview?"

"That's why I'm calling so early. He's leaving the country today for an extended period. He wants to interview you basically ...now."

"I don't get it," I said, already walking to my room to get dressed. "I thought you said he was in Kansas City. I can't get there immediately."

"He is," Professor Smithson said. "We're going to video conference with him from campus in fifteen minutes."

That sounded doable. Barely.

"You're not too hungover, are you?" Professor Smithson said more quietly. "Or still drunk?"

Wow. My lack of celebration turned out to be a boon. "Relax. I'm fine. I'll meet you in the conference room ASAP."

"Okay, see you soon." We hung up.

I quickly threw on a crisp white collared blouse, a fitted black blazer and a pristine new pair of jeans, figuring Dr. Tuche would only see me from about the waist up on the video conference.

While chugging the rest of my coffee, I realized I might have a transportation issue. "Mom?" I called out. I didn't even know if she was home or if she'd worked an overnight. She didn't answer.

I knocked on her closed bedroom door as I walked in. The

bed was made. Damn. What now? If I rode my bike at top speed, I might just make it on time, but I'd be sweaty and disheveled again.

I decided to see if I could get the phone number of that cabbie from yesterday; he could pick me up. I bet Mom had it. I went back to the kitchen to use the landline. Hurray, we still had the ancient thing. And hurray, Mom had taped 'Important Phone Numbers' on the wall. Since my cell drowned, the list was coming in handy. Hopefully, Mom would answer her cell. Sometimes she didn't when she was working. I dialed.

"What's wrong?" she asked.

"Nothing's wrong," I said. "Why do you think something's wrong?"

"It's not even six-fifteen in the morning. You've never been up this early before. Hey, how was last night? Did you and Crystal have fun? Who else was there? I bet your friends were impressed with your accomplishment."

I wish. "Mom, I don't have time to chat. I have to get to school for a job interview ASAP."

"A job interview now?"

"Do you have the number for that cabbie from yesterday?"

"Aref? Sure. But you can just take my car. The keys are on top of my dresser."

Even better. "You don't have your car? How did you get to work?"

"Aref was kind enough to give me a ride. I had a split shift, and we --"

I interrupted her. "Thanks for letting me borrow your car. But, I'm sorry, I have to go. Now." I hung up and ran for her bedroom.

I made it to the conference room with one minute to spare. I'd parked outside the building illegally but figured being punctual to a job interview was more important than avoiding a parking ticket. Plus, I knew work-study students were the ones who handed out parking tickets, and how many of them were up at this hour? Zero, I was betting.

Professor Smithson had beaten me to the nondescript room; it contained only a large table, tech, and a bunch of chairs.

He seemed to be fiddling with the equipment when I came in. He turned around. "Wow. You look surprisingly good. Rested. And when did you have time to take a shower?"

He did not look surprisingly good. He hadn't shaved, and his hair was sticking up in the back. His clothes appeared clean; he wore his favorite tweed suit but no tie, and his shirt was wrinkly. I'd never seen him so disheveled. It was kinda cute.

I debated what to say and decided against telling him he looked bad or asking why he was surprised I'd taken a shower. I forced a smile as I sat down at the conference table. "Thank you for meeting me here so early. And for setting up this opportunity for me. I appreciate it."

Before he could respond, the video conferencing software buzzed.

"That must be him," Professor Smithson said, reaching for the equipment.

An older distinguished man appeared on the screen. Was he European? I'd thought Professor Smithson was dapper, but he looked like a country bumpkin compared to this guy. "Good morning? Is anyone there?" He had an American accent.

"We're here, Ryder," Professor Smithson said.

"Oh, hi," Dr. Tuche said. "I see you now, Caleb. Is that your student Ella there?"

"Hi, Dr. Tuche." I waved my hand around. My heart started hammering--a feeling I was getting all too used to lately. It just hit me that I was in an important interview. Right now.

"Oh, there you are," he said.

"It's nice to meet you, sir," I said. "Thank you for this opportunity."

On the screen, he beamed at me. "You're welcome, young lady." He turned to Professor Smithson. "I must admit I appreciate a polite young person. You just don't find many of them anymore."

Professor Smithson yawned and nodded.

I smiled and nodded.

"So, did you get the thesis I emailed you?" Professor Smithson asked.

"I did." Dr. Tuche picked up the papers before him and paged through them. "Very impressive." He leaned forward. "And you truly built a working quantum computer prototype?"

"Yes, sir," I said.

"Very impressive, young lady."

So far, this interview was going great. I relaxed a little and leaned back in my chair.

There was a loud cracking sound.

Suddenly, I was on the floor. I felt dizzy. What happened?

"Where'd she go?" Dr. Tuche asked.

"Ella?" Professor Smithson leaned down over me. "Are you all right?"

I wasn't sure what I was. I sat up. "Uh, I think so. What happened?"

"What's going on over there?" Dr. Tuche asked.

Professor Smithson straightened and faced the screen. "Ella's chair broke." He helped me to my feet. "But I think she's okay. Right?"

I nodded--which made me a bit dizzy again. Had I hit my head? "Yeah, I guess so."

Professor Smithson pulled over another chair for me and pushed the old one out of the way. "That was unlucky."

When I finally sat down again, Dr. Tuche had an odd expression.

Oh, no. He didn't like clumsy young people? Had I just blown my only job opportunity? I tried to smile. I don't know how it came off.

"Ella would be happy to answer any questions about her quantum computer," Professor Smithson said. "Right?"

"Yes, sir," I said.

It sounded like Dr. Tuche's cell phone rang. "Just a minute." He answered his phone and did a bunch of nodding. Finally, he said, "No. Really? Now? All right. I'll be right there." He grimaced as he hung up.

He stood. "I'm sorry, I have to go. There's an emergency." He ran out of the room-- with him my only job prospect.

Professor Smithson and I looked at each other. What just happened?

What was with my luck lately?

Chapter Four

In the conference room, Professor Smithson didn't seem to know what to say to me after my aborted job interview.

In all fairness, I didn't know what to say to him either. "So, uh, thanks for the opportunity, sir."

"You're welcome, Ella." He yawned. "I'll let you know if I hear anything."

"If?" I didn't quite screech. I didn't have any savings, so if I didn't get this job, I was screwed.

"When," he said. "I'll let you know when I hear back from Dr. Tuche." He paused. "Are you coming in to work today, then?"

I thought I was. Did he know something I didn't know? "Aren't you paying me to come to work today?"

"Yeah." He dipped his head.

"Well, then I'm coming in." However, since it was still around 6:30 a.m., I didn't think I needed to rush to the lab. I needed to move my mom's car.

"I'm going home to take a shower. And eat breakfast," he said.

"All righty then," I said. "Have fun. I'll see you later."

He gave me a funny look, like I was trying too hard to be positive and then strolled out of the room. He knew me pretty well. In fact, he might be the only man that knew me well.

I'd miss him. But I wasn't going to get sad. We'd stay in touch at scientific conferences and stuff.

I sat back in the unbroken chair for a moment. I still couldn't believe I'd fallen on the floor. During an interview. Damn. What were the odds that my chair would break right at that moment? I tried to compute the odds but didn't have enough info.

Why had so much weird stuff been happening lately?

CONSERVATION OF LUCK

What were the odds I'd be awake and dressed at six thirty in the morning and just happen to get a job interview then? It was about nine-thousand-to-one.

That seemed like some very good luck. Sweet. I rubbed my hands together. I should try to find a poker game somewhere. Sadly, few people played cards at this hour of the morning.

Of course, the only reason I'd been awake was none of my friends could party last night, and the bar was flooded.

Weird.

I glanced down at my arms and legs. At least I wasn't injured when the chair broke. And that made me think of Mom, the night shift nurse, and her car. If there hadn't been that traffic accident yesterday, Mom wouldn't have made friends with Aref, and her car wouldn't be home this morning when I needed it. Actually, if the security guard hadn't had a heart attack, I wouldn't have needed to take a taxi home from the hospital, so they wouldn't even have met.

I was having an unusual string of good luck, even for me.

But speaking of Mom's car, I needed to move it before it got a ticket. I levered myself up.

Unfortunately, the car was not there when I got to the parking space. Damn.

I walked around and looked at the various 'No Parking' signs and discovered I'd left the car in a tow-away zone. There was a helpful phone number on the sign that I could call to find out where the car went, but, of course, I didn't have my cell phone. Damn.

So, my lucky streak was over already? Damn.

I needed to quit thinking, 'damn.'

Back in my lab, I called the towing company's number. It went to voicemail. No doubt, it was too early for the office to be open. I sighed.

I turned my attention to the quantum computer. I'd accidentally left it on since the demo yesterday.

But, it didn't seem the worse for wear, humming along quietly, waiting to compute something.

I should really put it through its paces. What was the most complicated calculation I could get it to do? Now, that was an interesting question...

"Ella?" Crystal's voice interrupted me as she walked into my lab. "I've been calling you, and it keeps going straight to voicemail. I finally called your mom, and she said you were at work already."

I felt a smile break out. "Hi, Crystal. How's it going?"

"Why didn't you answer my calls? You aren't pissed that I couldn't go out last night, are you?"

"No," I said. "I'm not pissed. Why would I be pissed? I know you had to work." Unlike grad students in the physical sciences who got jobs at their universities, students in the medical field had to support themselves. Most of them took out ginormous loans, but Crystal was trying to avoid that. She was smart.

I still owed money from my Bachelor's degree. "Say, you don't know of any job openings at the hospital, do you?" I needed a backup plan in case the thing with Dr. Tuche didn't work out, and I was betting it wouldn't.

She walked over and sat down next to me. "Job openings? I thought Professor Smithson was lining something up for you."

"He did. I had an interview this morning, but it was cut short. Something happened to the guy. I'm not sure what."

"Bummer." She looked at the floor, not at me.

"So, job openings at the hospital?" I asked again.

She glanced up at me. "Oh, honey, I'm sorry. You aren't qualified to do anything at the hospital."

Quantum computing was very specialized. Was it too specialized?

She added, "Why don't you go on for your Ph.D.?"

"I'm sick of school, and I'm sick of being poor." The university may have given me a job, but it didn't pay well. "So there's nothing? Not even an orderly or anything? I need to bring in money for rent and my minimum loan payments while I'm looking for something related to my degree."

"Well, maybe an orderly, janitor, or something like that." She wrinkled her nose. "Are you sure you want to do that?"

I nodded. "It beats starving to death."

"I guess I can look into it. Anyway, that's not why I stopped by. Why haven't you been answering your phone?"

"I wrecked my phone," I said. "Didn't I tell you? It fell in my

Big Drink the night before last."

"What?" Her eyes opened wide. "Oh, right. How'd you manage that?"

"It was when the security guard shot at me."

She jerked. "What! Someone shot at you? Why? That's horrible. Why didn't you tell me?"

"It's been a busy couple of days."

"I'm glad you're okay." She leaned over to hug me. "I don't know what I'd do if something happened to you." Her voice was full.

I got a little misty-eyed. "Thanks. Likewise."

She eventually released me. "So, anyway, I've been calling to tell you I wanted to take you out tonight to celebrate your degree. Can you come?"

This was more like it. My old friend Crystal was coming through. She cared about me just like I cared about her. "That sounds great."

"Meet at my place around 7:00 p.m.?"

"Sure. Oh, shoot." I'd forgotten about Mom's car for a few minutes.

She laughed weakly. "Somehow, the word shoot is taking on a whole new meaning now. What's up?"

My face morphed into a scowl. "I managed to get Mom's car towed this morning."

"Yikes," Crystal said. "She's not going to like that. But maybe she won't have to find out about it. Can I give you a ride to go get it?"

"That would be awesome. I haven't managed to get a hold of the towing company yet, though. Just a sec."

I dialed the number of the towing company again.

"AAAA Towing. This is Savannah. How may I help you?"

I resisted the urge to say something snarky about why there were so few A's. "My car was towed this morning, and I need to know where to pick it up."

"I can help you with that," she said. "Where was the car towed from? And what was the make and model? And the license plate."

"It was about 6:30 a.m. from the University of Kansas campus. It's a fifteen-year-old silver Prius. And I don't recall the license plate offhand."

"Let me check our records." She paused, and I could hear typing noises in the background. Finally, she said, "Oh, no. I, uh, can't help you. Let me transfer you to my manager. Just a moment."

Crystal poked me. "What's taking so long?"

"She's transferring me to her manager."

"That's odd."

It was odd. I started to get a bad feeling.

"Put it on speaker," she said.

I did.

After several moments, a man came on the line. "Is this the owner of the silver Prius?"

Crystal looked at me and nodded vigorously.

"Yes," I said.

"I'm sorry, but there was an accident with your vehicle. It was totaled."

"Oh, no," I said. Mom was going to kill me.

Crystal gasped and then put her hand over her mouth.

What was with all the car accidents lately in this town?

"We are prepared to replace the vehicle," he said. That sounded good. "You just need to bring the pink slip to our garage."

Mom was getting a new car? Wow. That sounded good. Maybe my lucky streak wasn't over.

At dinnertime that night, Mom was pretty excited about her new car.

I was excited about my new job possibility and scared I wouldn't get it at the same time.

The two of us were sitting at the table when the landline rang. We both jumped.

"Good grief," she said. "I forgot that thing was even there." That was ironic since she'd been the one that insisted we needed it. (She said it was safer because it still worked even if the power went out.)

She walked over and answered it. "It's for you. It's Crystal." She held out the phone.

"I thought I was going to help you celebrate," Crystal said.

"You're supposed to be here."

"I, uh, am having a transportation problem."

"Don't you usually take the bus?"

"Yes. I can do that."

She expelled a burst of air. "That will take too long. It was supposed to be a surprise. I planned a surprise party for you."

"You did?" I felt my eyes fill. "That's so nice. Thank you, Crystal. You're awesome."

"We need to figure out a way to get you over here quickly. I'll call around and find someone to pick you up. See you soon."

"Thanks, C."

As soon as I put the phone down, it rang again. Wow, this thing was getting more use in a few days than it had ever gotten. "Hello?"

"There you are, Ella. It's Professor Smithson."

I recognized his voice. "Yes, sir. Can I help you with something?"

"I finally heard back from Dr. Tuche. He wants you to join his company, Qubyte Inc., in Kansas City."

"That's awesome!" I jumped in the air. "When do I start?"

"Monday. Congratulations, Ella. I have to go. I'll see you at work tomorrow."

"Thanks. Do you have any more info about the job?" But he'd hung up.

Then I heard a car honking out front. Could Crystal have found a ride for me so soon?

I hurried outside. A familiar face was parked in a car at the curb. It was a handsome face attached to a hot tattooed body, and it said, "Green pepper beer!" It was the bartender from Freestate.

"Zander? What are you doing here?"

"You're Ella? I didn't know we knew each other. A woman named Crystal asked me to come to pick you up and take you to a party. I love parties." His grin was mesmerizing. "And beautiful young masters. Come on, get in."

Wow. This day was really looking up. What would happen next?

Chapter Five

Walking down the hall of the apartment building with Zander, I could hear the buzz of conversation and music from Crystal's apartment. The building was a bit worse for wear since it was popular with university students, smelling of stale beer and the struggle to get ahead. The carpet was an unfortunate shade of brown--presumably chosen so it wouldn't show stains.

It was warm and humid inside Crystal's place, jammed with people, smelling of beer and something spicy. Crystal'd pulled out all the stops for this party.

I ran over to her immediately for a hug. "Thank you for this!" I said in her ear to be heard over the ambient noise. "You didn't need to go to so much trouble."

"Of course, I did, Ella," she said in my ear. "You're my best friend."

I was so grateful to have her in my life. "Likewise." I was going to miss her when I moved to KC. I held her tight. "I didn't get a chance to tell you yet, but I got the job."

She jumped up and down, which felt weird since I was still holding on to her. "Yeah!" she said. "Yippee! Congrats, Ella! I knew you could do it."

"Thanks, Crystal. I appreciate that."

"So, are you moving then? When?" she asked.

"Yeah, I start on Monday," I said. "I'll sure miss you. I know we'll keep in touch, but it won't be the same."

"No, but it's only an hour away," she said. "We'll stay friends. I'll make sure of it."

We eventually separated. "So, how was the ride?" she asked. "Is the guy here? How was he?"

"He's probably still by the front door. Wait," I said. "You don't know Zander? How exactly did this ride come about?"

She shrugged. "It was a ride-share app."

"You got a random guy to pick me up?" I didn't like the sound of this. "What if he was an ax murderer?"

"Oh, come on," she said. "When was the last time someone got ax-murdered?"

She made a good point. "That's not the point."

Someone put his or her hand on my shoulder, and I jumped.

"Here you are, Green Pepper Beer. I was wondering where you'd got to. Can I procure you a frothy beverage?"

Crystal's eyes opened wide, and she mouthed, 'Who's he? He's cute.'

Zander laughed. I guess he could read lips. "Hi," he said. "You must be Crystal. I'm Zander, the guy you asked to pick up the lady of the hour."

"You're the ride-share guy?" Her mouth hung open. "I should ride-share more often."

He smiled. "So, Ella? Beer?"

He had a hot smile. He might be hookup worthy. "Yes, please."

He looked around the room. "Which way?"

"The keg's in the kitchen." Crystal pointed to the kitchen, right past a huge 'Congratulations Ella!' banner.

We watched Zander elbow his way through the crowd.

"The banner's great," I said. "And a keg? This is quite a party. Thank you."

"You're welcome," she said. "Did that Zander guy say something about pepper? What's going on with you two?"

"Yeah, he called me Green Pepper Beer."

"You guys have pet names for each other already? That must have been quite a car ride over here."

I chuckled. "No. I met him last night at Freestate. He's a bartender there. He served me a green pepper beer. He's just joking around."

"You already met the guy? Then why were you busting my balls about the ride-share?"

"It's the principle of the thing."

She grabbed my arm and walked me through the crowd.

"Hey, Ella, congratulations!"

"Thanks," I said.

"Congrats, Ella."

"Thanks." The room was so crowded that I couldn't really tell who was talking.

At the sofa, she pulled me down to sit next to her. "Tell me everything," she said into my ear. "What happened yesterday with Zander? And, hey, I thought you said you didn't go out partying last night. What's up?"

I sighed. "Sadly, I told you everything already. He served me beer. And there was some kind of freaky accident, the place got flooded, and I ended up going over to Hannah's and having pizza with her and her mom." Hannah's congrats had been sweet. "I did get free beer at Freestate. That rocked."

"I want him," she said.

"What?" I asked.

"You owe me. From the other night, the taser thing. I want Zander."

I was surprised. Crystal tended to go for more square guys. But I did owe her. "Are you sure? He doesn't seem like your type."

"Yeah, I'm sure. Give him to me."

I laughed. "I'm not sure about the morality of 'giving' him to you. But, sure, okay. I'd do anything for you, Crystal." We looked at each other. Our eyes might have gotten a little misty for a second, but we got over it.

"Good." Crystal gave me an appraising look. "What was that about a freaky accident? You've been having some bad luck lately."

"It's weird, right? It's almost like I'm cursed."

"Yeah." She nodded vigorously.

"But, it's actually good luck. It seems like it's bad luck at the time, and then it turns out to be good luck."

"Say what now?" she said.

"Okay. Take when I got Mom's car towed. That seemed bad."

She nodded, furrowing her brow.

"And then when it got totaled, it seemed really bad. But now she's going to get a brand-new car out of it. It ended up being good."

"That is good," she said. "When did all this freakiness start?"

I considered. "It's been going on today, yesterday, and the night before my defense. I guess it started then: with the security guard when he took a shot at me."

"Did anything else happen around then that was out-of-the-ordinary?"

"No." I shook my head. "I was just working in the lab. That's not right. It started when I finally got the q-computer to work. That was different."

"Huh. Could that have something to do with it?" she said.

"I don't know," I said. "I don't know what else it could be, but how could my computer affect luck?"

"There you are." Zander interrupted us. "You should think about becoming a professional magician--you keep disappearing." He laughed at his joke. It was cheesy, but Crystal and I couldn't help joining in. Hot guys always seemed funnier, didn't they? "Here." He handed me a big cup of beer.

"Thanks." I took a sip. "Ad Astra Ale? My favorite. Yum. Thank you. Zander, did I ever tell you how awesome my friend Crystal is?"

"I can see she's pretty awesome," he said, scanning her. "She put this party together for you, right?"

"Yes. She's an awesome friend and a great person," I said. "She's a nurse, and she helps people. And she's super-fun."

He glanced from me to Crystal and back again. He'd have to be an idiot not to know I was telling him to pursue her rather than me. "It's a real pleasure to meet you, Crystal. I'm drawn to nurturing women like you." He gave her his sexist smile. Whoo. It was pretty powerful. I was starting to regret my giveaway.

Crystal seemed mesmerized. "Likewise, Zander," she stuttered.

"Oh, I see people I know," Zander said. "I'm going to go say hi."

"Speaking of which, I should make the rounds and say hi to everyone," I said. It looked like Crystal had invited all the grad students from the physics department and the computer engineering department to the party. I wondered what a convention of nerds was called? A con? Heh, heh. I wondered if Malik was here.

She nodded. "Sounds good."

It was past midnight, and all the guests had gone home. (Malik had been here, but we hadn't had a chance to make out; it was too crowded.) I'd offered to stay and help Crystal clean up. So had Zander. I wasn't sure what to make of that, but since he was my ride, I wasn't going to complain.

"Gosh, Zander," Crystal said, "thanks for staying and helping clean up." Her small apartment looked like it had been hit by a tsunami of disposable plates and cups.

I was shoving paper plates, cornstarch cups and silverware into a big compost bag. "Yeah, thanks," I said. "We appreciate it."

"No problem," he said as he filled his own big compost bag. "I'm usually up this time of night, anyway. In fact," he set his bag down. "The night is young. What would you lovely ladies like to do next?" His cheesiness was wearing on me, but in the kitchen, Crystal laughed.

"Do you want these leftover nachos, Ella?" she asked. Speaking of cheesy...

"I was so busy talking with people and then dancing that I didn't get much chance to eat." I strolled into the kitchen, crumbs on the linoleum crunching under my shoes. "What about we finish them off?"

"I can always eat," Zander said.

Crystal stared at the platter, biting her lip. I knew she was trying to watch her weight. "Oh, what the hell. You only graduate once, right?"

Close enough. "That's the spirit," I said.

Zander had walked into the kitchen and stood near the keg. "Is there any beer left?" I asked him.

He leaned down and gave the top a pump. "I think so." He grabbed a cup.

"Is that a good idea, Ella?" Crystal asked. "You seem like you've had quite a bit."

I was tipsy, but as she said, you only graduate once. "Hey, I resemble that comment. Ha. Ha." I laughed at my joke.

"Three beers coming up," Zander said. "If it wasn't for the beautiful company, I'd think I was at work." Yeah, he was trying too hard.

But Crystal laughed a little as she handed me a little paper plate, and I loaded it up.

"Here you go." Zander passed me a cup.

I sat at the kitchen table. "Mmm. Nachos and beer, my favorites." When I tasted them, they were even better than they looked: crispy tortilla chips, melted cheese, salsa, beans, guacamole, sour cream, and jalapenos. "Crunchy, gooey, spicy. Yummy." I glanced over at her. "I'm so lucky to have a friend like you."

"Me, too," she said.

"I'll tell you what wasn't lucky," Zander said around a mouthful of nacho. "That flood last night at the brewery was not lucky. A bunch of unlikely things went wrong at once."

Why was he talking about luck?

"What happened?" Crystal asked.

"Our biggest fermenter tank lost integrity along one of the seams, a washer in the building's plumbing system broke, all the drains in the room were plugged--"

"All that stuff happened at once?" she asked.

"Yeah. Crazy," he said.

"When Ella was there?" She stared at me.

Zander shrugged. "I guess."

"How long were you at the brewery, Ella?" she asked.

I knew what she was getting at. She thought I was cursed. "I don't see how it could be my fault there was a flood."

"You have to admit it's suspicious," she said.

"What are you guys talking about?" Zander said.

I gestured towards Crystal with my fork. "She thinks I'm under a bad luck cloud." I thought I was under some kind of cloud, but I wasn't sure if it was bad luck or good luck.

"You have to admit a lot of weird stuff has been happening," she said. "You admitted it earlier!"

"I admit weird stuff has been happening," I said, "but it's been both good and bad. Yes, the brewery flood was bad, but getting to know Zander has been good, right?" We both glanced at him. "And that wouldn't have happened if the flood hadn't happened."

"That's true," he said. "If it hadn't been for the flood, I would have had to work tonight, and I couldn't have come to this fine party."

"See," I said. "Something good happened." I took another sip of beer. "In fact," my brain was zinging with creativity. I waved my fork around more. "I used to think there was no such thing as luck, but now I wonder..."

"How much have you had to drink?" Crystal asked.

"A lot," I said. But I thought I was on to something. So much had happened in the last couple of days, both really good and really bad. My brain tingled. It did all start when I got my q-computer to work.

"Sounds cool to me," Zander said, finishing his nachos.

"Sounds like it's a good thing Ella has a designated driver," Crystal said. She'd already demolished her snack. "Should we get back to work?"

"Okay," he said.

"I need to think," I said. I felt like I was on the verge of discovering something important.

"You said you'd help clean up." Crystal didn't look happy.

"And so I did." She went to a lot of effort for this party. The least I could do was help. "Sorry," I said, getting up from the table. "You're right. This might be the last party we have together."

Zander's phone pinged. He looked at it. "Well, shit." He sort of sagged.

"What's up, Zander?" Crystal asked. "Is everything all right?"

"Not really," he said. "I just got fired. In a text. After midnight."

"Ugh," I said. "That's awful, Zander. I'm sorry."

"That's horrible," Crystal said. "Their loss if they don't appreciate you. You deserve better."

He straightened. "You're right. That stupid flood wasn't my fault. It was just bad luck. Screw them!"

"Bad luck? You don't say." Crystal stared at me.

I felt a little weird and didn't think it was because of all the beer.

Chapter Six

Zander seemed to be trying to make the best of his unemployed status and offered to help me move to Kansas City. Crystal was helping, too, and we were making a day of it. I wasn't entirely sure Zander's classic Tesla was up to the task, but I guessed we'd find out.

So, Sunday morning found the three of us driving east on Highway 70. I'd carefully packed up my q-computer; it and the rest of my worldly possessions surrounded me in the back seat. It was a good thing my worldly possessions didn't amount to much.

I had managed to buy a replacement phone with my credit card. Ouch. The poor little card didn't have much credit left on it.

"Let me tell you again how much I appreciate this, Zander." The wind from the open window blew my hair. "What with my no-car status, I don't know how I could have gotten to my job in time without your help. And thanks, Crystal. I appreciate your help, too." I figured this trip would make or break them as a couple--it involved moving, after all. Mom always said doing something unpleasant with someone taught you who they truly were. They'd come out of it dating or hating.

"No prob, Ella," Crystal said. "Should be fun." Since when was moving fun?

Zander glanced over at her. "So far, so good." So far, dating. Check. I was happy for them.

The miles piled up behind us as we listened to Zander's music--hip-hop jazz fusion. The scenery was boring, unending crunchy brown dead grass. I wasn't totally sorry to be leaving Lawrence; I was ready for new challenges and a change of scene. The only things I was sorry to leave behind were Crystal and Mom. They would only be about an hour away, but it wouldn't be the same as living in the same town. And Professor Smithson, I'd miss him too, but hopefully, we'd see each other at quantum computing conferences and stuff.

I was a little surprised Mom hadn't seemed super-sad when we said goodbye. I'd been more upset than her. "Was it my imagination, or did my mom not seem that sad to see me go?" I asked.

Crystal looked back at me. "I think she'll survive without you."

"But, it's just been the two of us for a quarter century. I've been her everything, her whole family. She's been taking care of me all these years. What's she going to do now?"

"Have fun?" Zander said.

Crystal giggled. "I'm with Zander. You're great and all, Ella, but your mom deserves a break. She deserves to live her life for herself. I hope she does have fun."

"You make good points," I said. "I hope her odds for fun are one hundred percent."

I must have dozed off because the next thing I knew, we were pulling into the parking lot of a fifties-style diner. "Where are we? What's happening?"

"Lunch!" Zander said.

I realized I was very hungry. "Good. And get whatever you want--it's my treat." I owed them for helping me. And, anyway, that's what credit cards were for, right?

"I'm glad you're awake," Crystal said as Zander parked and turned the car off. "We've been having a disagreement. Zander asked me about all the bad luck lately, and I told him about your q-computer. He said he didn't believe it."

We all got out of the car.

"You don't believe I have a quantum computer?" I asked, standing in the parking lot.

"The luck stuff," Crystal said. "That a computer could affect luck."

"No offense, but is luck a real thing?" Zander asked.

"Good question." I remembered thinking I was on the verge of an epiphany at the party. But so far, it hadn't come back to me. No epiphany. Could it have been the beer talking? "I was pretty drunk," I said. "In the light of day, it does seem unlikely that I could flip a switch and affect luck."

"Hey!" Crystal said.

"But," I said, "A lot of weird stuff has been happening. If it's not my q-computer, it's a big coincidence. How about this? How about an experiment? I'll turn on the q-computer, and we'll see if anything unusual happens."

"Good." Then Zander shrugged exaggeratedly. "I mean, as long as you're buying lunch, I don't care what you do."

"Let's do it," Crystal said. "It'll be fun."

"Okay," I said. I carried my q-computer with us into the restaurant. I'd put it in a sturdy metal-sided suitcase I'd found at the Goodwill store.

The diner was in full-on retro fifties mode with booths, a checkerboard tile floor, and a big counter. "What'cha got there, kids?" the middle-aged waitress at the door asked. The half-full diner smelled of greasy burgers and fries. Yum. My mouth watered.

"Just a computer," I said. Close enough.

She led us to a booth, and I slid in first. Zander and Crystal ended up sitting next to each other across from me.

Zander checked out the menu. "I think I'm going to get a double-, no a triple-burger, and chili-fries, and a shake."

Crystal peered at the menu in his hands.

My stomach growled, and I picked up a laminated menu, too. It had pictures of all the meals, and they all looked good.

The waitress brought us waters, paper placemats, silverware and paper napkins, and we all ordered.

Zander ordered what he'd already mentioned, the heart attack waiting to happen.

Then, me and Crystal got the same thing: single burgers, side salads, and iced tea.

"So, fire the q-computer up," Crystal said. "Let's see what happens."

"Yeah," Zander said.

I was nervous all of a sudden. A lot of low-probability things had happened since I'd gotten the q-computer to work, but exactly how could a computer affect luck? My heart started pounding like I had a royal flush.

"Come on," Crystal said.

"Go ahead," Zander said.

"This is exciting." I carefully pushed my glass of water aside, opened the case and lifted out my laptop and the q-computer, setting them on the table. I turned them on. Nothing happened. "Nothing's happening."

"Give it a minute," Crystal said.

We gave it a minute, and then we gave it several more minutes.

"Boring," Zander said.

I knew I didn't know him very well, but he seemed quite disappointed. And a little annoying.

We gave it a few more minutes.

The waitress brought our food and the bill. I slid down to the other end of the booth, leaving the q-computer on. We all dug in. As advertised on the menu, it was quintessential diner food, greasy and delicious. It hit the spot.

After we all gorged ourselves, we leaned back.

"I'm sorry to say, the q-computer doesn't seem to do anything," I said.

Crystal waved a stolen (from Zander) fry at the q-computer. "Maybe it's because you're not computing anything? Didn't you say something about that at some point?"

I didn't recall that, but who knew? Crystal and I had discussed my master's project many times over the last few months. "I guess that could be," I said. I asked the q-computer to compute fifteen percent of our bill.

It output four dollars. That agreed with the calculation I'd done in my head.

Nothing else happened until the waitress marched over. "Give me that bill back. Your food is on the house. You're the ten thousandth customer this year. Congratulations!" She smiled.

"Yay!" I said.

"Woo hoo," Crystal said.

Someone knocked over a huge glass of something at the table behind us. I turned around and saw a little girl getting inundated with ice water. She started crying.

"Free food. That's what I'm talking about." Zander handed the bill back to the waitress.

CONSERVATION OF LUCK

Our waitress rushed to the next table to help clean up the spill.

Could I have stolen that family's luck? Suddenly, the greasy food wasn't sitting so well in my stomach.

"I wonder what happens if I turn off the q-computer?" I powered it down.

Nothing further happened.

"Nothing's happening," Crystal said. "Does that prove anything?"

"You can't really prove a negative." My mind was reeling. "But science is supposed to be repeatable. I'll fire it up again, have it compute something, and we'll see if anything freaky happens. The free food might have been a coincidence."

I powered up the q-computer again and repeated the fifteen percent calculation.

Crystal started coughing. Did she need the Heimlich? She managed to croak, "I'm okay. Water down the wrong way."

My hand hovered over the power switch on the q-computer.

But Crystal got a hold of her coughing. Phew.

The waitress came back. "Well, now you've won a free dessert. I've never seen anything like it."

"What are the odds?" Very, very long, I was guessing. "Thanks."

"Do you know what you want?" she asked.

Zander's cell rang.

"Give us a minute," I said.

Zander hung up his phone. "I have to move out of my apartment for a while. Mold. They're doing a mitigation thing." Uh oh. He scowled.

"Turn it off." Crystal jabbed her finger towards the q-computer. "Turn it off."

Shaking a little, I punched the power button on the q-computer and shut it down. So, that happened. I was excited. I was nervous. I also felt a little guilty.

How could a computer, even a quantum computer, affect luck?

"She proved her quantum thing is freaky," Crystal said.

"Is that why I have to move?" Zander asked. "Well, shit."

The waitress came back and topped off our drinks.

"Anything else for you then?"

"Is it free?" Zander asked.

She nodded. "Yep."

"I'll have some pie, then," he said. "Apple."

"Me, too," Crystal said. "Ella?"

"No." My stomach was still unsettled. "None for me." They continued to chat, and I continued trying to understand what was happening.

I stared at the q-computer.

Crystal and Zander started exchanging their life stories. I sipped my iced tea and tuned them out.

Who could help me understand this? Professor Smithson? I dialed him with shaky fingers.

He answered. "Ella? Are you on the road? Did something happen?"

"Uh, no, I mean, yes," I said. "Sort of."

"Are you all right?" he asked.

"Sorry. We're all right." I gathered my thoughts. "So, is there any chance the quantum computer could affect luck?"

"What? No." He sort of laughed. "Luck isn't a real thing."

That's what I used to think. "But the q-computer's based on probabilities and entanglement, right?"

"Yes." But he said it like he wanted to say 'no.'

"My quantum computer isn't the first quantum computer, right?"

"Right."

"Have any of the others reported any unusual phenomena?"

"What? Like luck?" He laughed again. "No." He paused. "Are you sure you're all right?" He sounded concerned--like he was worried I'd lost my marbles.

If one of the world's experts on quantum computing didn't know anything about it, how could there be anything to know?

"Yes, sir. I'm okay. Sorry to bother you." We hung up.

What the hell was going on?

Chapter Seven

When we pulled into the Plaza neighborhood of Kansas City, Zander was driving, and Crystal was looking for cheap hotels on her phone. My new job was supposed to be in the area. There were a lot of large green trees and flowers and elegant old brick buildings. The green foliage was a dead giveaway that rich people lived here.

I was nervous about my living situation. I was essentially homeless. That was a first for me. All I had was my credit card and a couple of hundred bucks in my checking account. Damn. I wished I'd won that money the other night. How was I going to pay first and last month's rent?

"Sorry, Ella," she said. "The cheapest I can find is a hundred bucks. This town is expensive."

I sighed. "Well, I don't have a car, so I have to stay in the area, at least for now."

"This Plaza Bed and Breakfast looks nice, and it's pretty cheap." She held her phone out for us to check it out.

"Whatever," I said.

"It looks romantic," Crystal said. Romantic? They just met.

Zander smiled at her. "Hey! An ad just popped up. Does anybody want to go gambling?"

"Uh." Crystal glanced at me. "I'm not sure that's a good idea."

Gambling. That was an awesome idea. I could win rent money. "I'm in. Sounds fun."

Crystal typed furiously on her phone. "Looks like we have a lot of choices, Harrah's, Ameristar, Odyssey."

"Why so many casinos?" Zander asked. "I thought gambling was illegal."

Supposedly my dad worked at a casino at some point, so I knew about them because Mom told me. "Here in KC, it's officially riverboat gambling," I said, "so it's not technically in the state. But what they really do is build a big casino near the river and then surround it with a little moat. They call it 'boat in a moat.'"

"That's funny," Crystal said. "But, uh, still maybe not a good idea."

Zander stared at me in the rearview mirror. "You know we have to go--with your q-computer. We could get really lucky."

He read my mind. I was so going to win big. I needed to win big at this point.

"Huh," she said. "I'm not sure."

"Come on, Crystal," he said. "I thought you were fun. Aren't you fun?"

"Uh." She stared at him. I knew what she was thinking. She liked him, and she wanted him to like her, too. She wanted him to think she was fun.

"I thought you had to get back to Lawrence, Crystal, for work," I said.

"Come on, Crystal," he said. "Don't be a spoil-sport."

"I could call in sick," she said. "I am feeling under the weather." She fake-coughed.

He grinned at her. "You poor thing."

She grinned back.

"But let's drop my bags off at the hotel first," I said. A car crammed full of stuff in a casino parking lot was just begging to be robbed.

We found the bed and breakfast, a colorfully painted old Victorian house, and pulled into a parking spot right in front. There were a lot of pots filled with colorful flowers. Pretty.

"Nice parking spot," Crystal said. "Lucky."

I knew for a fact the q-computer was off.

We grabbed some of my bags and tromped up to the front door.

Zander threw it open. "Hello? Anyone home?" The old-fashioned Victorian furnishings inside matched the exterior. It was beautiful, in a fussy kind of way.

A thin, white-haired older woman appeared from

somewhere in the back. "Hello. Welcome to the Plaza Bed and Breakfast. Would you like a room?"

"Yes." Zander put the bags he was holding on the floor inside the front door.

"My, you have a lot of stuff." The woman stepped up to the counter and typed on her computer. "I'm sorry. We only have two rooms right now."

"How unlucky," Zander said, grinning.

"We only need one," I said. "I'm the only one staying. These guys are going back to Lawrence."

"Aw," Zander said.

Crystal gave Zander a look like she wanted to spend the night with him here at this B & B. I was all in favor of fun, but this Zander guy was not her usual type. I was a little worried about her.

"Oh, you're from Lawrence?" the proprietress asked.

"Yep." I fished out my credit card and handed it to her.

She happily took my card. "You should go down to Country Club Plaza for dinner," the woman said. "We have many excellent restaurants, sushi, Thai food, Asian fusion, vegan, Hawaiian." She ran my card through her machine. "And, of course, barbeque and steak--that's what Kansas City's known for." She handed me an old-fashioned-looking key. "Let me show you to your room. Right this way." She stepped out from behind the counter. "Do you need help with your bags?"

She pulled out her phone and made a call. "Jeremiah? Where are you? We have guests. You need to get the bags." She paused. "I really must insist." She paused. "It's your job." She held the phone away from her ear. "Jeremiah?" She frowned and put the phone away.

"So, can I get your bags for you?" she asked and smiled.

We all stared at her. Did she seriously think we would make an elderly woman carry the bags?

"I'm not as young as I used to be, but I'm a yoga master," she said.

"Thank you, ma'am," I said. "But we can get the bags." She didn't even know these weren't all of them.

We followed her up the creaky stairs to the second floor. She pointed inside an open doorway. There were flowers everywhere in the room, on the carpet, drapes, wallpaper, and bedspread.

"It looks like a garden puked in here," Zander said.

The proprietress frowned.

"It's pretty," I said quickly.

"Yeah, very pretty," Crystal said.

I sauntered inside and turned and smiled. "Thanks. I think we've got it from here."

"Breakfast is served from eight o'clock to ten o'clock. Let me know if there's anything else you need. I'm Mrs. Flores, and my apartment's in the basement." I resisted snickering about Mrs. Flores and her massive number of flowers.

She started walking away.

Oops. I needed to find an apartment ASAP. I called out to her, "Is there a wifi password?"

She stopped and pointed. "Yes. It's on the piece of paper on the desk, near the room key and the front door key."

"Thanks," I said. I could look for an apartment later after I'd won tons of money.

"Let's get the rest of my stuff out of the car so we can go to the casino," I said.

I was going gambling with my q-computer.

What was the worst thing that could happen?

The drive to the gambling joint was uneventful--except for the roller coaster of my nerves. Would the q-computer work and give me good luck?

We finally got there and pulled in and parked. The parking lot was enormous.

"I feel lucky!" I said. 'Fake it 'til you make it,' was one of my philosophies.

"I'm not so sure about this," Crystal said.

"We're here now," Zander said. "Might as well go in."

"You all right, Ella?" Crystal asked.

"Sure! I feel lucky!" I grinned at her.

"I feel lucky, too." Zander exited and closed the car door. He popped the locks closed as soon as I grabbed the small suitcase and closed my door.

"Woo hoo!" I said.

Crystal didn't say anything.

"All right, here we go," Zander said as he pulled open the door. "Let's fire that baby up."

From the outside, the casino was a giant box painted with garish colors. From the inside, it was cold, dark and noisy. I reveled in the cool temperature. It also smelled of cigarette smoke--which was a good trick because cigarettes had been outlawed for years.

A large variety of bells, jingles and pings washed over us. There were also a shitload of people inside standing in front of many, many slot machines. It reminded me of some kind of playground for adults. The sense of hope and excitement was palpable. So far, I loved KC

I squinted, trying to make my eyes adjust to the lighting change. "Where's a good spot?" I couldn't see much of anything.

"What's security going to think of you trying to use a computer on the gaming floor?" Crystal asked.

I frowned. "Nothing good. I guess poker or other games of skill are out." Damn. I'd always wanted to hold a royal flush. So, that left games of non-skill?

Zander frowned. "I want to get out on the gaming floor."

"I'm not saying you shouldn't gamble," I said. "Go for it." I waved in the direction of the tables. "You might win big."

"What are you going to do?" Crystal asked.

"Slots, I guess," I said. "First, I need to find a non-obvious place to use the q-computer."

"Should we stick together?" she asked.

"No," I said. "Three people are more obvious than one person. I don't want to draw attention to the q-computer. Plus, don't you guys want to play poker or something?"

"Yeah," Zander said.

"All right, I guess," she said. "But we should at least meet for dinner."

Zander looked like he wanted to say something but kept quiet.

"Sure. Text me at dinnertime," I said.

They wandered off together.

I walked around for a while, trying to find a place to play where I could use my q-computer. I managed to find a snack bar and bought a bottle of water. Where was a good place to try out the q-computer, where security might not freak out?

A table near the half-wall that divided the snack bar from the casino looked promising. I sat down, opened my water and took a big swig. Nothing to see here, Security. I glanced around and didn't see any security cameras nearby.

I was going to use my q-computer, which would make me lucky. I would win a lot of money. I started to feel excited.

The folks in the casino around me seemed to be having fun. They were pumping a lot of money into the slot machines, anyway. Each time they pressed a button, hope seemed to light up their faces. This time, they'd win big.

Me, too.

I set up my computers, the q-computer on the bench next to me and the laptop on the table in front of me.

"Excuse me, ma'am," a large man in a large suit said. "What are you doing?" He pointed at my laptop. He looked like a former pro wrestler.

"I'm just checking my email," I said.

"Computers aren't allowed on the casino floor," he said.

"I'm not on the casino floor; I'm in the snack bar." I stared at him.

He stared back.

"Is there something wrong?" I finally asked. Did he think I looked like some kind of cheater?

"I guess not," he said. "Don't take the computer out onto the floor."

I opened my eyes wide in an attempt to look innocent. "I wasn't planning to." Any more. I had been considering it.

"Okay, then." He turned and walked away.

In case they had me under surveillance, I went ahead and checked my email.

Professor Smithson had sent me one. It was a much longer reply to my question about the q-computer affecting luck, complete with links to scientific papers about q-computers. But, the bottom line was the same: he thought it was impossible for my q-computer to do anything to luck.

I didn't know what to think. I'd seen things, strange things. But I respected Professor Smithson and his wisdom. I was confused.

"What'cha doin', Girlie?" A gravelly female voice interrupted my reading spree. At the slot machine right on the other side of the half wall, an ancient-looking skinny woman toting an oxygen tank sat on the stool. A thin air hose from the tank led up to her nose.

"I'm checking email."

"Glad to meet you, Checking, or do you prefer Miss Email? I'm Gladys." She guffawed at her joke so exuberantly I couldn't help joining in.

"Nice to meet you, Gladys," I said. "How are you doing? Winning anything?"

"Win a little, lose a little," she said. "How 'bout you? How come you're not playing?"

"I will."

She stared at me like she didn't believe me. Finally, she said, "You should try to have fun when you can, Girlie. You never know when a day might be your last." She had to stop to catch her breath. "Look at me; I'm on borrowed time. Emphysema. Stage four."

How horrible. "That's rough. I'm very sorry to hear that, Gladys. Can I do anything? Do you want to talk about it?"

"The doc said I'd die months ago, so everything I get now is gravy." She grinned.

I wasn't sure what to say. Finally, I decided on, "You have a good attitude. I'm impressed."

"You should play," she said. "Why come here if you're not going to play?"

"You talked me into it, Gladys." Yeah. What was I waiting for?

I repeated the fifteen percent calculation from the diner on my q-computer.

She turned back to her machine. "I'm feeling lucky." If she could enjoy herself, more power to her.

"Good luck." I was just about to get up and go to the slots when Crystal texted me.

I texted her back to meet me in the snack bar.

When Crystal and Zander appeared, they seemed to be in a good mood.

"You guys must have gotten lucky," I said.

Zander laughed.

After glancing at him, Crystal laughed, too. "Yeah, you caught us, Ella. We've been filling up the slots."

"Filling them all up," Zander said. "Filling them up to the brim."

Zander's sexual innuendos were annoying. Maybe because they were aimed at Crystal? I glanced around. At least no other gamblers were near us to overhear them. "I meant at the machines."

"Yeah," Crystal said. "I won ten bucks, and Zander won fifty bucks."

"But we've been giving it back since then," he said, still snickering.

I hadn't spent much time in casinos, but from my brief observations of Gladys and others, I was guessing that was usually the way it went.

"Have you tried it yet?" Zander asked.

"I'm just about to," I said. "Crystal, will you watch my stuff?" I pointed at the computers.

"Okay." She nodded and took stepped toward the snack bar.

I stepped over to the empty slot machine next to Gladys.

She nodded and said, "That's more like it, Girlie."

"Let's go," Zander said and rushed over next to me.

"I'm putting in the maximum bet," I said. And it was a progressive machine. Sweet.

"Is that a good idea?" Crystal asked from the snack bar. "Maybe you shouldn't--"

"Too late," Gladys said. "Money's in there."

"Go, Ella," Zander said.

I punched the button, my heart pounding with excitement.

I watched the slot machine with bated breath.

It stopped on...jackpot jackpot jackpot.

"Oh, my God! I won! Yes!" The machine lit up and started beeping and clanging. It was like a miniature circus. My heart pounded like it never had before. This was fucking awesome. "Yes!"

"Yes!" Gladys yelled. "You go, Girl!"

I couldn't even tell how much I'd won. The numbers were

still going up on the machine. The bells and whistles were still clanging.

"Yes!" Zander yelled.

"Wow," Crystal walked over and then she doubled over. "Oof." The next thing I knew, she was vomiting. Luckily there was a trash can right there.

The numbers continued to go up. "Crystal? What's wrong?"

"Must be food poisoning," Crystal managed to say between heaves. Poor thing.

I did keep an eye on my slot machine while worrying about Crystal.

I noticed Zander did not help her. He was entranced with the slot machine.

People started rushing our way from around the casino.

"Good job," Gladys said but started coughing. It was hard to hear her over the continuous clanging of the machine.

"You all right there, Gladys?" I asked.

Crystal stopped vomiting. Thank goodness.

Zander just stood there, staring

People continued to walk over. "How much did she win?" was a common refrain.

Gladys fell on the floor.

"Gladys?" I asked. Crystal seemed a little better; she was vertical anyway. "Crystal, can you check her? Do you feel well enough?" She was a nurse, after all.

Crystal nodded and kneeled next to Gladys.

I should check on them, but I couldn't leave my machine. I knelt in front of it.

"What's..." Zander tripped over Gladys' oxygen tank and landed on the floor.

A crowd of people surrounded us. "What's happening?" "Did she win?" "How much?" "Is she hurt?"

A very large security guard making his way through the crowd tripped over Zander, still on the floor, and landed on Zander's leg.

Zander screamed. "My leg!" he yelled.

Crystal said, "Zander? Are you all right?"

And then my friend, still kneeling over Gladys, said, "I think Gladys is dead."

Chapter Eight

In the casino, the numbers on the machine stopped ascending at $4,500. I couldn't seem to stop looking at them. I should be more worried about Gladys and my friends, but I'd never won anything like this before. It was going to solve all my problems.

"Get out of the way!" a paramedic said, practically shoving me.

I moved away from my machine, giving them space.

The two men turned their attention to the old woman lying on the floor. One quickly took her pulse and then shook his head. One started CPR. They kept attending to her, but from what I could tell, she didn't react at all. All of us in the crowd froze as we watched the scene. Somehow, the continued clanging and beeping of the slot machine made it kind of surreal.

After several minutes, one of the EMTs said, "She's gone. There's nothing we can do for her." He covered her with a sheet.

Now I couldn't stop staring at her. She'd been fine, or almost fine, just a few minutes ago.

They turned their attention to Zander.

He lay on the floor, moaning and clutching his leg.

Crystal was crying and hovering over him in a very non-nurse-like manner. I guess it's different when someone you know gets hurt.

The suited casino employee who'd been hassling me earlier had also joined us and conferred with the security guy. The suit did something to my slot machine that made it quit making so much noise.

We all watched the paramedics work. "What's your name, sir?" one said.

He grunted, "Zander."

"It looks like your leg might be broken, but you're going to be all right. We're going to take care of you." They got a gurney ready for him.

"I'm very sorry for your loss," the suited casino employee said. "And I'm sorry you got hurt, Sir. My name's Mr. Hernandez. I'm the assistant manager here. Can you tell me about the decedent?"

Neither Zander nor Crystal was paying any attention to him. I said, "We just met her. Her name is Gladys." A lump grew in my throat. "I mean, her name was Gladys."

I couldn't wrap my mind around it. She'd been alive, and now she wasn't. She'd been a person, and now that person was gone. Before the paramedics covered her, it'd been clear no one was there anymore. "I don't know anything else."

As the paramedics reached for Zander to put him on the gurney, he said, "Wait. What are you doing?"

"We're taking you to the hospital, Zander," one of the EMTs said. "You need an x-ray. Your leg might be broken."

"Do I have to go with you?" he asked.

"Yes, you need to go," Crystal said.

"I don't have any health insurance," Zander said. "I can't afford a fancy ambulance ride, and who knows what. Can't you fix me up here?"

The two EMTs glanced at each other over his body like they'd been asked this before.

Finally, the chunkier one said, "No, Zander. You need an x-ray and a cast if it's broken."

"Can I ask, who's the lucky winner?" Mr. Hernandez said, pointing at the machine.

I opened my mouth to say 'me.'

"Me," Crystal said, beating me to the punch. Whoa. "And I'll help with your medical expenses, Zander. Please go with the paramedics."

I was too stunned to talk. I'd never seen Crystal lie before.

I could tell Mr. Hernandez was studying the situation. But Crystal was standing right in front of the machine now. He talked quietly with the security guy that was first on the scene. The guy that broke Zander's leg.

"This employee here was the one who broke my friend's

leg." I pointed at the security guy. "Shouldn't you guys pay medical expenses if it was your fault?"

"I didn't do anything, boss," the security guy said. "I don't know how this guy hurt himself."

"That's not right!" Crystal said.

"Don't you have security footage that you can check?" I asked.

"Of course we do, ma'am," Mr. Hernandez said. "In the meantime, I cannot authorize your medical expenses, sir."

Zander moaned.

Crystal turned back to him. "I'll pay! Go to the hospital, Zander."

Zander nodded, and the paramedics lifted him onto the gurney.

"We'll follow you to the hospital," Crystal said. "Wait. We need the car keys."

He fished them out of his pocket and handed them to her as they started wheeling him away.

"What about Gladys?" I called after the paramedics. They'd just left her lying on the floor.

"Someone will come to pick her up," they called back.

The crowd dispersed as quickly as it appeared, all except for me and Crystal, Mr. Hernandez, and Gladys, of course.

"So, Miss ...?" Mr. Hernandez said.

"Miller," Crystal said.

"Miss Miller, can I get a cashier's check for you?" he asked.

"Wait a minute," I said, holding up my hands.

Crystal ignored me and said, "Yes," to the Hernandez guy.

"You will have to fill out tax forms," he said.

"Fine," she said. "Just hurry up. We need to get to the hospital."

"Right this way." He pointed at the cashier area.

The two of them started traipsing away.

"Wait a minute," I said. "Crystal, I need a word. Now."

She held up her finger to the employee and stepped back to me.

"What the hell are you doing?" I whispered. "That's my money." I paused. "And are you all right? That was a lot of vomit."

"You don't deserve the money," she whispered. "You cheated."

I reeled back. "What?"

"Don't you get it, Ella?" she said. "Your q-computer did something, something bad." She didn't wait for my answer; she rushed back to Hernandez's side.

She wasn't right. I deserved the money. Especially if my q-computer was responsible for the win.

Was it my fault Gladys died? Maybe it wasn't. Maybe she would have died today anyway. But my feeling of dread and my upset stomach didn't seem to agree.

I was still reeling from everything that had happened. Finally, I called after them, "But what about Gladys?" Were they just going to leave her there? Alone? On the ground?

They stopped.

"Are you coming, Ella?" Crystal asked.

They were going to leave her lying there. "No. Someone needs to stay with Gladys. I'm not just leaving her here alone."

"I need to get to the hospital," Crystal said.

Mr. Hernandez watched the two of us like we were playing in a tennis match.

"Then I guess you better do what you need to do." I was not cool with her calling me a cheater, stealing money from me, or leaving an old lady like old trash on the floor. "I'm staying here with Gladys. I'll meet up with you at the hospital."

Crystal and Mr. Hernandez turned and walked away.

I sat on the carpet next to Gladys and leaned against the half-wall. I couldn't believe the way Crystal was acting. How could she say I was a cheater?

How could she take my money? I won it. Surely, the security footage would prove that. And then she'd be in trouble, but she'd made her own bed.

Did she take the money for Zander? Maybe she thought he wouldn't get help if she didn't take it? Could she be falling for him already? We'd only known him a few days.

Or maybe I'd never really known Crystal. Maybe she wasn't a good person. But that didn't feel right.

I sat on the floor and watched the hubbub of the casino continue as if nothing had happened.

I turned to Gladys. "I'm sorry you died, Gladys," I said. Was it my fault? Me and my q-computer? It couldn't be. "Really sorry." So, why did I feel sick? Maybe I had the food poisoning Crystal had?

I'd been trying to deny it, but... If I had never come here today, would Gladys still be alive? My eyes filled.

What if it was my fault?

I stood up and walked to my q-computer, still in the snack bar. I picked it up and seriously considered smashing it on the table.

But I couldn't do it. I'd devoted years of my life to creating it.

Mr. Hernandez rushed up. "Are you all right? What are you doing?"

"What am I doing?" I put the q-computer down. "What are you doing?" I said. "Is someone coming for Gladys?" Whatever else I felt, I definitely felt bad Gladys had died.

"I came to tell you, they're right outside, pulling up now." That was a relief, at least. "I can get one of our employees to give you a ride to the hospital." Watching me closely, he sat down on the stool nearest Gladys.

I put the q-computer and my laptop back into the case and returned to stand by Gladys.

Sure enough, another couple of men with a gurney ran up, gently placed her on it, and rolled her away.

"Bye, Gladys," I whispered. I watched her until I couldn't see her anymore.

"What's going to happen to her now?" I asked Mr. Hernandez.

"Her next of kin will be notified, and they'll plan a memorial service," he said. Right. A memorial. Crystal should pay for the funeral with 'her' winnings. We had a lot to talk about.

"What about the security footage?" I asked. "Did you see how Zander hurt his leg?" Or how I won the money--but I didn't say that.

"Unfortunately, the closest security camera malfunctioned. In the best of circumstances, the coverage right here on the edge of the floor isn't great, and the crowd of people obscured what happened."

"Really?" I couldn't get a read on him to tell if he was lying or telling the truth. Was he trying to protect his employee from being sued? Or to protect the casino?

And did that mean he didn't see exactly who won the jackpot?

Did the camera malfunction because of luck?

"Yes. My boss isn't happy about it either," Mr. Hernandez continued. "Again, I'm sorry all this happened. Is there anything I can do for you?"

"I'd like to know about her memorial," I said. "Do you have a card or anything? Can I give you my phone number?"

"Sure." He handed me a card and entered my number into his cell. "Fred, please drive Ms. Hote to the hospital." When did I give him my name?

"Hote?" Fred, apparently, said, startled. I hadn't even noticed him joining us.

At the hospital, Crystal was the only one sitting in the small waiting room they'd directed me to. From the outside, the hospital had seemed huge, but most of it was dark now. This little emergency area was the only part that seemed open at this late hour.

I sat down next to her. "How's Zander?"

"I don't know," she said, staring at the floor. "They wouldn't tell me anything. I'm not family."

I'd been fuming about her behavior the whole drive over, but I decided being belligerent probably wouldn't accomplish anything. "I'm sorry he got hurt. How are you doing?"

"My stomach is better, but I'm freaked out." As she faced me, I saw tear tracks on her cheeks. "I can't believe Zander got hurt. I can't believe that poor old lady died. And I can't believe I essentially stole the money. I've never done anything like that before, I swear. You have to believe me."

The Crystal I thought I knew would never do anything like that.

"Are you going to give it back?" I asked.

She started crying. "It's just that Zander needs it."

I needed it.

She continued. "He has to pay the bill here."

"It's nice that you care about him so much," I said. "But

Zander isn't your responsibility. He's an adult. He can take care of himself."

"Come on. You know this is your fault," she said.

"I don't know that." It was likely my fault, but we didn't know it for a fact. I didn't know much, but I knew this whole situation was bad.

"How would I even give the money back at this point?" she asked. "I filled out a bunch of official forms, including IRS forms."

"I don't know." Very bad.

We sat there for quite a while. I was regretting the whole casino q-computer debacle from start to finish. I didn't know what Crystal was regretting. We didn't talk.

Eventually, a nurse carrying crutches wheeled Zander out in a wheelchair. "Who's here for Zander Jones?" He was wearing a brace around his ankle and looked out of it.

Crystal jumped up. "Me. Us. I'm here."

The nurse wheeled him over to us. "We're releasing him with the caveat he has to stay off his feet. We gave him instructions. It's a bad sprain. Be careful; he's a little out of it. We gave him painkillers."

I stood. If they were releasing him already, he must not be that hurt.

"Hi," he said, sounding groggy.

"Did you take care of the billing situation?" the nurse asked.

"Yes," Crystal said. So, the money was gone already?

"All right," the nurse said. "Please bring your car around to the main entrance. I'll wheel him out."

Crystal and I got his car and drove it to the entrance. The nurse wheeled him out, gave us the crutches, and helped him get into the back seat with his leg up on the seat. We took off back to the B & B, with Crystal driving.

"I'm so glad you're not hurt worse, Zander," Crystal said. "I was really worried."

He didn't answer. When I turned around to look at him, he was asleep. "They gave him painkillers."

"What are we going to do, Ella?" she said.

It was after 2:00 a.m. "We're going to go back to the B & B and take it one step at a time," I said. "We need to get some sleep. And I need to start my new job tomorrow." I absolutely couldn't afford to mess that up.

Frankly, I was a little afraid of what might happen next.

Chapter Nine

Monday morning, as I entered my new workplace, I wiped the sweat from my face and smoothed my blouse. Yeah, I was nervous.

At least nothing seriously bad had happened in the last few hours. Last night, we'd had to wake Mrs. Flores, the proprietor of the B & B, to get another room for Zander. Mrs. Flores took pity on us and didn't charge us. I was pretty surprised when Crystal said she'd stay in Zander's room to take care of him. I hadn't even seen them this morning before I left for work.

I squared my shoulders and smiled my most confident smile as I walked into the lobby of Qubyte, Inc. It was about thirty feet by thirty feet with lots of windows and green plants. I walked right up to the receptionist's desk. She had short, brown hair and some kind of high fashion outfit I couldn't afford. She looked like she should be working in New York City or something.

"Can I help you?" she asked.

"Hi. I'm Ella Hote, reporting for duty."

She looked blank.

I had a second of panic. Had my job fallen through? That was the last thing I needed. I plowed ahead. "I'm a quantum computing expert. I have a master's degree." That sounded good, really good. "Dr. Tuche hired me."

"Dr. Tuche is out of town," she said.

"I know. He hired me before he went out of town."

She started punching keys on her keyboard. "Can you spell that?"

"Sure," I said. "E-l-l-a."

Some middle-aged men entered the lobby and headed straight for the elevator.

Her lower lip curled down. "I meant the last name."

"H-o-t-e," I said.

More employees streamed in and went to their offices or labs.

"I'm Avery, by the way." She typed some more. "Oh, there you are. I have paperwork for you." She printed pages, which she handed to me. "I need your signature."

"How old-school." I grabbed a pen from the holder and started signing.

"Yeah, Tuche is old," she said. "He can't seem to let go of paper."

"So, how many people work here?" I asked, still signing.

"About fifty," she said. "Dr. Tuche likes to keep things pretty small."

"This building seems pretty big for fifty employees," I said.

"Oh, yeah. We rent out the extra office spaces. For example, there's an accounting place and an eye doctor on the top floor. We don't have a cafeteria in the building, but the coffee shop next door is pretty good. They serve breakfast and lunch stuff."

As I handed her the papers, I caught sight of a hot thirty-ish guy who looked like he could bench press me coming in. I smiled confidently at him.

He smiled back. His smile made promises, promises that he knew how to satisfy a woman, promises I wanted him to keep. "Wow."

"He's the optometrist, Dr. Sanchez," the receptionist said.

I stared at her. "Seriously?" I had no idea optometrists could smile like that.

"Yep." She nodded and turned back to her computer.

At the university, the administrative assistants knew everything about everything. "Do you know if anybody around here enjoys games of chance?" I asked.

"What? Like poker?"

"Yes," I said. "Exactly like poker."

"If they do, I haven't heard about it." She shrugged. "So, you're in Dr. Macuill's lab. He's really nice."

Nice sounded ugly.

"He's on this floor, down the hall." She pointed.

The lab in question was crammed with high-tech instruments, some of which I couldn't even identify. The furniture, lab tables, desks and chairs were much fancier than I was used to at the university. It looked like they'd purchased it all recently--from an actual furniture store. Nice. At the university, our furniture was literally over a hundred years old or stuff someone had found on the side of the road.

A dark-haired head popped out from behind electronic equipment in the corner. "Are you Ella?" The mystery head appeared to be in its late twenties.

I nodded. "Yeah, Ella Hote. Nice to meet you."

The man crawled out of the corner and stood up--but not before checking me out, I noticed. Of course. Who wouldn't want to check me out? So, while he was at it, I checked him out. He looked pretty fit if a bit on the skinny side. I didn't see any tats. Frankly, he looked nice, aka boring, aka Crystal's usual type. Based on Avery's comment, this must be Dr. Macuill.

"Hi, I'm Jayden Macuill." I stepped closer. He had the most amazing long eyelashes I'd ever seen. Hmm.

My heart started beating like I had four-of-a-kind. "Hi, I'm Ella Hote." I held out my hand for a shake.

He chuckled. "Yes, I know." When our bare hands touched, I couldn't seem to look away from his eyes. Who was this guy? I usually didn't like boring guys.

"Are you feeling all right, Ms. Hote?" he asked.

Get a grip, Ella. I backed away from him. How old was he? Twenty-seven? Twenty-nine? "I'm fine," I managed to eke out. Still reversing, my backside hit one of the lab tables. Something fell off the table behind me and clunked on the floor, spraying coffee everywhere--including all over my pants.

Jayden suppressed a laugh. "Oops. You're not having a very lucky first day, are you?" He took a step toward the door. "I'll go get paper towels."

I held up my hand. "No. I did it. I'll go." I headed for the door. I needed to pull myself together and quit acting so goofy, anyway. It was out of character.

Of course, I couldn't find any paper towels or any restrooms. I had to go back to the front desk and ask the receptionist where they were. "Hi, Avery, remember me?" I smiled widely. "I just asked you where the quantum computer lab was."

"Like a minute ago?" She smiled and nodded her head. "Sure. Hi, again. What can I do for you?"

"I need paper towels. Where's the ladies' room?"

She gestured back the way I'd come. It must be further in the building.

"You don't happen to know anything about that guy Jayden, who works in the quantum lab, do you?" I asked casually.

Her eyes lit up. "Oh, Dr. Macuill? Yeah, he's a real sweetie. He brings me coffees."

I felt my lip curl. Sweetie sounded boring.

I successfully found the ladies' room and a bunch of paper towels.

Back in the lab, I successfully mopped up the spill.

As I tossed the remnants of the mess in the trash, I said, "So, I'm guessing I owe you a coffee."

Jayden shrugged. "It's okay. You don't have to if you don't want to."

But I wanted to make a good first impression--or at least a good second impression. "It's no problem," I said. "Avery said the place next door was pretty good?"

He nodded.

"What do you want?"

"If you're sure, I'll just take a regular black coffee." He smiled, and it lit up his face, making him almost handsome. Okay, so maybe not super boring. "Thanks."

"I'm sure," I said. "I'll be right back."

KC Cafe next door had a huge line in front of their long front counter. I sighed. That would teach me to do a good deed. The cafe itself was huge with wood-and-aluminum panels and furniture giving it an industrial chic vibe. It smelled nice, though, like cinnamon. When I finally got to the front, I ordered two regular coffees. They had several cinnamon rolls in their front pastry case. Sadly, I couldn't afford one.

The employee said, "Eighteen dollars."

"Say what?" I said.

"Eighteen dollars."

"Maybe you didn't hear me right. I just ordered two regular

coffees. Plain. No espresso. No shots. No syrup or anything."

"I heard you." She was skinny and freckle-faced. She looked like she should be in algebra class. "Eighteen dollars."

Prices here were much worse than at home in Lawrence. "How about one coffee?"

"Nine dollars."

I handed the nine bucks over.

As she took the money, she stared at me, eyebrows raised, somehow conveying disdain without saying anything.

With regret, I handed her another dollar for a tip. I needed to find a game and win some money ASAP. My resources were quickly approaching zero dollars; how was I supposed to pay for rent and food?

She smiled. "Thanks." She put the money in the register. "Yeah; we just had to raise prices because of the drought."

The midwest had been suffering a wicked drought the last few years. I knew the drought was bad, but I didn't know it was this bad.

The morning passed without any further incidents or goofiness on my part. Jayden asked to see my q-computer, and I told him I'd left it at home--which was even true if home was the B & B I was staying at.

He asked me to bring it in after lunch.

Crap. I didn't want any more weird stuff to happen.

Or anyone else to die.

Wait. What was I thinking? That was crazy.

After lunch, I gingerly placed my q-computer prototype on the lab table. I'd debated bringing it in but decided to throw myself on the mercy of the court and tell Jayden I didn't want to turn it on.

I hadn't seen Crystal or Zander at the B & B, but Mrs. Flores said they hadn't checked out yet. Where were they? What were they doing? I thought they both had to get back to Lawrence.

But enough of that. I needed to focus my attention on work.

Where was Jayden, er, Dr. Macuill? He might be hiding behind equipment, for all I knew. "Dr. Macuill? Are you here?"

I pictured his chocolate-brown eyes framed by those luscious lashes. I pictured him leaning toward me, lips slightly open...

"Ms. Hote?"

I jumped. "Yes, sir, Dr. Macuill. I mean, what, Dr. Macuill?"

"Please call me Jayden. We're going to be working long hours together, getting Qubyte's quantum computer off the ground." He smiled, displaying tiny laugh lines around his eyes.

They made him look even more delicious. I shook my head. What was with me? "Okay, Jayden. Call me Ella."

"Okay, thanks, Ella." He smiled at me, and I deliberately didn't smile back. "Is this your thesis project?" Jayden pointed at my prototype.

"Yes. You asked me to bring it in. It's my quantum computer."

"Yeah, I figured. Should we fire it up?"

What to say? I didn't want to tempt fate by firing it up. "No." Jayden and I weren't going to hook up, but that didn't mean I wanted him to die. "Uh. It broke."

"It doesn't look broken," he said. "I'd been hoping to see it in action. We've got a q-computer prototype here," he waved his hand ambiguously behind him, "but we haven't turned it on yet."

"Of course, you wanted to see it in action. That's why you asked me to bring it in." Maybe I could distract him? "Do you know how a quantum computer works?"

He smiled. Finally, he said, "I think we can assume I know how it works, but I'd like to see how much you know, so pretend I know nothing." He sat on one of the lab stools.

"Okay." No pressure--just a pseudo-job-interview after I'd already gotten the job. "A quantum computer works like a normal computer except it has quantum bits, qubits, instead of regular bits."

"And what's different about a qubit?" He put his hands on his thighs and shifted on the lab stool.

"Regular bits have only two possible states; they can either hold a one or a zero. But a qubit can hold a one, a zero, or a quantum superposition of these."

"Superposition?" His eyes were still smiling.

"The superposition is important because it means the quantum computer has way more states to work with," I said. "An old-fashioned computer can only be in one of two states at any one time, but a quantum computer can be in up to two-to-the-nth states simultaneously. Entanglement is involved, too."

"And how does the superposition work?" He leaned forward slightly.

"Quantum mechanics," I said. "But, to be honest, that part always seems a little confusing." A little late, it occurred to me that I probably shouldn't be so honest with my new boss. "Uh, but I know it has to do with probabilities."

"Don't worry about it," he said. "Quantum mechanics has boggled several of the best minds in history--like Einstein." He smiled again. Damn, it was a nice smile. "The states of the quantum computer are represented by wave functions which specify probabilities. So all these different probabilities each attack the computer task at the same time."

"Like parallel processing," I said.

"Exactly. And when the calculation finishes, the quantum states collapse to a classical state, and we have the answer."

"I must admit that's the part I don't get. How do all the states 'collapse'?"

Jayden leaned toward me and whispered, "I don't really get that part either."

I did not sniff his hair.

He straightened. "But the physicists say an observer instantiates the new reality."

"Not totally helpful," I pointed out.

He laughed. "I agree."

His laugh was so infectious I had to laugh with him.

He pointed at my prototype. "Did you ever try it out? You must have."

Forty-five hundred dollars! A dead woman! But I said only, "Yes. I had to do a demo for my master's defense. Of course, I only have eight qubits in here."

"I know." He showed off his laugh lines again. "A qubyte. It should be interesting."

What did that mean? Did Jayden know something about luck? And how a q-computer screwed with it? "Oh? Interesting how?"

He shrugged. "Just interesting." I couldn't tell if he knew something or not. "So, are you going to turn it on?"

"No." Not if I could help it. "Do you want me to turn it on?"

"Sure," he said.

Damn. "I'd rather not. Right now."

"Why not?" he asked.

What to say? I had a brainstorm: he could tell me about his computer. "Show me your q-computer. It's different than mine. That's what we're going to be working on, right?"

"Yes," he said. "Good idea."

Jayden showed me his prototype in great detail. It was fascinating. I couldn't believe I would get to work with such a machine. It utilized much more sophisticated active-quenching circuits with superconducting flux qubits--he said. I didn't totally understand it, but I didn't admit it to him. See, I was getting better.

"Have you tried yours yet?" I asked after the tour.

He grinned and pressed the power switch. LEDs turned green, and there was a whirring sound as if a fan had started.

If his machine was like my machine, just turning it on didn't do anything. "So? Is it working?"

Jayden shook his head. "It's on, but it's not calculating. We've done tests with a few qubits, but Dr. Tuche thinks we should do more simulations before operating with a qubyte or more."

Hold the phone! Did Dr. Tuche know about the weird effects on luck? "Did Dr. Tuche say why?"

"No," Jayden said.

"So, Dr. Tuche is your boss. Are you my boss?" I asked.

"No," he said.

I digested that for a moment. I didn't want him to be my boss.

"Simulations sound interesting," I said. "Maybe you could show me?"

"I could. But actually, I've been dying to see a q-computer in action. There are only a dozen operating q-computers in the world, and I haven't seen one work in person." He shot me what might be construed to be a mischievous grin. "And there's no time like the present. Your computer's right here. And Tuche didn't say we couldn't use yours."

"I'd really rather not." The odds were low that something

bizarre would happen, but why risk it?

He gave me an odd look.

"I just think we should do what Dr. Tuche says," I said.

"I'm tired of waiting," Jayden said.

"I don't think we should do it. I'm new; I need to do what my boss says."

"Is there a reason you don't want to do it?" He stared at me.

I didn't think he'd believe the reason. "Uh." I debated arguing with him, but his mind seemed made up.

And somehow, he was affecting me more than most guys did. On some level, I wanted to do what he said. I wanted him to like me.

Jayden sat back on the lab stool and grinned. "Come on. Please."

"It's broken." With great difficulty, I managed to stand still instead of doing what he wanted me to do.

"You don't seem all that convincing." He stared at me with those gorgeous long-lashed eyes.

"Well, maybe we could run it for a couple of minutes..." I said.

"What about ten minutes?"

Ten minutes wasn't very long. Probably ten minutes wasn't enough time for anything bad or weird to happen.

"Please." He had a great smile. I felt myself wavering.

"Okay. Ten minutes would probably be okay." I hooked it up to its monitoring computer and turned them both on. I typed code to control how long the q-computer was on.

Jayden stared at the monitoring computer. "Nothing's happening."

"You have to give it a calculation," I said. Maybe this was a mistake. "But maybe we should turn it off."

He frowned. "I don't understand. Why?"

I didn't know how to answer that without sounding crazy. And I didn't want to sound crazy. Quickly, I typed in '1 + 1 = ?' and pushed enter.

Probably nothing would happen, right?

Chapter Ten

In the quantum computing lab, I caved and turned on my q-computer and ran a calculation.

Nothing strange happened. Phew. I couldn't believe I'd sort of believed my q-computer affected luck. I sighed in relief.

"Weird," Jayden said, peering at the monitor.

I jerked. "What's weird?"

"There are more states in play than I would have expected from this little test," he said. "Did you see that before?"

Before I could reply, a loud rumbling noise erupted outside. "What was that?" I said, walking over to the window. It had gotten quite overcast, and we hadn't even noticed.

The noise, thunder, boomed again, followed closely by large drops of water falling from the sky. "It's raining." I turned around to look at Jayden. "It hasn't rained here in weeks, maybe months, has it? It hasn't in Lawrence, anyway. I want to get a closer look." I ran for the door.

"Wait for me," Jayden said.

We weren't the only ones wanting to experience the rain first-hand. The area was chock-a-block full of people standing outside looking at the sky, mouths hanging open in surprise. The temperature must have gone down by, like, twenty degrees, too. The whole thing was great.

And then, as quickly as it began, it stopped. Within a few minutes, even the gray clouds dissipated.

"Huh," Jayden said. "Rain wasn't predicted for today, was it?"

"I doubt it," I said. I didn't even remember the last time rain had been predicted. "But the drought must be over! It's awesome! We should celebrate!"

"If the drought is over, that is huge." Jayden grinned. "Let's celebrate. It's almost five o'clock. You wanna get a beer?"

I should go back to the B & B and check in with Crystal and Zander, but I wanted to drink a beer with Jayden. Did that make me a bad person? "I'll be right behind you," I said. "I have to send a text." I sent Crystal an update.

She didn't text me back.

A few minutes later, at the Lucky Star, the bar across the street from our office, Jayden sat nursing a cold one and chatting with the bartender. The cool darkness of the bar felt great. The building was an old wooden A-frame you had to step down to enter. It seemed ancient, but that didn't dissuade the clientele; there were a lot of people sitting at tables drinking beer in the late afternoon.

I slipped onto a stool next to Jayden. "Hey, Jayden. How's it going?"

He shook his head.

"Aren't you excited about the end of the drought?" I asked.

"Of course. But I checked my q-computer when you were texting. Remember, I'd turned it on? It was acting unusual during our test of your machine. A bunch of probability states were born and died--even though I didn't do any computations."

"Mysterious." I nodded at the bartender. "I'll have what he's having."

Bob, according to his name tag, placed a frosty mug in front of me. "Tough luck, Jayden," he said.

Bob seemed to know Jayden. "Been here before?" I asked, taking a sip of my frothy beverage.

He nodded, staring into his beer. He seemed to be in a bad mood. Why? Did something bad happen to him? Had he been experiencing bad luck? When? We'd only been separated for a few minutes, and I didn't see anything.

We sat there in silence for a few moments. I noticed the news on the TV in the corner. It showed a weather map with the logline 'Freak Cold Weather.' "Hey, turn that up," I said.

The bartender complied, and we were serenaded with, "The big news: parts of KC-metro were subjected to unexpected cold weather, complete with rain." The weatherman continued. "It's too early to tell for sure, but if this keeps up, it looks like there's a chance the drought is over!"

Everyone in the bar cheered.

The camera went back to the news desk and the male anchor mock-shivered and said, "Brr, it was cold, but at least it only lasted for ten minutes."

Something about that statement seemed important, but I couldn't quite identify it.

The female anchor giggled and said, "Yeah, if it had kept up, we could have forgotten about global warming."

Both anchors laughed.

Just about then, Bob managed to knock over an entire pitcher right in front of Jayden. The beer tsunami washed over him, drenching him.

He belatedly jumped up off his bar stool. "Shit!"

I jumped up as well, worried about any stray rivulets. "Are you all right?" Suddenly I realized what was important about the newscast: we'd run my q-computer for exactly ten minutes and ten minutes of weirdness ensued.

"Wow, buddy, it's not your night, is it?" Bob said.

Jayden gave him a dirty look--which I thought was very restrained given the circumstances. Bob should apologize.

"Uh, Jayden," I said. "I have to tell you something."

Now he gave me a dirty look. I guessed I couldn't blame him since he was soaked with beer, but I didn't do anything.

"What?" he asked.

I didn't have the heart to tell him my q-computer might have caused the rain shower and his beer tsunami. It just sounded too strange.

Back at the B & B, Crystal and Zander were waiting for me in the living room.

"There you are!" Crystal said. "We waited to leave so we could say goodbye."

Now I felt bad that I hadn't rushed home after work. I reached out to my best friend for a hug. "I'm going to miss you so much, C. Thanks for coming out here with me." She felt warm and homey in my arms.

"I'm going to miss you, too," she said. "We'll have to v-chat. A lot."

We separated, and I nodded. "Sounds good."

"Bye, then, Ella." Zander struggled to get to his feet and stumbled. He shot me a split-second scared look. We were both probably wondering if his stumble was bad luck.

"Bye, Zander," I said. "It was nice getting to know you better." Was it? I was kind of ambivalent about it. "Thank you for the ride out here. Sorry, you got hurt." Talk about being punished for a good deed.

He shrugged. "It's okay." He hobbled to the front door, smacking one crutch on the doorway.

Crystal and I had another quick hug, and then she headed towards the door.

I decided not to bring up the money again. What's done is done. "Bye."

In the doorway, she turned and said, "Bye, E."

"Bye, C." I walked to the open doorway and watched them get in the car. I watched them back out and drive down the street. Nothing bad happened.

Now I was on my own in a strange new city.

I tried not to feel sad. It was an adventure, right?

"Ella?" Mrs. Flores said from behind me, making me jump. "Are you staying another night?"

Shoot. I needed to look for an apartment. "Yes." Ouch. My poor credit card.

Later that night, I got a text from Crystal that she and Zander got home safe and sound with no bad luck. That was a relief.

I did not get a text from my Mom, and I resisted sending her one. I was trying to take Crystal's advice and give Mom space. She'd been taking care of me a long time and deserved a little-- no, a lot--of 'me' time after all these years.

I texted Hannah a 'hurray the drought might be over,' and she texted me a 'hurray' back. She also asked when I'd be back in Lawrence to visit. I didn't answer that one because I didn't know what to say.

I started looking for an apartment I could afford.

KC sure was expensive, at least in our area.

I was pretty nervous about going to work Tuesday, but it

was only my second day on the job, so it wasn't like I could call in sick. Plus, I wasn't sick.

Would Jayden be suffering from bad luck? If so, was it my fault?

At the lab, I talked to the receptionist Avery for a while, trying to decipher if Jayden was still having bad luck and where our boss Dr. Tuche was. Could Tuche be having bad luck? If so, why? Exactly how far did bad luck spread?

And did Tuche know quantum computers could affect luck?

Unfortunately, Avery didn't know anything, or if she did, she wasn't saying.

At about nine-thirty, Jayden finally appeared at the front entrance, limping and bleeding a little, with a torn pant leg.

"Jayden!" I said. "Are you all right?"

"Dr. Macuill!" Avery said.

He scowled and limped past us. "I'm all right." Did he direct that scowl at me?

"You don't look all right," Avery said.

"I'm all right!" he said.

She flinched as he yelled at her. "Can I get you a coffee or anything?" she asked.

"No," he said. "Come on, Ella. I have some questions for you."

I gulped. What did that mean?

Avery stood up at her receptionist's desk and watched the two of us walk, or limp, as the case may be, back to the lab.

Jayden dropped his backpack onto his desk and sank onto the chair. "All right, Ella, what do you know?"

"Uh, Jayden, what do you mean? Know about what?" At least I wasn't attracted to him when he was so grumpy. He wasn't my type, so I don't know what that was about anyway.

"Why didn't you want to turn on your q-computer yesterday?" he asked.

"Why do you ask?"

He raised his eyebrows. "You would not believe the string of mishaps I've experienced since I saw you last."

"I might," I said. "Why don't you tell me?"

He shook his head. "I don't want to get into it. Just tell me what you know."

I didn't want to get into it. I just stared at him.

He stared back at me. Then he shook his bloody leg at me and said, "Please, Ella. If you know something or even suspect something, please tell me."

"I don't know anything for sure," I said. "But after I turned on my q-computer and did calculations, I started experiencing strange things. But I asked my advisor, Professor Smithson, about luck, and he said the q-computer couldn't be doing anything."

"Anything else?"

"Well, some other people also experienced things."

"What?" He shook his head. "You better start at the beginning." He pointed at the lab stool next to his chair.

So much had happened in the last few days I wasn't even sure I could remember it all. "It's pretty crazy. Are you sure?"

"Yes. Start talking."

"Let's see. It all started last week when I finally got my q-computer to work. A security guard shot at me--"

"What? Why?"

I kept going. "And my phone broke, and then the security officer almost died. There was a huge traffic accident, and I got covered in blood helping my mom triage and was late for my master's defense. Professor Diaz missed my defense because of a family emergency, and his replacement, Professor Chan, almost flunked me, but I passed by the skin of my teeth." Damn. I probably shouldn't have said all that. This guy apparently still discombobulated me.

Jayden frowned.

"I tried to celebrate my degree at a bar, but it flooded, so I went home early. I got a surprise job interview first thing the next morning, during which my chair broke, and Dr. Tuche had a personal emergency. My mom's car got towed, but it was totaled while in the towing company's possession. Dr. Tuche gave me the job, and my best friend had a party for me."

I took a breath. "But the party's probably not relevant." When I glanced at Jayden, he seemed surprised.

"But the bartender from the flooded bar gave me a ride to the party, and he and my best friend may be falling for each other, and they gave me a ride out here, and we won a lunch at a diner." I took another breath.

Jayden's mouth had fallen open.

"And the three of us went gambling and sort of won forty-five hundred dollars, but Gladys died, and Zander sprained his ankle. Yesterday it rained, and maybe the drought is over, and you had a pitcher of beer spilled on you. And somewhere in there, my mom started dating the cabbie, and ..." I wound down. "Whatever happened to you this morning."

He just looked at me. Frankly, now, he looked discombobulated.

"But it might not all be related," I said.

Finally, he cleared his throat and asked, "Who died?"

"Gladys. She was an elderly woman we met at the casino." She'd told me she was sickly. She probably would have died anyways. Maybe.

"And how long did all this take? How long has this streak of unlikely stuff been going?"

"Since I got my q-computer to work."

He raised his eyebrows again to say, 'How long?' It was weird how I could understand him so easily since we had just met.

"Uh." I tried to think back. "It's been since last Wednesday night, so, like, five days."

Now he looked a little scared.

We stared at each other some more. I wondered if my expression also conveyed fear.

He winced as he gingerly leaned over and touched his bloody leg. He straightened, sighed and said, "I owe you an apology, Ella. I shouldn't have made you turn on your q-computer when you didn't want to."

"Thanks for saying that, Jayden."

Avery breezed into the lab, carrying two paper cups. "I thought you guys could use some coffee."

"Maybe stay where you are," I said. "Near the door."

At the same time, Jayden said, "Thanks, Avery," and held out his hand.

Avery listened to him. His injured leg was extended into the middle of the room, right where Avery should walk. And she did, tripping over it and spilling the cups all over Jayden's lap.

He jerked back.

Only a few assorted drops landed on me.

"Ow!" he said. "That's hot!"

"Oh, no, Dr. Macuill," Avery said, righting herself. "I'm so sorry."

I backed away from them.

"I'm so sorry, Dr. Macuill," she said. "Let me get paper towels."

"No!" he said, glancing my way. "It would be safer if you went back to your desk."

I nodded.

"Are you sure?" she asked.

"Yes," he said.

"Thanks for the coffee, Avery," I said. "Some of the paper towels I got yesterday should still be around here somewhere."

As soon as she left, Jayden turned to me and said, "Help! I believe you, Ella. You have to fix me."

I stepped over to my desk, grabbed paper towels and handed them to him. As he blotted, I said, "I'm not sure how to fix you, Jayden. I don't understand what's happening."

He glanced up at me. "You must have ideas."

"Well..." I felt like anything I had to say might be considered crazy.

"Please, Ella." He looked so pathetic I felt sorry for him.

"I don't know much." I sighed. "I might have been sort of lucky. It seems like people near me might be sort of unlucky."

"So, what? Bad luck is contagious?"

I slowly nodded. "Maybe not bad luck per se, but, yes, improbabilities are contagious." Poor Gladys. "And I think it gradually wears off?" Crystal and Zander seemed back to normal now, didn't they?

"Are you asking me or telling me?"

"I'm hypothesizing. Hmm. I'm not sure if people have to be literally near my computer in space or if they can be causally connected." What did happen to Professor Diaz? And Dr. Tuche, for that matter?

"Where's Dr. Tuche?" I asked. "And what happened to you this morning?"

Jayden ignored my questions. "To be clear, you're

saying you think your q-computer is doing something no other q-computer has done? Including the rain yesterday? How did it cause that?"

It did sound very grandiose when he put it like that. "I'm not sure." We didn't know much of anything when you came right down to it.

As a scientist, I learned things via experiments. "Is there a chance we should do some experiments?"

"Whoa." He jerked back again. "You'd risk maybe screwing up probabilities on purpose?"

"I'm not sure. But how else are we going to get to the bottom of this? Do you have any other ideas?"

He shook his head.

I had a brainstorm: Jayden had said they had a simulation of their system. Maybe we could study this phenomenon using that. "What about your simulations? Have you ever seen any strange probabilities?"

"No." He glanced at his computer. "But of course, we don't have planet Earth and all its people and the weather in our computer model. Or probabilities. How would we even quantify that?"

Damn. "Yeah, I don't know." I paused. "What do you suggest? I guess we could just not ever use a q-computer again." That's not what I wanted, but I didn't want to endanger people.

"So, we both quit our jobs?" he asked. "And let the poor saps who come after us figure it out? What if they get hurt?"

When he put it like that, it didn't sound fair. "Could we somehow stop the whole project?"

"What? I don't see how. Sabotage?" he asked. "That's crazy. And Tuche has a lot of documentation and equipment. How would we get rid of that? Plus, our group and others have published papers about this."

"I'm not advocating sabotage." Or was I? No. It'd be too hard to make sure the project ended. And what about the other q-computer projects in the world? There's no way we could affect them all. My brain tingled. There was something interesting there...

"Shit," he said. "I guess we should experiment."

"Maybe we could even figure out how to turn off or cancel the effect," I said.

"That would be great," he said.

"Yes!" My brain was tingling again. "Like two waves interfering and canceling each other out? Oooh. They do talk about probability waves..." For the first time, I didn't feel totally confused about this stuff.

I felt full of excitement.

And, at the same time, full of dread.

Chapter Eleven

"Before we do any more experiments, we should ensure we're not duplicating what others have done," Jayden said.

"That's a good idea," I said. "What do you suggest?"

"We should do literature searches," he said.

"Good idea." We were stalling. I knew it, and Jayden knew it. I didn't want to kill anyone else. I don't know what his excuse was.

So, we did some lit searches.

Eventually, Jayden pushed back the chair from his computer monitor. "I can't find anything."

"Me neither," I said. "There's nothing on the Web of Science."

"Maybe the scientific journal referees are rejecting articles that have to do with luck?" he said.

"I would," I said. "Wouldn't you?"

"Yeah," he said. "At least until this week."

"Do you know any other people working in this area?" I asked. "Professor Smithson said q-computers don't affect luck. But maybe you could ask some people?"

"It's worth a try," he said and returned to his keyboard.

I did some random internet searches but didn't find anything. If I was being honest with myself, though, I was just avoiding doing an actual experiment with my q-computer.

After several minutes, Jayden pushed himself back from his keyboard again. "So that's that." He looked over at me. "We'll have to wait for their response."

Waiting sounded good to me.

"So, every time you've used your q-computer, something weird's happened?" he asked.

I thought back over the last several days again. "I think so. Yes." I shook my head. "And I hypothesize all your bad luck over the last two days has been because of it."

"And the rain?" he asked. "Do you think that was from the q-computer?"

"Well..." I drew the word out. "Considering we turned the q-computer on for ten minutes, and it rained during those exact same ten minutes, I hypothesize yes. The q-computer made it rain." I stood up and walked over to the window, and looked out. No sign of rain now.

"But that's big. A lot has to happen physically. The atmosphere has to have moisture, and the temperature has to go down. How could all that even be related to luck?" He paused and shook his head a little. "What is luck?"

He raised a lot of good questions. "I don't know," I said, turning around. "We should try to figure out exactly what luck is. It's related to probabilities, right?"

"I guess," he said. "Good luck is when improbable things help a person?"

I shrugged. "I guess. Then bad luck would be when improbable things hurt a person?"

"It's as good a hypothesis as any," he said.

"The only way to be sure something real is going on is to repeat the experiment with exactly the same conditions and see if we get the same results."

"Did you affect the weather with your q-computer before?" he asked.

I shook my head. "No. And that does seem like a big effect."

"I might believe the q-computer affects little things like spilling beer or having a bike accident--only because I've experienced them myself. I'm having trouble believing your little computer can affect the weather."

"You hypothesize it won't affect the weather," I said.

"Yeah," he said.

"So, what happened yesterday?" I asked. "We turned my computer on for ten minutes and started a calculation."

"Why are you telling me?" he asked. "I was here."

I was stalling some more. "I'm gathering my thoughts. Maybe we should duplicate the experiment from yesterday and see if we get the same results."

He looked a little worried. "I guess that makes sense." He rubbed his injured leg. "Maybe we should work up to it."

Yay. More stalling. "I like the sound of that," I said.

Over the next hour or so, we mapped out a plan that started with me turning my q-computer on for one, two, and so on, up to ten minutes and observing the results. I liked the plan because I thought nothing would happen until we actually did a quantum calculation.

We implemented the plan.

My hypothesis was proved.

"Why are you smiling?" Jayden asked. "Nothing's happening."

"We're safe," I said. "Why aren't you smiling?"

"If we can't duplicate yesterday's results, what are we left with?" he asked. "We're crazy?"

"Hmm. Good point," I said. "I, uh, think I know why nothing's happening."

"Why?"

"I hypothesize we have to do a calculation to put the quantum states in play."

"What do you mean?" he asked.

"I don't know for sure, but I think we have to expand the wavefunctions, get all the entangled wavefunctions working, doing something, for the probabilities to be affected."

He stared at me like he was saying, 'Now you tell me.' Finally, he said, "Well, let's do that."

"Okay. But let's take a break." I was sick of being here in the lab. We'd been in this room all day.

Jayden nodded. "Fine."

I strolled out of the lab. My feet led me up the stairs. It felt good to move around. I found myself outside the Hot Optometrist's office. I peeked in through the window but didn't see him.

Reluctantly, I walked back down to the lab and entered.

"Ready?" I asked.

Jayden nodded again.

"Here goes," I said. "But, I'm only going to run it for five minutes." I input my favorite '1+1=?' calculation.

My palms were sweating, and I had to keep wiping them on my pants.

I was watching the clock. I wasn't sure what Jayden was doing.

I heard a pop and the tinkle of glass. Nervous, I turned off my q-computer. "What happened?"

"The light bulb burned out." He pointed to the ceiling over by the lab door. "This is not the drama I was expecting."

I didn't say anything.

"You're smiling again."

"Yes, I am."

We spent the rest of the day running my q-computer for longer and longer periods and doing calculations.

Several minor unlucky things happened, including the mysterious Dr. Tuche calling but only saying, "Oh, no, I'm losing serv--" At least we knew he was still alive.

The rest of the light bulbs in the ceiling fixtures burned out. Avery spilled a coke on Jayden--much to her embarrassment. I got a big zit on the end of my nose.

I don't know how much of what happened was due to the q-computer.

I do know we did not change the weather.

Finally, at dinnertime, Jayden said, "I don't get it. Why isn't it doing what it did yesterday?"

"Is there something different?" I asked, having the feeling something was different.

"I don't know what that would be," he said.

I wracked my brain. "I know! You had your q-computer on too yesterday."

"I think you're right." He stood up and limped to his q-computer. "Shall we?"

"Uh, it's late," I said. "Maybe we've done enough today."

"All right." He seemed relieved.

I know I was.

That night I couldn't sleep, thinking about the impending luck experiment. What would we do? How would we do it? What would happen? Would anyone get hurt?

I finally dozed off right before my alarm went off.

Tired, suffice it to say, I wasn't at my best when I showed up at the lab Wednesday morning.

It turned out I was better than Jayden, though, because he didn't show up at all. I couldn't call him because I didn't know his number. And there was no sign of Dr. Tuche as usual. After puttering around the lab for a while, I went looking for Avery.

She was right where she was supposed to be, at her desk. "Hey, Avery. How's it going?"

"It's going good, girl." She smiled. "Where's that sweet Dr. Macuill today, anyway?"

Sweet? Were Avery and Jayden dating? Ugh. Why did I care? I couldn't believe the thought of them dating made me envious; I barely knew Jayden. "That's what I'm wondering. I was expecting him. Did he call in sick or anything?" I hoped he wasn't sick. Would it be unlucky if he was?

She shook her head. "No. I haven't heard anything."

"No texts? No voice mail?" I asked. "No email? No v-chats?" I hoped he wasn't worse than sick.

She glanced at her desk phone and computer screen and shook her head. "Nope."

"Can you give me his number?" I asked.

She frowned. "I don't think I should."

"It's just that I could have sworn he said he was coming in bright and early this morning," I said. "I thought we were going to do some experiments." Not that I necessarily wanted to do them. I was worried someone would get hurt. Did Jayden get hurt?

I had a bad thought: were employees disappearing from Qubyte Inc.? What happened to Dr. Tuche anyway? I never did get a straight answer about that. "Maybe Dr. Tuche knows? Maybe we could ask him? Where's he again?"

"Heh, heh," Avery said. "Nice try. I'm not at liberty to divulge that information. He's on travel." She pointed at my cell. "You could try contacting Dr. Tuche yourself. I assume you have his contact info."

I examined my phone. Professor Smithson did give me his email address. But maybe it wasn't my place to ask my boss-- who I hadn't even met in person--where he was.

And as far as Jayden went, what if I emailed Tuche about Jayden being late to work, and it ended up getting Jayden in trouble? Somehow, I didn't think getting Jayden in trouble with his boss would result in a decent working relationship.

"So, you think Jayden's sweet?"

She laughed. "Don't you? All the girl nerds around here swoon over him."

Oh no. I looked around the building's foyer. I didn't see any girl nerds. "Is that a lot of people?" Wait. Why did I care? I didn't care.

"No." She smiled.

Was Avery being cagey? Did she have a crush on Jayden, too, or not? "So, you're into Jayden?"

Avery held up her hand, showing off a large diamond engagement ring. "Observant much?"

For a second, my heart stopped as I thought she meant she was engaged to Jayden, but that didn't make any sense. She called him Dr. Macuill.

I came to my senses. "Wow. That's a gorgeous ring. Tell me about your fiancé." I'd never been much interested in rings or fiancés. Until now. Now, they seemed fascinating.

Avery wanted to talk about her man, Liam. A lot. She went on and on. I interjected a "Nice," "He sounds great," or "Lucky you," periodically. She seemed genuinely happy. Good for her.

I hoped I'd feel that way about someone someday--which sort of surprised me. Mom and I seemed to do fine without a steady man around.

Eventually, Avery wound down. Jayden still hadn't shown up. I was getting very concerned. Could he have been trapped or hurt in an unlucky freak accident? If so, what could I do about it? It wasn't like I could call the police and ask them to check on him because I thought he was having some bad luck.

"Thanks for chatting, Ella," Avery said. "None of the scientists around here ever want to talk with me. It's almost like I'm a piece of furniture or equipment or something."

"I've enjoyed chatting with you, too," I said. I meant it. She was my only possibility for a friend so far in KC

"Dr. Macuill's MIA?" She scrunched up her nose.

"Yes. And I'm a little worried." I was a lot worried.

"That's not like him. He's kind of a workaholic. I'm not comfortable giving out his number, but I can call him."

She grabbed her cell and punched a button. She listened for a few moments. "Straight to voicemail. Huh."

She looked at me like she was starting to get worried too. "I suppose I can give you his home address if you want to go check on him." She turned to the computer and started typing. "But don't tell anyone you got it from me."

Jayden lived in an apartment building close to our lab. As I walked up, I didn't see anything amiss; at least the building wasn't on fire or anything. It was a four-story boxy red-brick building with exterior stairs and looked like it might have once been a motel.

When I got up the stairs, however, I made a discovery. Jayden stood in the hall very close to his front door, wearing only a towel and flip-flops.

When I got closer, I realized the towel was stuck in the door.

I tried not to ogle him, but it was tough. He was surprisingly fit for a nerd, trim but with well-defined muscles.

"You're not Mike," he said.

I had to fight not to grin. "Nope, not Mike." Whoever Mike was. We stared at each other for a few seconds. "I was worried something might have happened to you when you didn't show up for work," I finally said.

"I'm fine." He did not open the door. He did clutch his towel and hold it more firmly around his waist.

"Are you sure you're all right? You aren't being held at gunpoint, are you?" I glanced around but didn't see anyone. "Are you some kind of hostage?"

"No. Why would you say that?"

"You're acting odd," I said. "Why are you just standing here? Why are you wearing a towel? What's wrong?"

"I'm fine. I'll be at work later." He gritted his teeth. "Or, at least I better be. Damn Mike."

"Who's Mike?" I asked.

"He's my roommate," Jayden said. "And the super of the building."

I was starting to understand. Jayden had locked himself out of his apartment. Wearing only a towel. How unlucky.

I had to struggle not to giggle. "So, ah, did you call him?"

97

"Yes!" Jayden clenched both fists, and his towel started to unwrap from his waist.

I froze, staring at his midsection.

He grabbed it before it fell. I felt a split-second of disappointment before I chastised myself. Bad, Ella. I tried to put myself in his shoes ...or his towel. No giggling! No ogling!

"With my neighbor's cell," he said, "but he was late for work, and no one else has come by."

"So, ah, I have my cell. Do you want to try calling Mike again?"

"Yes!" He managed to hang on to his towel this time, as he exclaimed.

I got out my cell, he gave me the number, and I dialed. As it rang, I handed it to him, and he took it carefully with one free hand.

"Never mind who Ella is," he said. "Where the hell are you? I've been waiting here for, like, an hour."

He listened.

"What do you mean you can't come! You're the super! It's your job to come!"

He listened.

"What--" Jayden stared at the phone. "The asshole hung up on me!" He was shaking and turning red. All over.

Look away, Ella. But I didn't want to look away.

He had a nice body, plenty of muscles, with not much body hair. Maybe he was a little bit my type. I resisted the urge to ask him if he worked out. Yay, me.

I tried some more not to stare and managed to look away. "How can I help? I'm here to help."

"Actually, you can help." He held up his forefinger, and the towel started to slip. He grabbed it. "I did laundry last night but fell asleep before retrieving my clothes from the dryers. This morning I just thought I'd pop down to the laundry room, but my towel got stuck in the door."

Poor guy. "Do you want me to get your clothes from the laundry room?"

"Yeah."

"Okay. Where's the laundry room?"

"In the basement." He pointed down the stairs. "Laundry

basket's still down there."

I went down to the basement. Sure enough, there was a bunch of clothes in a pile on a table near the dryers. I recognized the shirt Jayden was wearing when the pitcher of beer doused him. I put them all in the basket and brought them upstairs.

"Here you go," I said.

"Thanks a lot, Ella." He reached for the basket, but his towel started opening. "Maybe just put it down in front of me."

I put it down.

"Thanks," he said. "So, see you at work later. Goodbye."

I could take a hint or a blatant message. "Sure." I took a step down the hall.

"Could you not mention this to other people?"

Who would I even mention it to? Mrs. Flores? Avery? I did sort of want to mention it to Avery. "I won't mention it to anyone."

"Hey, how did you know where I live?" he asked.

"I can keep a secret." As I walked down the hall, I smiled.

Jayden and I were finally in the lab, ready to work after lunch.

He'd seemed genuinely embarrassed by the events of the morning, so I resolved not to mention them again.

I tried not to think about them again. Why was I wondering so much about what was under that towel?

We both sat down on stools near the two q-computers.

Jayden turned on his q-computer.

I turned mine on and typed in '1 + 1 = ?'

I pressed enter.

Chapter Twelve

Jayden and I had just turned on our q-computers and were waiting with bated breath for something to happen. I glanced around the lab. No light bulbs broke, and no coffee spilled. Nothing seemed to be happening. Jayden and I looked at each other. I didn't know about him, but at this point, I thought something would happen.

He said, "Well, that was anti-clim--"

He was interrupted by a loud crash of thunder.

We rushed to the window.

Black clouds roiled towards us. I'd never seen clouds move so fast.

I was torn. We still needed the rain, but that looked dangerous. "Uh, maybe we should turn it off," I said.

"Yes, let's," he said.

We both ran to our machines and powered them off.

With a final burst of thunder, the black clouds dissipated as quickly as they appeared.

I was shaking. Did we do that? We must have done that. But how had we done that?

Avery walked in. "Hey, why is it so dark in here?"

"The bulbs burned out." Jayden pointed at the ceiling.

"What is going on with the weather around here?" She walked towards my q-computer.

I shrugged exaggeratedly. "Don't know." I noticed she was not carrying any beverages. Good.

"Gosh, beats me," Jayden said. Gosh? Who was this guy?

We stared at her. No one said anything.

Awkward.

"You guys are acting weird," she said, staring at us. She

held up a forefinger. "Wait a minute. Is there something going on between you two?"

Jayden and I both said, "No!" simultaneously.

"They doth protest too much." She smirked. "Ha. I knew it. I knew when you got his home address from me, there was some kind of hanky panky going on."

Avery apparently could not keep a secret. "Nothing was going on," I said.

"No hanky," he said.

"Or panky," I said. Why were we so in sync?

"She didn't see me naked," he said.

"Nope," I said. "Not naked. No nakedness." Technically, he'd been wearing a towel. I also couldn't help remembering his smooth skin, his well-defined pecs...

"Jeez," Avery said. "I was just joking around. You guys did it already?" She turned to me. "Wow, you go, girl. You move fast."

Both pairs of eyes were on me. I felt embarrassed. It wasn't like me. "I move fast, but no, we didn't hook up. Jayden should be so lucky." I grinned.

He looked surprised.

I was a master. I should take control of this conversation. "Anyway, this all seems workplace-inappropriate. Did you want something work-related, Avery?"

She paused for a moment. "I wanted to ask you about the weather." She put her hands on her hips. "But now I want to know what's going on between you two."

I glanced at Jayden. He was blushing. "Nothing," I said.

"We're busy," Jayden said. "We need to get back to our work, our important work."

"Very important work," I said.

"Very important sounds interesting," she said. "Let me help." She caressed my q-computer.

Who knew how the good or bad luck transferred? "Don't touch that!" I said.

She frowned but turned and traipsed towards the door.

"Please close the door behind you," Jayden said.

She did.

Jayden and I did not look at each other. Had I just said I wanted to hook up with him?

All right. I needed to get past this awkwardness between Jayden and me. I had scientific expertise, and I needed to use it. "We need to be more methodical with the experiment."

"I agree." Jayden dipped his chin. "What do you suggest?"

I wracked my brain. We needed something we knew was affected by probabilities, like gambling. Poor Gladys. Was it my fault she was dead?

"Ella?"

"Right. What about tossing a coin?"

"What? Like heads or tails?"

"Yes. If we flip a coin, there are only two possible outcomes, heads or tails. And both outcomes are equally likely."

"And each flip is supposed to be an independent event," he said.

"Right," I said. "So, we could study the number of outcomes, accumulate the statistics and see if they agree or disagree with the theory when the q-computers are on and off."

"That's great, Ella!" Jayden said. "We can prove one way or the other if the q-computers affect probability. It's quantitative, which is exactly what we want."

"And hopefully not dangerous," I said. Hopefully.

"All we need is a coin," he said.

I didn't have any coins. "Do you have any coins?"

"No. Who uses coins these days?" He stood and walked to the desks against the wall. "But I'm pretty sure I saw some pennies once in one of these desk drawers." He pulled out the center drawer of the center desk. "Yeah. Here we go."

We quickly devised a protocol to use. Since my q-computer could be turned off and on via my laptop, we decided to automate that process by running it for five minutes at a time. We wouldn't even necessarily know if it was on as we experimented, so it was sort of like a double-blind study.

For calculations, we decided to add prime numbers.

Jayden's computer had to be turned on and off by hand, so he was manning that.

That left me to do the actual coin flipping.

Later, we'd compile the data and determine if a particular coin flip corresponded to zero, one, or both q-computers being operational.

"All right," Jayden said, rubbing his hands together. "This is going to be good. Are you ready?"

I suddenly felt nervous. What would happen? "I'm ready. Are you ready?" I wiped my sweaty palms on my pants and picked up the penny.

"I'm ready," he said. "Go!"

I initiated the calculation on my q-computer. "So, we have a fifty percent probability of heads and a fifty percent probability of tails." I balanced the penny on my forefinger and thumb and flicked my thumb up. The penny flew up into the air.

And across the room.

I didn't even see where it landed. "Damn."

Jayden laughed.

Eventually, after many, many coin tosses, I'd mastered my technique. I could flip the penny about two feet above me and catch it. My thumb even started cramping.

My phone rang.

"Just a sec." I answered my phone.

It was Mrs. Flores. She plunged right in. "Hi. It's Mrs. Flores. I wanted to ask you if maybe you wanted to stay here at the B & B and work as the manager."

That sounded great. I hadn't gotten anywhere in my apartment search. I was so surprised I didn't answer immediately.

"I can't afford to pay you a salary, but I can forgive your bill, and I won't charge you going forward."

That sounded even more great. "Wow, Mrs. Flores, that sounds very generous." Considering I had no money, was this good luck? Could I stop thinking about luck?

"Will you think about it?" Could she be worried I wouldn't take the job?

"I will think about it," I said. "Can you tell me more about what's involved?"

The lab door opened, and Avery led in a guy in coveralls. "Greg came to change the light bulbs." He was a tall, trim older man, and I could tell he'd been lethal to the ladies when he was younger. Heck, I had half a mind to ask him out now myself.

I said on the phone, "Can we talk about it tonight, Mrs. Flores?"

"Sure," she said. "I'll see you then." We hung up.

Greg wrangled a cart with tools and supplies and carried a large ladder--which made sense because the ceiling was high. As he entered, he let go of his cart and twirled, checking out the ceiling. "Whoa. What happened to all the light bulbs?" The ladder swung around in a circle.

Jayden jumped up from the stool in front of his q-computer. "Please be careful." He reached for the ladder. "We have sensitive equipment in here."

"It looks like a bunch of computers," Greg said.

"Yeah..." Jayden said.

Greg started setting up his ladder.

I flipped the penny.

In the meantime, Avery had sidled over to me. "What are you doing? Flipping a coin? I thought you had such important work to do. That doesn't look important." She was clearly annoyed with us.

"I'm sorry if we offended you earlier," I said. "But this is work. We're testing probabilities with the coin tosses."

"Really?" she asked. "How does it work?"

I started giving her the run-down.

And then I'm not sure what happened.

Suddenly Avery was on the floor, under the ladder, and Greg.

Greg grunted and then said, "Ow. That hurt."

Avery didn't say anything.

I crouched down. "Avery? Are you all right?"

She didn't move. She didn't even seem to be breathing.

"Oh, no," I said. "Greg, get off her."

Jayden helped him up. They both lifted the ladder off her. She still didn't move.

"Avery?" I checked her for a pulse. I couldn't find one. I wished my mom or Crystal was here with their medical expertise. "I think she's seriously hurt. Call 911!"

I sat on the floor next to her. Oh, no. Not again. Did we do this to her? Did my q-computer do this to her? It got darker and darker in the lab, reflecting my mood.

Would she be okay?

I had a thought--optometrists were doctors, right? I jumped

up. "Stay with her!" I yelled at Jayden and Greg on my way out the door. I ran up the stairs to Hot Optometrist's office, aka Dr. Sanchez--which I'd just happened to scope out earlier.

The glass doors were open, but there was no receptionist at the front desk inside.

"Hello? Dr. Sanchez? We've got a medical emergency downstairs. Avery's hurt."

"Avery?" Dr. Sanchez appeared from the back. "Oh, no."

"Yeah, come on." I turned and ran back out the door, down the stairs and into the q-computing lab.

He followed me.

"Here." I pointed, a little out of breath.

In the q-computing lab, nothing had changed.

As the doctor knelt over Avery, he said, "Avery? Are you all right?" He put his head down near her mouth.

Jayden said, "Who the hell is this guy?"

Greg said, "The optometrist from upstairs."

"How do you know him, Ella?" Jayden asked. Interesting. He was acting like he cared like he was jealous.

I heard the ambulance siren approaching.

"I'll go meet the EMTs," I said as I ran out the lab door again.

I ran to the lobby, through the lobby, and held open the front doors as the ambulance drove up. "This way. Please hurry."

The EMTs jumped out of their rig and ran inside.

"Come on." I ran back to the q-computing lab, through the doorway, and pointed.

Dr. Sanchez was still leaning over her. Jayden and Greg still looked worried.

Dr. Sanchez said, "She's not responsive. I'm not sure what's wrong."

"Greg and the ladder fell on her," Jayden said. "It was a freak accident."

I didn't say anything. I needed to catch my breath.

One of the EMTs, a guy, took the optometrist's place, leaning over her. He glanced up at the female EMT. "Gurney."

She nodded briefly and turned to the door.

"Do you need help?" I asked.

"Sure," she said. "You can hold the door again."

I did so, and soon the two of us were back in the q-lab. The two EMTs loaded Avery onto the gurney.

I had to sit down. I was still breathing hard.

The male EMT said something to Dr. Sanchez, and he nodded. The two EMTs ran off with Avery.

I tried to catch my breath.

"Are you all right?" Dr. Sanchez asked.

"Yes, thanks," I said. "I'm just not used to so much running around." Or possibly injuring people with q-computers. Had I done it again?

"I think you helped her," he said. "Nice job. You're a good friend."

But I didn't feel like a good friend.

"What hospital did they take her to?" Jayden asked.

Dr. Sanchez replied, but I didn't catch it. Then, he said, "I'm sorry, I have a patient coming in, and my receptionist is out of the office."

"Thanks for your help," I said.

"Yeah, Dr. Sanchez, thanks," Greg said.

Dr. Sanchez left.

Jayden and Greg, and I were left standing in the lab. I was kind of stunned.

"Are you sure you don't need to get checked out, Greg?" Jayden said.

"I'm okay," he said. "I'm sorry about what happened to her. She's a real nice young lady. It was a freak accident."

Thunder boomed outside.

I understood why the room was so dark all of a sudden. "Jayden, is your q-computer still on?"

"Shit!" He raced over and turned it off.

The dark clouds outside dispersed.

"We should go to the hospital," I said. "But I don't have a car."

"I didn't drive today," Jayden said.

"I can give you guys a ride," Greg said.

"Okay," I said.

As we passed Avery's desk, I said, "Wait. I want to get her purse for her. And her phone. We should call her fiancé."

"She has a fiancé?" Jayden and Greg both said.

"Yeah." I couldn't help thinking of Gladys lying dead on the floor of the casino.

I hoped Avery'd still be alive for her wedding.

Chapter Thirteen

Greg, Jayden and I entered the hospital. The unique odor of chemical cleaners, bodily fluids and desperation assailed my nostrils. The KC hospital was considerably larger than the one I was used to in Lawrence. The front entrance atrium was huge and filled with people bustling around.

It also had a lot of green plants; that was a luxurious touch. I touched one, and they were real. Wow. It took a considerable amount of water to keep all these plants green.

We waited in a large waiting room near the front doors, but the doctors wouldn't tell us anything. I felt guilty. I hoped Avery was okay, or at least soon would be.

After about twenty minutes, a thirty-ish balding man ran in. "Where's Avery Rodriguez? I'm her fiancé. How is she?" He seemed very worried.

The admitting nurse spoke to him immediately. Unfortunately, we couldn't hear what she said.

The nurse whisked Avery's fiancé through the 'No Admittance' doors. We nodded as he passed us, but he just looked confused.

We waited some more. I was upset. Why didn't they tell us anything? Was she going to be all right?

Greg finally stood and said, "I have to get going. Can you guys let me know how she is?"

We nodded.

"Sure, Greg," Jayden said.

Greg left.

After what seemed like a long time, the fiancé came back out. He sat down next to us.

"Liam?" I said. "Are you Avery's fiancé?"

"Yes," he said. Up close, his eyes looked red, like he'd been crying. "Do I know you?"

"No," I said. "I'm Ella. I'm the one who called you on Avery's phone. And this is Jayden." I'd given Avery's stuff to a nurse earlier.

"Oh." His gaze drifted away.

"How is she?" Jayden asked.

"Yeah," I said. "Is she going to be okay?"

I was filled with a sense of dread. What had my q-computer been responsible for now?

"Thanks for calling me," he said, blinking rapidly as if fighting back tears. "She's not out of the woods yet." Oh, no. My heart went out to him.

He continued. "They said she was unlucky. The EMTs reported it was a freak accident. She's in a coma."

Unlucky? I recoiled. A coma? That sounded horrible. "Oh, no."

"I'm very sorry to hear that," Jayden said.

Liam turned to him. "You're Jayden? You work with her, right? What happened?"

"We aren't sure what happened," Jayden said.

We had a good guess, though. Q-computers happened.

"What do you think happened?" Liam asked.

"Our handyman, Greg, accidentally hit her with his ladder and then it, and he fell on her," Jayden said.

"How did all that happen?" Liam asked.

Jayden held up his hands and shrugged.

I started shaking. We turned on the q-computers, and we shouldn't have. I didn't know what to say. Now, it was my turn to fight back tears.

We sat there quite a while with Liam. I couldn't tell if we were helping or not.

Eventually, Liam said, "You guys might as well go. I can call you when I get more info."

I wasn't sure if we should leave or not. "We would appreciate any updates," I said.

"Yeah," Jayden said. "We can give you our numbers." We all exchanged numbers.

"I can stay longer," I said.

"Yeah, me, too," Jayden said.

Liam said, "Go."

"Are you sure?" I asked.

He nodded.

"I'll pray for her," I said.

"Okay," Liam said.

"Me, too," Jayden said. He started walking for the door.

"We're so sorry Avery got hurt," I said before I turned to leave. "We'll be hoping for her quick recovery."

Liam just nodded.

I followed Jayden outside. The sun was about to set. There was no sign of any clouds. "Uh," I said. "Now what?"

"Yeah." He was subdued. "How do we get back to the lab?"

Right. Greg had given us a ride here. "Cab? Uber?" I said, but I didn't want to spend the money.

"Well, that's neither here nor there."

Those words seemed incongruous coming out of his mouth. "What?"

"Sorry." Jayden shook his head. "My mom used to say that a lot. When I get upset, I seem to say things she says." Ah ha.

"Do you have any buddies that can come pick us up?" I asked.

"Don't you?" he asked.

"I just moved here, remember?"

"Right." He pulled out his phone. "Mike should be able to come. He better. He owes me."

Was this the notorious MIA super? I'll say he owed Jayden. Of course, after getting a nice eyeful of towel-clad Jayden, perhaps I owed Mike? In other circumstances, I might have grinned.

Jayden got a hold of Mike, and we waited for him in front of the hospital. Personally, I couldn't wait to get a look at the guy.

"All this luck stuff has thrown me for a loop," Jayden said.

I raised my eyebrows.

"Yeah, Mom again. It's like my whole paradigm has been turned on its ear."

He wasn't the only one.

An older dinged-up two-door something screeched to a stop in front of us. I couldn't decipher the make or model.

"Come on, already," the man inside yelled.

Jayden sighed as he opened the passenger door and gestured to the back seat.

"Why do I have to get in back?" I asked. "You guys need to drop me off at the lab first."

Mike snickered as Jayden got in the back.

I got in. Mike was a surprisingly tall redheaded, freckled-covered guy--sort of like a giant leprechaun. I couldn't help grinning. "Hi, Mike. I'm Ella."

"So, you're Ella! Hi, Ella." He screeched away from the curb. The inside of the car smelled like stale beer.

"Does this run on gas?" I asked. It looked old enough. "How do you afford it?"

"I know a guy," Mike said. "I have a gasoline-tax-exemption card." He grinned.

Wow. I'd thought those cards were hard to come by, very hard.

"Yeah, Mike knows a lot of guys." Jayden did not sound happy in the back seat.

"Jayden said you were smoking hot, but he didn't do you justice," Mike said as we narrowly missed an ambulance turning into the parking lot.

Wow. Jayden thought I was hot? I clutched the door handle. "What?" It wouldn't hurt to hear again.

"Smoking. Hot," Mike said.

Of course, he'd think that. Everybody thought that. I was smoking hot.

"Hey, don't mind me, buddy," Jayden said. "Just say whatever the hell you want."

Mike twisted his head around to look in the back seat and threw Jayden a mischievous grin. "Okay. Jayden here is horny for you. He told me himself."

"Hey!" Jayden said. "I did not say that. I wouldn't say something like that. It's disrespectful."

We careened around another curve. "Maybe you could slow down a bit." I glanced back at Jayden, and he was blushing. I was torn between wondering if blushing was sweet or if we were going to crash to our fiery deaths. "Maybe focus on the driving."

"Ooh! She's a bossy one," Mike said. "A little spitfire. You didn't mention that, buddy." For his part, Jayden didn't mention how super annoying this guy was, but I should have figured it out from what happened to him earlier. I was beginning to think walking back to the lab would have been the better choice.

Especially considering how unlucky people around me had been lately. I clutched the door handle harder. Were we about to die? I pulled out my phone and dialed Mom.

She answered. "Ella? What's up?"

"I love you, Mom. If something happens to me, please know that."

"What's going to happen?" she asked.

Next to me, Mike said, "Give me a break." But he slowed the car down.

I stopped feeling like I was going to die any second. "I don't know, er, think, anything's going to happen, Mom. I just miss you."

"I miss you, too, sweetheart," she said. "But I'm here with Aref. We're about to leave to go out to dinner."

"Okay. Have fun. I'll text you later." We hung up.

Before I expected, we were back at my workplace.

I jumped out of Mike's car as soon as he stopped. Even though I'd found out some juicy info about Jayden, I was very ready to get out of that car. "Thanks, Mike. Bye, Jayden. I can make sure the lab is locked." I didn't tell him I was going to take back my q-computer. If there was any more trouble, it wouldn't be because of me. I closed the car door.

"Wait, I want to get in front," Jayden started to say.

But the car zoomed off, so I couldn't hear what happened after that.

As I ran through the lobby, Avery's empty desk gave me a queasy feeling. I speedwalked back to the lab, and sure enough, the door was wide open. The ladder was still lying on the floor. I quickly approached Jayden's q-computer. It was off. Check.

My q-computer, on the other hand, was not off. Hell.

I powered it down.

As soon as I entered the front door of the B & B, Mrs. Flores said, "Oh, Ella! There you are! It's so nice to see you again."

I liked her. She was a good judge of character. "Likewise,

ma'am."

"So, have you given any more thought to my job offer?"

"Thank you for the generous offer," I said. "Can you tell me a little more about what it entails? You know I'm usually over at Qubyte during business hours."

"Yes. I know that. It's fine. Should we discuss it in the parlor?" She pointed at the room nearest the front door. I didn't think I'd ever been in a parlor before. It was full of delicate antiques and knick-knacks. It was the way I'd imagine a parlor to look.

"Actually, can I put my stuff in my room and change clothes first?" My stomach rumbled.

She laughed a little. "What would you say to supper?"

"I'd say, 'Hello supper, nice to meet you.'"

She laughed again. Easy crowd. "Okay. Meet me in the kitchen in a little while. But I have to warn you, it won't be anything fancy."

"I love not-fancy," I said and started up the stairs. In the flower-explosion room, I quickly slid my q-computer under the bed and put on jeans and a t-shirt.

Back in the kitchen, Mrs. Flores was making supper. Something delicious simmered on the stove. She'd gotten out some homemade-looking bread and cheese and butter and was busy slicing the bread into even slices.

"Can I help with something?"

"No." She gave me a mischievous grin. "I'm trying to bribe you with food. Sit down." She pointed at one of the stools around the generous kitchen island where she was working.

I sat. "I estimate your odds of success are good." Odds. Crap. What were the odds Avery would be okay?

She looked up at me. "Are you all right, dear?"

No. But I tried to buck up. This was a job interview, after all. "Sure."

She smiled and continued making sandwiches. "So, as an employee, you'd get free room and board. You could use the kitchen whenever you want."

"So far, so good," I said.

"I wouldn't mind help with the grocery shopping, however. Or at least unloading stuff from the car."

"Still good."

"The main duties would be keeping an eye on things upstairs at night and seeing to any guest needs. My hearing isn't what it used to be, and I don't always hear guests when I'm downstairs in my apartment."

"Still sounds good."

"It'd be great if you could do jobs that involve the stairs, like carry up clean towels and sheets from the laundry room in the basement. And luggage, if you're available. I'd also like help with the breakfasts. I try to do some food prep and baking the night before. Can you wash dishes if you're here?"

"Yes. All that sounds doable." All that sounded great. "But, as I said, I do have a day job. I can't be here during the day."

"I understand." She paused from ladling some of that great-smelling soup into bowls. "What do you say?"

"I say thank you for this opportunity. I'm grateful." Phew. So, I wasn't homeless after all.

We had a friendly dinner. The grilled cheese sandwiches and homemade soup were the best I'd ever tasted.

Afterward, I said, "Can I clean up?"

"I don't mind if you do," Mrs. Flores said. "I'm going to make myself some tea. Would you like some?"

"No thanks." Under her direction, I cleaned up the kitchen as she sat at the kitchen island.

"I'm already very glad I hired you, Ella," she said.

"I'm glad you're glad."

"I have a favor to ask," she said.

"Shoot."

"Can I get you to change rooms?" She looked uncertain. Uh oh. Usually, at this point--just when you relaxed your guard--something bad happened. "It's just that the garden extravaganza room is one of our most popular among guests. I have a very nice small room on the top floor."

I'd been worried all this niceness was about to come crashing down. "Of course, I'll change rooms!"

"It doesn't have all those pretty flowers," she said.

Sounded like a win, win. "I'll try to manage," I said gently.

When she said top floor, she meant top floor. The room was tiny but very cute, on the fourth floor, hidden under the eaves. It had a single bed against one wall, with what looked like a homemade nature-themed green-and-brown quilt. The little window over the little desk looked out over the whole Plaza neighborhood. It was perfect. Mrs. Flores told me the little bathroom across the hall was for my private use. She gave me a set of keys and asked me to keep an ear out for the front door.

During all this, in the back of my mind, I was worried about Avery. What if she died? How evil was my q-computer? But I kept shoving it down.

I dragged all my stuff up to my new room. Then I made the bed in my old room with fresh linens and replenished the towels in the adjoining bathroom. It felt good to accomplish practical things.

Back in my room, I sat on my bed and called Crystal to v-chat.

She answered right away. "Ella? I don't see any flowers. Where are you?"

I couldn't help grinning a little. "I got a job at the B & B!'

"That's great! What does it pay?"

"I get free room and board."

"That sounds pretty good." She nodded. "And it works around your Qubyte schedule?"

"Yep."

"Well, then, congratulations. I guess it's lucky we found that place, then, huh?"

We both froze as we realized she'd mentioned luck.

"Not that it's because of your q-computer..." She petered out.

For my part, my heart was pounding like I was in the finals of the World Poker Tournament.

After a few moments, she continued. "It's weird to think that somehow your q-computer could be controlling me. I don't think I like thinking that."

The disaster with Avery came rushing back despite my efforts. I pictured her lying on the ground, not moving. My eyes felt heavy. I pictured her being rushed away by the EMTs. I blinked back tears as I remembered her fiancé blinking back tears at the hospital. I cleared the lump in my throat.

"Then, don't," I said. "Let's not think about my q-computer.

How are things going with you and Zander?"

"They're still going," she said, but she didn't smile. "He's asked about you a few times. It's a little weird. You don't think he likes you more than he likes me, do you?"

I cut her off. "Of course he likes you; you're awesome. What's not to like?"

She nodded. But I could tell from her expression she wasn't convinced. "I don't suppose you've looked into Gamblers Anonymous? You know they have a lot of info online. I looked it up."

"Bless you for thinking of me, but I don't need Gamblers Anonymous," I said.

I heard a knocking sound on Crystal's end. "I think that's Zander, now," she said. "I gotta go." Zander got around pretty well for a guy with a sprained ankle. She logged off.

"Okay, bye," I said to no one. And then there I was in a strange room, in a strange city where I didn't know anyone.

I started thinking about Avery again. How was she? I could text Liam and ask, but that might be annoying. Instead, I said a quick prayer for her and then texted him, 'I'm praying for you and Avery.' I stared at my phone, willing him to text me back.

He didn't.

I wanted to talk to Jayden. I wanted him to tell me the accident today wasn't our fault, wasn't my fault. But I wasn't sure he'd say that. What if he said it was my fault? Ugh.

I clicked around on the internet and, just for the heck of it, did find the Gamblers Anonymous site. Nah. It wasn't for me.

But it did decry multiple online gambling sites. That made me curious, very curious. It wouldn't hurt to investigate...

Chapter Fourteen

As I played online poker in my room at the B & B, my phone beeped at 10:00 p.m. I didn't recognize the number, but it was local. I was ahead a hundred dollars; maybe it was time for a break.

"Ms. Hote?" a man asked. I didn't recognize his voice.

"Yes," I said. "Who's this?"

"Mr. Hernandez." Was that supposed to mean something to me? "From the casino," he added.

My heart started pounding. Would he accuse me of killing Gladys? Logically, my brain knew that didn't make sense, but my heart evidently had a mind of its own. Or was there trouble with Crystal's winnings? Was Crystal going to jail? "Yes?"

"You'd asked me to call you to tell you about the memorial for Gladys Meyer?"

"Right." My heart settled a bit. "When is it?"

"It's tomorrow morning at 9:00 a.m. at the Saint Martin Senior Living Community."

"All right," I said. "Thanks for the info." We hung up.

I immediately called Crystal. "Hi Crystal. I found out Gladys' memorial is tomorrow morning at nine here in KC. Can you come?"

"No," she said. "Sorry. I feel like I should go, but I can't."

"No?" I was so surprised I couldn't talk for a moment. She should go. "What do you mean 'no'?"

"I can't make it," she said. "I can't come all the way over there. I have class at nine, and I have to work right after."

"But..." How could she not come?

"I'm busy right now. I'm on a date, remember?"

"But..." We were the reason Gladys died. "You could invite

Zander?" That sounded like an odd idea as soon as it left my mouth.

"I want to go to the service, Ella," she said. "I'm sincerely sorry, but I can't. Now, I have to say goodbye." She hung up.

"But..." I stared at my phone. I had to go to the memorial. It wasn't even a question. But I didn't have a car and didn't want to go alone. I barely knew anyone in town.

I pondered the situation for a few minutes.

I could ask Jayden to go with me.

I dialed him.

"Hi, Ella," he said. "Did you hear something about Avery?"

"No," I said. "I texted Liam, but he didn't write back. Did you hear something?"

"No," he said. "Why are you calling? I hope nothing new is wrong." I did seem to interact with him during emergencies.

"No, nothing *new* is wrong," I said. "I have to go to a funeral tomorrow morning, and I was hoping you could come with me."

"Hmm," he said. "Well, you did save me with that clothes situation the other day." Oh, yeah, the naked situation. "I guess I owe you. Sure. Text me the when and where. I'll come to pick you up."

"Thanks."

Jayden picked me up punctually at 8:00 a.m. From the outside, his car was a well-used Prius. From the inside, it was filled with fast-food wrappers. On the plus side, it smelled good, like burgers and fries.

"Morning," I said as I got in the car. "I really appreciate this."

"What do you hear about Avery?" he asked.

"Liam texted 'no change,'" I said.

"So, whose funeral is it?" His brow was furrowed. "I thought you didn't know anyone in town."

"It's Gladys Meyer," I said as we pulled away from the curb.

"The name is vaguely familiar."

"I told you about her. Gladys is the woman who died when I was using my q-computer in the casino." I thought about arguing that it'd been a coincidence, but I didn't have the heart. I didn't think it was a coincidence.

"Oh, no." He looked horrified. "That sucks."

118

"Yeah." That about summed it up. We drove quietly for a few minutes.

Jayden glanced at me. "I know you live at a place with breakfast in the name, but I don't. Is it okay if we stop for coffee?"

"Sure," I said. I could afford it now that I didn't have to pay rent. And I had a new hundred bucks thanks to internet gambling. "Whatever you want, my treat. Coffee sounds great. I didn't get any this morning."

"How is that possible?" He paused. "Bed and breakfast." He emphasized the 'breakfast.'

"When I got out my black suit and dress shirt, they were very wrinkly. It must have happened in the move. And I don't have an iron."

"That sounds kind of unlucky." He frowned.

"Mrs. Flores said I could borrow hers, but we both got caught up in helping guests." I did not regale him with the tale of all the minor mishaps at the B & B this morning. "So, by the time I could iron, I had to choose between getting coffee and ironing." Ironing had seemed more respectful to Gladys.

"Well, you look good," he said, "not wrinkly at all."

"Thanks." He wore a dark suit as well. "You look nice, too. Not wrinkly either."

"I think that's the first time I've been told I'm not wrinkly." He chuckled. "What do you say we go through a drive-through?"

I was depressed about Gladys. Some coffee might perk me up. On the other hand, I might end up spilling it all on my non-wrinkly outfit. "I wouldn't want to put you out," I finally said. "But that might be nice. I can pay."

He turned and glanced at me. "Or, I could pay. You're on your way to a funeral, after all. You need something to cheer you up."

"Thank you. That would be nice." Any doubts I'd had about Jayden were evaporating. He was a nice guy and so not my type in terms of romance. But he'd make a great friend.

As he drove, I surreptitiously checked him out. He had a strong jaw and was more clean-shaven than I'd ever seen him. His usually unruly hair was combed neatly. I knew from before that his eyes could be kind of mesmerizing. Overall, he had a nice face. Trustworthy. Not my type at all.

"Why are you looking at me like that?" he said.

So much for surreptitious. "Like what? Uh, no reason." I quickly turned to look out the window, but not before I caught his grin.

We zoomed through the drive-through of a certain global-dominating coffee chain. After my first sip, though, I said, "Ah."

Jayden nodded. "See, I know what I'm talking about. That hits the spot, right?" He sipped his own.

I couldn't disagree. "You do know what you're talking about," I said. "Thank you very much. I really appreciate all this."

We made it to Saint Martin's senior living center without spillage or other mishaps.

Why hadn't there been mishaps? I'd have to ponder it later.

A giant mural of 'Saint Martin the Horse-Rider' greeted us from the wall near the receptionist's desk. According to the inscription, he was the saint of luck charms. I felt uneasy. Apparently, one day while riding his horse, Saint Martin came upon a naked beggar and cut his cloak in half to give the man something to wear.

"Saint Martin, do you know him?" An elderly woman interrupted our mural considerations. She was all decked out in a sparkly tracksuit, including sparkly shoelaces. Her hair was a pretty but unnatural shade of lavender. I wondered if it was intentional or some kind of accident.

"I can't say I've had the pleasure," Jayden said.

"He's the patron saint of those who hope a stranger will aid them," she said. "People say he's the patron saint of good luck."

"Uh." I felt a chill. This all seemed like too much of a coincidence. What were the odds Gladys would live in a place named for this guy?

Jayden glanced at me. "You don't say?"

"Yep," she said. "So, what are you folks doing here? We don't get many visitors--not that I'm complaining."

I found my voice. "We came for Gladys Meyer's memorial. I hope that's okay."

"Oh, my gosh! You must be Ella!" she said. "After she met you, Gladys texted me about you. I'm her best friend, Betty."

We shook her hand.

"Gladys, uh, texted you?" I felt pressure in my chest and eyes. Being reminded of how vibrant and special she was made me miss her.

Betty reached into her fanny pack and pulled out an iPhone. "Yep. She said she met the nicest young lady at the casino. Oh, I have to text the rest of the girls that you're here." Her thumbs flew over the screen.

I was torn between being amazed Betty was such a good texter and trying not to cry. Why did Gladys' death affect me so much? I didn't know her.

Jayden reached for my hand as if he sensed how I felt. "So, the memorial service--where is it?"

"The chapel," Betty said. "Down the hall. Follow the signs; you can't miss it. I'll see you there."

We left Betty texting in front of Saint Martin.

The chapel was almost full--mostly with senior citizens. It looked like the very old chapel you'd find in a monastery or nunnery or something, with high arched ceilings, big colorful stained glass windows on three walls, a white marble floor, and old wooden chairs set up in rows. "Wow, this isn't what I expected from the rest of the building."

"They must have built the old folks' home around this existing chapel," Jayden said. "It looks at least a hundred years old."

"At least."

Mr. Hernandez from the casino stood near the back and nodded to me as we went in.

I nodded back.

Jayden and I found seats on the side, and the service soon started.

I hoped I wouldn't have to go to a funeral for Avery soon.

They played some kind of pretty but sad instrumental music.

I kept checking my phone for new texts from Liam, but there was nothing.

"Pachelbel's Canon," Jayden said.

The minister, a very old man with a full head of wavy white hair, stood up in the front. "Beloved friends, it is not difficult for me to sympathize very deeply with you because I believe that in the departure of our dear sister, Gladys, I am as great a loser as anyone alive. I know many of you feel the same, and some of you asked to say a few words."

Betty made her way to the front. "I do agree with the minister here. I'll miss the old broad Gladys." I felt myself smile. Betty reminded me a lot of Gladys. "She was like a sister to me. She was a real pip, too, you know. The docs only gave her a few months to live, and that was two years ago!"

The congregation shifted and rumbled, leaving the overall impression they agreed that Gladys was a real pip.

"You all remember the time Gladys and I had fifty pepperoni pizzas delivered here, and poor Mr. Stuart, the security guard, didn't know what to do!"

I saw a lot of smiles around us. Judging from the crowd of white-haired heads, a significant portion of the home's population must be here. Wardrobe ran the gamut from nice suit and tie to sparkly tracksuit.

"And the time we got the real wine smuggled in for the so-called --," Betty made air quotes, " --wine and cheese tasting party." She chuckled. Others joined her. "And the time--"

A woman I couldn't see in the front row cleared her throat loudly.

Betty glanced her way. "Anyway, the point is: Gladys was a true friend, and she made the most of her life. She lived it to the fullest. I don't think she had any regrets." Betty turned her face to the sky. "Gladys, girl, get the party started up there, and we'll join you soon!"

Some of the other residents said, "Hear, hear!" and "Yeah!"

This made tears come to my eyes.

The minister stepped towards Betty. "Thank you, Miss Robinson."

Betty nodded and took her seat, her eyes shining with tears.

Overall, it was a very nice service with lots of music, hymns, heartfelt reminiscences from friends, and nice words from the minister. Gladys clearly had a lot of dear friends and was beloved by her community. She had a good life. I should be so lucky.

Afterward, as we all stood to exit, Jayden said, "Is it my imagination, or is that guy in the back staring daggers at you? Do you know him?"

CONSERVATION OF LUCK

I turned around. In the back of the room, next to Mr. Hernandez, a middle-aged man glared at me like he knew me and didn't like what he knew. Who was he? I gulped. If looks could kill, I would have been in grave danger.

"No one knows you had anything to do with Gladys' death, do they?" Jayden whispered.

People continued to file out of the chapel.

"No," I said. "Because I didn't." Maybe if I said it enough times, I'd believe it.

But the more I looked at the man, the more familiar he seemed. He was around six feet tall, with a thin build, tan skin and a hawk-like nose. The sense of familiarity made me feel weird. Prickly or something. I turned to face the front of the chapel. "Is he still looking?"

"Yeah," Jayden said.

I handed him my phone. "Try to take a picture without him noticing." I sat down.

Jayden did something, sat beside me, and handed me my phone.

I stared at the picture. He had a prominent chin and nose, intense black eyes, and tan skin. I felt like I should know this guy. He clearly knew me.

I sent my mom the picture with the text, 'Do I know this guy?'

My phone rang immediately. Mom.

Luckily, the chapel had mostly cleared out by this point.

"Mom?" I said. "That was quick. Do you know that guy? Do I know that guy?"

She didn't answer me immediately.

"Mom?"

Finally, she said, "That's your father."

Chapter Fifteen

I turned around and started shaking. I was staring at my MIA father across the chapel at a funeral. I couldn't believe it. I'd never seen him in person before.

"What's wrong?" Jayden asked.

The guy in question was still staring daggers at me.

What was he doing here? What did he want with me? Had he followed me somehow?

"Ella?" Jayden touched my shoulder. "Who's that guy?"

"My deadbeat dad. Supposedly."

The whole chapel had cleared out except for me, Jayden, my dad, and Mr. Hernandez.

"What?" Jayden asked.

Seemingly under their own volition, my feet started walking towards my dad.

"Where are you going?" Jayden asked.

I stared daggers back at the guy. How dare he follow me around! And he crashed Gladys's funeral. How creepy.

As I approached, Hernandez and Dad both took a step back.

"Ms. Hote," Mr. Hernandez said, "is there something we can help you with?"

"Gee, I don't know," I said. "Why don't you ask him?" I jabbed my finger in Dad's direction.

"You seem upset, Ella," Dad said.

My whole body shook. "Do you think so?" My voice shook as well.

"I don't understand." Hernandez's head ping-ponged between Dad and me.

"Me neither," Jayden said from behind me.

"Calm down, Ella," Dad said.

"You have no right to tell me to calm down," I said.

"Maybe we should go," Hernandez said.

"Yes, maybe that would be best," Dad said. They walked quickly toward the door.

"Oh, no, you don't," I said. "I have things to say, things I need to say to you."

They ignored me.

"You can't leave!"

They'd left. I just stared at the door.

"They're gone, Ella," Jayden said. "Maybe you should sit down."

I let him lead me to a chair. My whole body vibrated, and I felt nauseated.

"Are you all right?" he asked.

My phone rang. I absentmindedly answered it. It was Mom. "What happened? We got disconnected. What did your dad say?"

I deflated as all the energy collapsed out of me at once. "He said I seemed upset and told me to calm down, and then he basically ran away."

"I'm so sorry, Ella." She paused. "He's not the father you deserve. But you have to know it's not your fault."

"I know." Logically, I knew it. Emotionally was another matter.

"Do you want me to drive over there? I've been meaning to see your new place and meet this Mrs. Flores."

"That would be nice."

"I'll be there at five-ish."

"Sounds good." We hung up.

Yeah, I was a grown woman, and I wanted my mom. So what?

"Don't worry," I said to Jayden. "I'm okay. The episode is over."

"Are we staying for refreshments?" he asked.

"I don't think I'm up for it."

"Okay," he said very calmly like he was afraid to agitate me.

"Let's go." I led the way back to the car.

"Can you explain what just happened?" he asked.

"No," I said.

Once we were on the road, he said, "Where to?"

I didn't want to be alone with my thoughts or, more accurately, my feelings. "The lab?"

"Okay."

We drove for a while before he said, "So, do you want to talk about it?"

"Not really."

He opened his mouth. He closed his mouth.

"That was my dad," I finally said. "We've never met. He owes my mom many thousands of dollars of child support." I refrained from saying he missed all my ballet recitals, church choir performances and every single solitary one of my graduations--and there had been quite a few.

"I don't know what to say," he said. "Yikes."

"Yikes?" I felt the corner of my mouth turn up. "Is that your Mom's influence again?"

He snickered. "I guess so. Indubitably."

I snickered a little as well. Having a new friend was nice.

We drove in silence for a while more.

"What do you think he was doing there?" he asked. "Could it be another luck thing?"

I shrugged. "I have no idea. He did not seem to be there to see me."

"Who was that other guy he was with?"

"Hernandez?"

He shrugged.

"That was odd," I said. "Hernandez works at the casino where Gladys died."

Jayden glanced at me. "Yikes?"

I couldn't make heads nor tails of all this.

Yikes, indeed.

When we got to the lab building, I very carefully did not look directly at Avery's desk as we walked by.

"Have you heard anything new about Avery?" Jayden asked.

"No," I said. "Did you hear anything new?"

"No," he said. "But I'll try to find out." He pulled out his phone.

The door to the quantum computing lab was unlocked. So much had happened lately, I couldn't remember if I'd locked it yesterday when I left or not.

"I don't see your q-computer," Jayden pointed at the lab bench. "Did you take it home?"

"Uh..." I wasn't sure what to say. I did take it home, but I didn't want to admit it. What if he asked me to bring it back? I didn't want to bring it back.

In the meantime, Jayden glanced all around the lab. "It couldn't be stolen, could it?"

I froze. Stolen? I knew it wasn't stolen. It was under my bed at the B & B. But if Jayden thought it was stolen, that could solve my problems. I wouldn't be able to use it (in front of him, anyway), and thus I wouldn't be responsible for anybody's bad luck. Or death.

"Oh, no," I said woodenly. "You must be right. How unlucky. Gosh, darn."

He peered at me. "Are you sure you're okay?"

"Close enough," I said.

"We better call the cops about the stolen q-computer," he said.

"No," I said. "I don't think that's a good idea, what with bad luck and all."

"I'm not following," he said.

"Please just don't call the cops for now," I said. "Maybe it will turn up."

"It's your q-computer, so I'll hold off if you want. But what if the thief turns it on and does something dangerous?"

"Then it will be on my head," I said. If it had been stolen, that would be a serious problem. But it hadn't been, so it wasn't.

"I guess we should get back to work?" he said. "More coin tosses?"

Why was he asking me? He had more seniority than me. He had a Ph.D., for Christ's sake. I was in a bad mood. Take a breath, Ella.

"Good idea. It will be a good test to see if we need my q-computer." I put my stuff down, sat on a lab stool, and reached for the coin.

Flip. Flip. Flip. Flip.

After what seemed like an eternity, Jayden said, "I need a break. You want a soda or coffee or something?"

I was wearing my one-and-only nice suit that I didn't want to get drenched with soda or coffee or something. "I guess that would be okay if you turn off your q-computer."

He did so. "Good idea."

It turned out the little coffee place in the building next door, KC Cafe, was pretty deserted in mid-afternoon. The employees seemed bored to death.

Personally, I didn't see how they could avoid gorging themselves on the cinnamon rolls the place always seemed to smell like.

Jayden walked right up to the counter, ordered two coffees and paid before I quite knew what was happening.

I opened my mouth to object, but I didn't want to seem ungrateful. "Thanks a lot. I'll get the next one, buddy."

"Buddy?" He grabbed the cups, handed me one, and walked to the coffee station.

"What about buddy?" I asked. "Is buddy bad?"

He grinned. "Well, not many of my buddies have seen me naked."

"I, uh, didn't see anything much." I saw oh-so-much. Why didn't men walk around unclothed more often? All kinds of women wore skimpy tops and tight pants; why not men?

"Aw," he said, the corners of his mouth turning up. "That's kind of harsh."

"I mean, I saw much stuff, good stuff. It was good." Ugh. I was babbling.

"I'm just giving you grief, Ella." He laughed.

After a moment, I couldn't help laughing, too.

We sat at one of the little cafe tables. I focused on my coffee. Good grief, what was it with this guy that discombobulated me so much? Maybe it was bad luck.

"So are we going to go on a date or what?" he asked, eyes twinkling. Twinkling? Ugh. What was wrong with me?

Of course, he wanted to date me. The question was: why would I want to date him?

On the other hand, I didn't know eyes could actually twinkle.

"Uh."

"I'll take that as a yes," he said. "Tonight? We're already dressed for it, not wrinkly and all."

"I can't tonight, gosh darn," I said quickly. Yes, he made me very nervous. Saved by the mom. "My mom's coming in."

"Oh, good," he said. "I get to meet your mom."

"I don't think so." I put my coffee down on the table, and some slopped out. "We're not at the mom-meeting stage."

He got up and procured napkins, damn it. He wiped up the spill.

"Quit being so nice," I muttered.

"What was that?" he asked. "I didn't quite catch it."

"I said, thank you for cleaning up the spill. Let's put a pin in the date talk for now."

"Aw." He grinned. What grown man said 'aw'?

"It's been kind of a long day already. Can we focus on the experiment?"

"Yes." He sipped his coffee. "What do you think we should do next?"

"How about you do some calculations, like summing prime numbers, with your q-computer while I keep flipping the coin?"

"Calculations on my computer?" he said. "Dr. Tuche didn't authorize that."

"Where is Dr. Tuche?"

He frowned. "Avery would know."

I stared at him. Did he find out how she was earlier?

"I need to find out how Avery's doing." He pulled out his cell and stood up.

"I'll meet you back in the lab in a little while," I said.

He nodded.

I got up and walked up and down the block for a few minutes, trying to calm down.

I noticed there was a toy shop in the middle of the block, with a bunch of dice in the window. I went in. I bought dice. We could use them to test luck, right?

Walking past the coffee shop on the way back to work, I realized I didn't want to go back to work; I was sick of coin flips. There were still a few coffee-drinking souls inside. It was like they didn't have anything better to do. It was like they were looking for something to do.

I examined the small paper bag in my hand. I knew just what they could do. I went inside. "Anybody in here know how to play craps?"

Everyone glanced up with curiosity.

I pushed a big table against the wall, took the two dice out of the little bag and held them up. "So the idea is that the shooter rolls the dice on the table, and they hit the wall. We bet on the rolls."

One of the employees approached.

I braced myself for her to shut us down before we began.

The employee said, "Ooh. I played this in Vegas. Can I be the first shooter?"

I grinned. "Yes, you can." I handed her the dice.

"So, who thinks she'll pass on her first roll, which is rolling a seven or eleven, or crap out by rolling a two, three, or twelve?" I asked.

"I pass," the roller said. "For a dollar."

"I bet a buck she'll crap out," the guy with the beard said.

"Me, too," the skinny guy with the glasses said.

"Okay, I'm in, the crap thing," the woman who looked like a housewife said. "A dollar."

I rubbed my hands together. "Excellent. I bet all of you a dollar that she'll roll something besides two, three, seven, eleven, or twelve."

"Is that allowed?" the employee asked.

"We can bet anything we want," I said. My dice, my rules. This was gonna be great. They were all clearly inexperienced in craps.

"So I roll now?" the employee said.

I smiled. "Sure."

She rolled the dice and got a five and a four. "So, that's the point, right? My pass bet becomes a point bet?"

I smiled some more. "Yes. You want to roll nine again." I looked at them. "And you all each owe me a dollar."

They frowned but handed the money over.

I said, "All those crap bets are now bets that the shooter will seven out. So who thinks our lovely employee here can roll another nine?" I asked.

Unfortunately, my luck was not enhanced that afternoon--at least not in a good way. I ended up handing back the three bucks I won, as well as twelve more bucks. At that point, I shut it down.

"I saw you here earlier," the employee said, clutching extra bills in her hand. "Do you live or work near here?"

"Yeah," I said. "I work at Qubyte, next door."

"Well, you're welcome to come over and play craps any time." She grinned.

When I finally got back to work, only about an hour after I'd left Jayden, he relayed there was no change with Avery.

I suggested we try throwing the dice instead of tossing the coin, but he didn't go for it.

We spent a long afternoon working in the lab. If I never saw another coin again, it would be too soon.

I kept my eye on the clock, and at four forty-five, I stood. "Gosh, I need to go."

"What grown woman says 'gosh'?" he asked, smiling.

I tried not to let the fact that our minds worked similarly freak me out. "This woman, apparently. I'll see you tomorrow? Maybe we can start analyzing the data?"

"Okey-dokey." He grinned.

A strange car sat in front of the B & B when I arrived home. What now?

Chapter Sixteen

With some trepidation, I walked past the fancy new car and entered the front door of the B & B. It was a shiny bright red Kelvin, complete with the solar panel body.

"Oh, there you are, dear," Mrs. Flores called out. "We've been waiting for you."

Who was we? It couldn't be deadbeat Dad again, could it?

"Hello, Ella." Mom turned around from where she was sitting on the couch.

"Hey," Hannah said, smiling, sitting next to her.

I felt like an overcooked noodle for a second and leaned against the front wall.

"Are you all right?" Mrs. Flores asked.

What was wrong with me? "Yes." I straightened, quickly walked over to them and gave them each a hug. "Thanks for coming. You made great time."

"Yeah." Mom nodded. "We left Lawrence before rush hour."

"I had no idea your sister and your mom were so charming, Ella," Mrs. Flores said.

"I had no idea your boss was so charming," Mom said. It looked like I'd interrupted a mutual admiration society.

"Yeah, yeah, everyone's charming," I said.

Mom frowned. Except me, maybe. Maybe I wasn't too charming right now. Change the subject, Ella. "So, whose car is that outside? It's fancy."

Mom beamed. "It's mine! Isn't it pretty? I've never had a brand-new car before. It's solar Kelvin. I hardly ever have to use the battery. It turned out to be lucky that you totaled mine, Ella."

I felt my lip curl. I was sick of that word 'lucky.'

"You totaled her car?" Mrs. Flores asked. "That doesn't

sound good. You weren't drinking, were you?"

Mom and me and Hannah all stared at her. Drinking? Where'd she get that?

"Ella's not a big drinker," Hannah piped up.

I flashed her a smile, wondering if she realized she'd implied I was a small or medium drinker. The two of us had had quite a few discussions about alcohol. Seventeen years old was a tricky age. Legally, she couldn't drink. Realistically, everyone she knew at her high school did drink.

"Considering it was around 6:00 a.m. and she wasn't even driving," Mom said, "I'm pretty sure drunk driving wasn't a factor."

"I, uh, just hope no one was hurt." Mrs. Flores backpedaled.

"No drinking was involved," I said. "It was a parking incident."

"Parking?" Mrs. Flores asked. "How do you total a car in a parking incident?"

Mom glanced at me. "It's a long story. The point is it all worked out for the best."

I plopped down between her and Hannah on the couch.

"How did it go with your dad?" Mom asked.

"Bad," I said.

"You met your dad! Wow!" Hannah said. She knew I hadn't met him before. She hadn't met her dad either. That was something we had in common.

I nodded.

"What was that like?" Hannah asked. She was probably imagining it was a dream come true.

I felt my lip curl up. "Not great."

Mrs. Flores looked like she wanted to say something but didn't.

"I'm sorry you were surprised like that," Mom said. "I'd heard John was in Kansas City. I should have warned you. Where'd you run into him again?"

Yes, a warning would have been nice. "A funeral."

Mrs. Flores gasped. "A funeral? I'm so sorry for your loss."

"Me, too." Mom leaned in for a hug. I collapsed into her arms for a moment. It had been a stressful couple of days. Actually, since I got my master's, it had been stressful. I sat up. Actually, for that matter, since I'd gotten my quantum computer to work, it had been stressful.

"Do you want to talk about your loss?" Mrs. Flores asked.

"Not really." I leaned back on the couch. I basically killed a woman. I did not want to talk about that. I glanced at Hannah. Especially in front of my little sister, I didn't want to talk about killing people. Can you say 'bad example?'

"Are you sure?" Mom asked.

I nodded.

"Uh, okay," Mrs. Flores said. "So, what does this John do?"

"I heard he was into gambling," Mom said.

"That doesn't sound good," Mrs. Flores said.

No, it didn't. But..."Could he be working at a casino?" He was with that Hernandez guy from the casino, after all.

Mom nodded. "Yes. Maybe. That makes sense. His people are against gambling."

"So, how does that make sense?" I asked.

"He rebelled against the values of his people," Mom said.

"His people?" Mrs. Flores asked.

"Oh, yeah," Hannah said. "Ella's a First Nations People, er, person. It's super cool."

I flashed her a smile. She was sweet.

"John's Native American, Hopi," Mom said. She'd told me all this when I was a girl, but I hadn't thought about it in a long time. Technically, it meant I was Native American.

"I thought all Indians, er, I mean Native Americans, had casinos," Mrs. Flores said.

"Nope," Mom said. "The Hopi are the Peaceful People, and being civilized and peaceful is the Hopi way."

"Aren't all those tribes the same?" Mrs. Flores asked.

"*Ooooh!*" Hannah glanced at Mom and me. We'd had several discussions about people's preconceptions about Native Americans.

Now Mrs. Flores was in for it. I'd thought the same thing when I was young and ignorant--like twenty years ago. But Mom had set me straight.

"Of course not," Mom said. "Each tribe is like its own nation. Would you say the United States and Canada are the same?"

"Pretty much," Mrs. Flores said. "At least the Canadians wish they were the same as us."

134

"Don't let any Canadians hear you say that," I said, snickering a little. I'd had a Canadian friend at KU who hated comments like that.

"Or, are the United States and Mexico the same?" Mom said.

"Uh, no," Mrs. Flores said. "They have those cartels... Er, I mean, the people have darker, er... It's warmer down there."

The three of us stared at her again. Finally, Mrs. Flores said, "Nope. Of course, they're not the same. Totally different."

I suppressed a smile. So did Hannah.

"Anyway, the Hopi are against gambling," Mom said.

"How do you know so much about it?" Mrs. Flores asked.

"We visited John's family on the Hopi reservation in northeastern Arizona when we were first married. His mom was lovely. She's since passed."

I felt a wave of sadness. I never got to know my lovely paternal grandmother.

Mrs. Flores didn't react to the marriage comment. They must have had quite a discussion before I got here.

"I don't get it," Mrs. Flores asked. "John doesn't sound like an Indian; I mean Native American, name."

"His given name was Jolon," Mom said. "He goes by John. I don't know if he legally changed it or not. For that matter, I don't think Hote was his family's original surname."

"How did you and John meet?" Mrs. Flores asked.

"Haskell Indian Nations University," Mom said. "When I was going to KU, they had a program for students to interact with the Haskell students. We had dances and fun runs and stuff like that. I was curious because I'm one-sixteenth Wichita."

I'd heard all this before, but my circumstances were different now. "What does the Wichita tribe think of gambling?"

"They're all for it," Mom said. "They have a big casino complex in Anadarko, Oklahoma." Did that mean I had gambling in my blood from Mom's side? Ha! Take that, Crystal! Gamblers Anonymous, my ass.

Someone in the foyer cleared his or her throat. An older couple stood just inside the front door.

Mrs. Flores jumped out of her chair. "Are you checking in?"

"Yes," the man said.

I got up. "Do you want me to take care of it?"

"No, no," Mrs. Flores said. "You visit with your mom and sister."

"Okay," I said.

Mrs. Flores led the couple to the front desk and started checking them in. Their discussion was pretty loud as the proprietress regaled them with tales about how great the Plaza was.

In the lull in the conversation, I took a deep breath. I wasn't in immediate danger after all. That strange car out front was Mom's. Phew. I took another deep breath.

I needed to de-stress.

Of course, I had reason to be stressed. Avery. I checked my phone for messages. Nothing. Darn it.

"Are you all right?" Mom asked.

Not really. But I didn't want to get into it. Still standing, I nodded. "So, do you guys want to see my room?"

"Sure," Mom said.

"Definitely!" Hannah said.

We climbed all the way up the stairs, and I showed them my cute little room.

"Nice," Hannah said. "You have this all to yourself, huh?"

I nodded.

"And you don't have to pay rent or anything?" she asked.

"Nope," I said. "I help out around here." I knew Hannah was worried about what would happen to her when she turned eighteen and got kicked out of the foster care system.

I walked to her and put my arm around her shoulder. "Don't worry. We'll figure something out for you when you graduate. I promise."

Now it was her turn to nod.

Mom had sunk onto the bed, puffing. "I thought I was in good shape from running around at work, but maybe not." She breathed heavily for a few minutes.

To be honest, I was glad to get an opportunity to suck in some air, too.

Finally, Mom said, "This room is really cute." I knew she'd like it. "You've done well for yourself, Ella. I'm glad. I knew you didn't enjoy being kicked out of the nest, but it was time."

Damn. She was right. I was twenty-four and a half, after all. I sat down next to her on the bed. "I didn't want to go."

"No!" She expressed mock surprise. I ignored it.

"I don't blame you," Hannah said. "Your mom is so nice."

Mom turned and smiled at her. "Thanks, honey." She turned back to me. "I have a feeling you're going to thrive here, Ella."

"Thanks, Mom," I said. "But enough about me. How are things going with that Aref guy?"

She giggled. "Good. I really like him." I guessed so if she was giggling at her age. "I hope my issues with your dad haven't impacted your opinion of men. I may have complained about him too much. Not all men are bad, you know."

"I do have trouble imagining you with that John Hote," I said. "How come you don't have any pictures of him around the house?" I refrained from saying, 'he seems like a jerk.'

"It ended poorly," she said. "It was a whirlwind romance, very romantic and passionate. Love at first sight."

I could feel myself frowning. Passionate? Maybe I didn't want to hear about this.

"It didn't last, but I have no regrets. It gave me you. And you're the best thing that ever happened to me." She put her arm around me.

I looked at Hannah. "How about you, H? Any romance?"

She looked upset. "Sort of."

Cryptic. "Do you want to talk about it?"

She stared at me and my mom sitting on my bed. Mom still had her arm around me. "No." She looked down at the floor.

"Are you sure, H?" I asked. "I'm always happy to talk to you."

"I'm sure."

For some reason, I thought of Jayden for a second. Had I ever fallen in love? I wasn't sure. Crystal had told me if you weren't sure, you weren't in love. I didn't know if I agreed with her.

After Mom and Hannah had gone home and I'd cleaned the kitchen up after Mrs. Flores, I decided to try online gaming again. It had gone great last night, and nothing bad had happened. I debated it but decided to turn on my q-computer and do a little

'1 + 1' calculation. No one else was around, so what could go wrong?

I found the same site I played last night, put in my credit card info, and started playing poker. On my first hand, I got four of a kind, it was four threes, but it was still four of a kind. "Sweet!" This hand would be hard to beat.

And then the power went out in my room. "Crap!" So much for nothing going wrong because of my q-computer.

From down the hall, I heard a man say, "Help? Can you help us?"

It must be that older couple we'd checked in earlier. I thought they were the only guests right now, anyway.

I got my phone to use as a flashlight and went out in the hall and down the stairs, calling out, "Don't worry. We'll have the power on in a jiffy." Hopefully.

The power seemed out in the whole house.

From the basement, I heard, "Ella? Are you there?"

"Yes, Mrs. Flores!" I called down to her. "Just a minute!"

The older couple stood in the doorway of their room. "What happened?" the woman asked.

"Just a little power outage." I smiled. "Nothing serious. In the meantime, how about I get you guys some candles? It'll be romantic."

"Thank you," the man said.

I ran down the stairs.

Mrs. Flores had come up from the basement and now stood near the front door. "Oh, good. There you are, Ella."

"Does this happen a lot? Do you think we need to reset a breaker, fuse or something?"

"No. I can't recall this happening before " She pointed out the front window. "It's the whole neighborhood. What do you think happened?"

Oh no. I felt a chill slither up my back. Me and my q-computer. That's what happened.

The next morning, I was on pins and needles the whole way to work.

"What's wrong?" Jayden asked when I walked into the lab. "You look weird."

"Thanks," I said. "I love being called weird." Not.

"That came out wrong," he said. "Weird and beautiful too, of course."

"Thanks." It was cool being called beautiful. Of course, I did deserve it. I smiled. "I guess I'm still feeling the aftereffects of sort-of meeting my dad." And causing a power blackout. And hurting Avery.

"Any word on Avery?" I asked.

"Yes." He sat in front of the lab's q-computer. "Liam texted me that the doctors said she was improving and she might wake up soon."

"Way to bury the lead!" I said. "What a relief! That's great news. Tell me as soon as you hear more." So maybe I wasn't totally evil.

"Yeah, okay." He nodded. "How's your mom?"

"She's good," I said. "She has a new boyfriend." I paused for a moment. Did Hannah have a new boyfriend? Something was up with her.

"Ooh, la, la," he said.

That had to be his mom's influence again, but why would he be nervous now? I raised my eyebrows.

"Anyway, back to work!" he said too loudly.

"Yes, sir." I sat down in front of one of the lab computers.

"Are you sure about not calling the cops about your stolen q-computer?" he asked. That again?

"I'm sure," I said. "I have a feeling it'll turn up." It would turn up if I took it out from under my bed again.

"What's next?" I asked. "More coin tosses?" Lord, no.

"I can't face any more coin tosses right now," he said. Something else to be thankful for. "Let's start compiling the data we've got and see if there are any patterns."

"How do you want to do it?" I asked. "A timed series of heads and tails, and ons and offs? We could put time on the graph's horizontal axis and indicate everything that happened."

"Good idea," he said. "You could plot step functions. If the computer is on, the value is one."

"Yeah. I get it," I said. "If the computer is off, the value is zero. Similarly, if the coin is heads, let's call the value one; if it's tails, it's zero."

"And then we can compare the three different time series and see if any of the ones are coincident and how often." I would have said that if he'd given me a chance.

"I'll start with the data from my q-computer," I said. "Can you start with the data from your q-computer?"

"Yes, ma'am." Was he being polite or sarcastic? I glanced up at him. He wore a seemingly sincere smile. Polite. Huh.

We got to work.

The time series for my q-computer was trivial since it had been turned on and off on a regular schedule, namely, every five minutes. I just had to get the correct starting time, and then it was all automatic. I finished my plot before Jayden completed his.

I watched him work for a couple of minutes. He was very attractive in a nerdy nice way--which made sense since he was a nerd and nice. He was the kind of guy Crystal usually went for (Zander was not).

Could Crystal be right when she'd said I'd never been in love?

"What?" Jayden noticed me checking him out. Damn.

"I finished, boss," I said. "Should I start on the coin toss data?"

"What do you think?" he asked.

"I think 'yes.'" I got to work.

It was very tedious work because I had to extract the exact toss times from the digital record before I could plot them.

At about eleven thirty, my stomach growled.

"What was that?" Jayden looked around the room. "Thunder?" He was suspiciously straight-faced.

"You're joking, right?" I asked.

"You never know when a freak rainstorm might break out around here." He grinned. "But, yeah, I'm joking." He rubbed his forehead. "It is just me, or is this data analysis hideously boring?"

I needed a break. Desperately. "It's not just you."

"Lunch?" he asked.

"Definitely." I stood up.

"I think I'm going across the street to the Lucky Star. Do you want to join me?"

I stared at him. We'd been spending a lot of time together

lately. Maybe too much time. We weren't dating, after all. He wasn't my type, after all.

"I think I'll pass." I grinned to soften the blow. "I'm not much of a day drinker."

He seemed surprised for a second but only said, "Okay. See you back here at about one o'clock?"

I nodded. "Sounds good."

I needed some fresh air and sunshine. I decided to take a walk and look around for a new place to eat.

Outside it was already shaping up to be a scorcher, but the sunlight felt good on my skin.

I strolled a block over to the Plaza and then strolled along the sidewalks with the tourists. I pretended I was a rich tourist with no cares in the world other than spending my loads of money and having fun. Wouldn't that be nice?

My stomach growled again, and I stepped into a coffee shop. The glass case displayed a bunch of rolls and buns, and croissants. The shop smelled faintly of chocolate.

"Hello. Welcome. Where are you from?" the employee asked, smiling.

She thought I was a tourist from somewhere else? How fun. "Paris," I said with a fake French accent.

"Really?" she said. "Er, I mean, how wonderful. I'm guessing you want a croissant sandwich, maybe *avec jambon et fromage*?"

Huh? But everything tasted good on a croissant, right? "Yes, I mean, *oui. Jambon. Fromage. S'il vous plait.*"

"*Et cafe?*" she asked.

I guessed that was coffee and nodded forcefully.

She was smiling as she handed my lunch over, but if she thought I was lying about being French, she had the good grace not to say so.

I sat at one of the cafe tables in the front window and imagined I was in Paris. Some day I would be in Paris.

Jambon et fromage ended up being cheese and ham. It was yummy. I enjoyed my lunch and watched folks walk by.

And then I thought I saw a familiar face look into the cafe. Zander's familiar face, to be specific. But that was impossible.

As soon as whoever it was saw me, they jerked away.

I jerked back. Should I follow him? But I wasn't done with my lunch, so I decided against it.

When I finished up and bussed my table, the employee beamed at me. "*Merci beaucoup.* Would you like a complimentary chocolate? We make them on the premises using an ancient French recipe. It should remind you of home." What were the odds of free chocolate? Apparently, one hundred percent!

"Yes! I mean, *oui.*" I took the treat gratefully, and it was delicious. Not running after the mystery guy was definitely the right decision.

On my way back to the lab, I caught a weird reflection in one of the store windows. It appeared to be a familiar-looking guy on crutches following me.

I turned around. "I see you, Zander!"

He seemed surprised at my confrontation and started hobbling away. Quickly.

I took off after him.

Amazingly, the guy eluded me. How could somebody on crutches move that fast? The crowd thinned, and I couldn't see him anywhere. I was standing outside a fancy furniture store, however. Maybe he'd gone in there?

I entered. A woman glided up to me immediately. "Can I help you find something, ma'am?"

"I'm looking for, uh, a friend of mine. He's on crutches. Did he come in here?"

"I think someone on crutches did come in." She pointed towards the back. "He went out that way."

I raced in the direction she pointed. But when I got outside to the back alley, there was no sign of anyone.

Mysterious. What was he up to?

In the lab, Jayden was already working when I got back. "How was your lunch?"

"Mysterious." I sat down.

"Say what now? Mysterious how?" he asked. "Did something quantum happen?"

"No. I don't think so. Never mind. Let's just get back to work."

"I sent you the data from my q-computer," he said. "Can you combine all the times series into one big plot?"

"Yep." I'd already started working again. "Piece of chocolate..." I could still taste that delicious sweet, creamy chocolate.

"What?"

"I'm on it, boss."

I finished all three time series plots and then combined them.

I stared at the amazing final plot on my screen. "I'm done," I finally said. "Do you want to come and see?"

"Yes." Jayden quickly joined me in front of the screen. "Wow." He pointed as the ones lined up exactly. "Every time both the q-computers were on, we got heads."

"Yes," I said. "We should compute the correlations to prove it quantitatively."

"Wow," he said.

"Wow," I said, staring at the plot. I'd suspected the q-computers could affect probabilities, but seeing it in concrete, quantifiable data was something else entirely.

All my nervousness was justified. What had we discovered?

I had a sneaking suspicion there was no way to put the genie back in the bottle.

Chapter Seventeen

In the quantum computing lab, Jayden and I had just proved that q-computers affect probabilities.

"We can write a kick-ass paper on this!" he said.

My cell rang. It was Mrs. Flores. "Hold that thought, Jayden," I said.

"Hello, Mrs. Flores," I said. "Is everything okay? Did the power go out again?" It had come back on sometime during the night.

"No. Nothing like that. I'm sorry to bother you, dear," she said. "I have bad news."

Uh oh. What now? Did someone else die? Or end up in the hospital? My stomach sank. "Is my mom okay?"

"Your mom?" she said. "I don't know. Did something happen to her?"

In the lab, Jayden said, "Something happened to your mom?"

"Mrs. Flores," I said. "Why are you calling me? What's the bad news?"

"Sorry, dear," she said. "We had a break-in here at the B & B. I'm not sure when it happened. We just noticed."

"Now? During the day?" That was one balls-y burglar. "Is everyone okay?" I asked.

"Yes. No one was hurt."

"I'm glad to hear that." I paused. "Is there something I can help you with?"

"I'm sorry to say they broke into your room," she said. "I can't tell if they took anything or not. I'm about to call the police. You should be here."

My room? The thieves must be after my quantum computer.

Oh no!

Get a grip, Ella. I was getting ahead of myself. Run-of-the-mill thieves wouldn't be tempted by it--it didn't look like a regular computer.

I had a feeling in my gut, a bad feeling, that Zander was involved. I bet that it wasn't a coincidence that I'd seen him earlier.

"Ella?" Mrs. Flores said.

In the lab, Jayden asked, "Ella?"

"I'll be right there, Mrs. Flores." I hung up.

I stood.

"Where are you going?"

"I have to go back to the B & B. There was a break-in." I grabbed my purse.

"But we're right in the middle of something," he said. "Do you have to go right now?"

"Yes." I sighed. "I'll be right back." I walked to the door.

"What about the correlation analysis?" he called after me.

"It'll have to wait."

The police were already at the B & B. Mrs. Flores sat on the very edge of the couch in the front parlor, looking like a nervous wreck. Her color was off, and she kept fidgeting.

Two patrolmen stood over her. It was disconcerting seeing large men in the delicately decorated room. Somehow the spindly side tables, floral carpet, and antique couch seemed out of place. But, it was the cops that were out of place--with their uniforms and giant belts covered in equipment. Neither one of them had much hair. They must have shaved their heads. They could have been father and son. One looked about forty-five, and one looked about twenty-five.

"Are you sure I can't get you, gentlemen, coffee?" Mrs. Flores shifted on the sofa. "It'll just take a jiffy."

"Hello," I said, closing the front door behind me. "Mrs. Flores, are you all right?"

She jumped up. "Oh, Ella. Thank goodness."

The cops stepped toward me.

"Are you Ella Hote? The employee?" the older cop asked.

"Yes." I walked to Mrs. Flores and put my arm around her.

She was shaking.

"Oh, Ella," she said. "I'm so sorry. They got in your room. I was downstairs in my apartment. The last guests had gone out, and I was taking a little rest. I'm sorry." Her eyes filled.

"Please calm down, Mrs. Flores," I said. "It's not your fault."

"If you were in the basement napping, how do you know someone broke in?" the older officer asked.

"I heard a crash," Mrs. Flores said.

"What broke?" one of the officers asked.

She pointed at the remnants of a vase on the floor near the front door.

"Have you guys been up to my room yet?" I asked.

"No," the older one said. "We've been waiting for you."

The four of us climbed all the way up to my room. Mrs. Flores and I were the only ones breathing hard at the top of the stairs. I guess cops really did keep in shape. And, clearly, I'd been spending too much time in the lab.

The door to my room was wide open. I hadn't left it that way.

I stepped inside. The place was a total shambles. Every drawer had been emptied onto the floor. Everything from the closet had been thrown onto the floor. The mattress had been upended and leaned against the wall.

I threw myself to the floor and scooted under the bed, looking for the q-computer. But there was nothing there. It was gone. This was bad. This was catastrophic. A criminal had my q-computer. Who knew what he'd do?

"Ms. Hote," the older cop asked. "What are you doing?"

I scooted back out and stood up. "I was looking for my student project. It looks like the thieves took it." These were not your ordinary thieves. Zander must be involved, but how'd he get up here with his sprain?

"Was it valuable?" the younger cop asked.

That was a good question. It was very valuable--but only to people who knew what it was. "Well..." I said slowly. "I made it for my master's degree. I spent about two or three hundred dollars in parts." But those were raw materials. I'd also utilized thousands of dollars of university resources in terms of computing power and fancy microscopes, etc.

"Why did the crooks take it, then?" the older cop said.

"It was a prototype of a new type of computer."

"If it was valuable, why did you have it here in your bedroom?" the younger cop said.

That was a very good question. I'd thought I was protecting people. I was evidently an idiot. "I don't have a good answer for that."

"Do you have a picture of it?" the older cop asked.

I nodded and got out my phone. "Yeah. I can send you a picture."

He gave me his contact info, and I sent him the pic. He grunted when he saw it. "It's not exactly impressive looking. Who knew it was a new kind of computer?"

"Well, everyone at my master's defense knew about it," I said. "And there's another guy, Zander Jones, who saw it work. Here, I'm sending a picture of Zander, too." We'd taken plenty of pictures on our road trip to KC

I didn't mention luck at all. I didn't think the cops would believe me.

"We'll fill out a report and let you know if anything develops," the older cop said in a monotone.

The younger cop just shook his head.

I wasn't holding my breath.

I tried calling Crystal. No answer. I left her a voicemail asking if she knew how to contact Zander.

I called Professor Smithson to tell him what was up, i.e., that the prototype had been stolen. He didn't answer, so I also left him a voicemail.

Back at the lab, walking by Avery's still-empty desk, I felt sad and worried. Was she okay? She might be a casualty of my q-computer. I texted Jayden, 'Anything new on Avery?' He texted back: 'No.'

Did whoever took my q-computer know what they had? Probably. Otherwise, they wouldn't have taken it. I couldn't be one hundred percent sure it had been Zander.

Did they know how to use it? I was hoping not.

I called Crystal again as soon as I got into the lab and sat down.

"Hi, Ella," she said. "I'm at work. I can't really talk."

"This will be quick," I said. "I just need to talk to Zander. What's his phone number?"

She didn't answer me.

"Crystal?"

"Why do you want to talk to him?" she finally asked.

I didn't have the heart to tell her her boyfriend was very suspicious and probably had been following me, and he might be a thief. "I just do." I needed to get that q-computer back ASAP.

"Well, that's gonna be tough," she said. "He disappeared. He changed his phone number; I don't know the new one. I even went by Freestate Brewery, and his manager said he didn't leave any forwarding address, number, or anything." She sounded sad.

My heart went out to her. She didn't deserve to have her heart broken by him. "Oh, Crystal. Why didn't you tell me? I know you liked him."

"And I know you didn't like him," she said. "I didn't tell you because it's embarrassing. I was into him, and he disappeared like some kind of spy."

Or criminal. But I didn't say that. "I'm so sorry, Crystal," I said.

"Thanks. Who was he, Ella?" She made a sound like a sob. "The manager at Freestate said his name was Zander Smith, but he told me his name was Zander Jones."

Wow. He was even sketchier than I thought he was. This was hard on her. "We'll talk later, Crystal," I said. "I love you."

"Love you, too." She hung up.

I texted the cop this new info about Zander.

When I looked back at Jayden, he was holding up pieces of paper stapled together. "What's going on?"

"My q-computer was stolen," I said.

"Yeah, I know," he said.

"From the B & B," I said. "Today."

"I thought it was stolen the other day from here in the lab," he said.

"I know." When did I turn into such a liar? "I lied. I thought I was protecting people by not using it."

"I don't understand why you would lie to me. Not cool." Jayden's gaze had moved to the window. "Wait. Where did that storm come from?" He stalked to the window.

I followed him. Dark clouds roiled over downtown. Lightning flashed, and thunder thundered. "Oh, no!" The last time I'd seen a storm develop so suddenly, q-computers were involved. The thief must know how to use the stolen q-computer. And since the storm was in the area, the thief was probably still in the area.

Damn. We were so screwed. Who knew what he would do?

Get a grip, Ella. I tried to think. "Is your q-computer on?"

"Yeah." Understanding dawned. According to our recently-analyzed data, we saw the biggest effect with the coins when both q-computers were on. He ran to his q-computer and powered it down.

I should have thought of checking his q-computer as soon as I'd found out mine was stolen.

I stared out the window. Were the clouds falling apart? Yes. Phew. I unclenched. "I think that helped."

Jayden joined me at the window. "It looks a little stormy but just regular stormy." His expression when he looked at me was definitely on the stormy side.

"I'm sorry," I said. "I made a mistake. I shouldn't have lied to you. I definitely shouldn't have tried to hide my q-computer at the B & B. I screwed up." I wasn't used to screwing up. It was a weird new feeling. My eyes felt hot.

"Well, good grief, girl," he said. "You're not the devil. So, you made a mistake or two. As Mom would say, it's no use crying over spilt milk." He paused. "We all make mistakes. I've made mistakes. One time I managed to lock myself out of my apartment essentially naked. I had a towel, but it was locked in the door so that I couldn't move."

A burst of laughter escaped me. I couldn't help it. "Really? Wow. That sounds stressful."

"And my hot co-worker had to come to save me." Now he looked serious.

My heart pounded. I didn't know what to say. "Oh?" As Jayden would say, 'good grief, girl.' Why was I so emotional around him?

My phone rang. It was Professor Smithson. "Hi, Ella. What's up?"

"As I said in the voicemail, it looks like thieves stole my q-computer from the B & B."

"Why would they do that?" he asked.

I shrugged. I thought they wanted to control luck, but I didn't think Professor Smithson would want to hear that.

"Ella?"

"I'm not sure," I said.

"This isn't good," he said. "Technically, that q-computer is university property."

Ugh. I'd forgotten that.

"Do the police have any leads?"

"I told them about my master's defense and a couple of other people who knew about the q-computer, but they didn't seem too optimistic."

My facial expression must have been pretty bad because Jayden said, "What now?"

I held my finger up.

"Ideally, it will turn up," Professor Smithson said.

"Yes. That would be ideal." That would be good luck. I didn't know how realistic it was.

My mind was racing. Zoom. Zoom. "Uh, what if I built another one for you? To replace the original? Do you think that would be appropriate?"

Two q-computers working together had a stronger effect, according to the data.

Maybe two q-computers working against each other could cancel each other out or something? Maybe we could use a new q-computer to fight the effects of my old q-computer? I'd have to think about that for a bit.

After a few moments, he said, "That could insulate us. Do you think you could do it? Quickly? It took you almost two years to build the first one. We don't have that kind of time."

"I take copious notes and keep excellent records, Professor Smithson. I do think I can build another one in a few days."

Jayden scooted his chair right up next to mine. "What's happening?" he whispered in my ear. His breath felt warm on my face.

"Especially," I continued, "if I had some help from one of my Qubyte colleagues."

"That would be great, Ella," Professor Smithson said. "Should I plan on seeing you tomorrow in the lab?"

"Yes, sir," I said. We hung up.

"What's going on?" Jayden asked again.

"Well, to avoid getting in even more trouble, I'm going to Lawrence." I smiled at him. "Any chance you want to come along and help me build another q-computer?"

Chapter Eighteen

The next day found me getting into the passenger seat of Jayden's battered Prius. He'd cleared out the fast-food wrappers, but I could still faintly smell burger.

I'd talked to Liam on the phone, and he'd said the doctors were optimistic about Avery's recovery. Yeah, I was in a good mood.

I wished I could say I was surprised Jayden agreed to help, but I wasn't. I don't think I've met such a nice guy before. He probably deserved better treatment from me.

Well, there was no time like the present.

As we pulled out of KC, I said, "So, Jayden, thanks for your help. I appreciate it."

"You're welcome." He glanced at me.

"What's the Jayden story?"

"Huh?"

"I feel like I've sort of sucked you into all my drama. Who's Jayden? What's the Jayden drama?"

"Hmm." He stroked the steering wheel. "I'm not sure where to start."

"Start at the beginning."

"Okay," he said. "Here's the highlights: I was a late-in-life baby, a surprise. My folks, they were older than my friends' folks, treated me like I was a precious gift."

"Only child?"

"Yes. I grew up in KC. My dad died when I was in college at M.I.T." He paused for a moment. "I also got my Ph.D. at M.I.T. I've been at Qubyte for," he scrunched up his face, "three years. And then you showed up."

"I'm sorry about your dad," I said.

"Yeah. It was tough. The three of us were pretty tight."

"How's your mom doing now?"

"She had to move into an assisted living place, but she seems to like it pretty well. She's made a lot of new friends-- which is good for her."

"That sounds nice," I said. The miles were piling up behind us. "That was kind of a concise summary. Did you have any hobbies or sports or anything?"

"Well, I'm not going to tell you that when I was in school, I tried out for the baseball team every year and never made it on the team."

I snickered. "Yeah, better not tell me that."

I didn't hear anything about any girlfriends in that summary. "So, ever have any serious relationships?" I asked.

"You talk," he said. "Have you ever had a serious relationship?"

I hadn't considered it before. "Serious? No." Someone as hot as me couldn't be tied down, right?

"Fair enough," he said. "I was with my high school girlfriend for seven years."

"Seven years! That sounds serious."

"The first three years were great. But then we tried to do the long-distance thing when I went off to M.I.T., and she went to Mizzou. It didn't work. It would have ended earlier, but I leaned on her when my dad died."

I felt bad for the girl. After seven years, she probably expected a ring. "What happened?"

"She fell in love with a guy at Mizzou," he said. Okay, I didn't feel bad for her. "They're married with three kids now. I'm the godfather."

"Godfather? To the kids? You stay in touch?"

"Of course." He grinned. "I can't wait for you to meet them."

"You seem remarkably well-adjusted."

"Thank you." He seemed pleased--whether it was with himself or me noticing his mental health, I couldn't tell.

"I've sort of been seeing this girl Ashley," he said.

What did 'sort-of seeing' mean? I decided not to be nosey. What did I care, anyway? I didn't. I didn't care at all.

"So, why quantum computing?" I asked instead.

"I wanted to pioneer a new kind of computer and change the world. Make the world a better place."

Wow. That was a good answer.

"How about you? Why quantum computing?"

"What you said," I said. It was my new official answer to that question.

We were quiet for a while.

"You said we could stay with your mom, right?" he asked.

"Yep. Right." I couldn't afford to stay anywhere else.

He grinned. "So, now we're at the mom-meeting stage?"

"Apparently so." I grinned back. He was pretty funny.

"Thanks for helping me," I continued. "If there's anything I can ever do for you, don't hesitate to ask. You've been a true friend."

He looked at me out of the corner of his eye.

Was friend a bad thing? Had I just insulted him? "Not that you are friend material, er, only friend material," I said. "I like you."

He glanced at me and smiled. "I know."

"What?" I sputtered. "What do you mean, you know?" I barely knew; how could he know?

"It's obvious," he said. "You're nervous around me."

And here I thought I'd been playing it pretty cool. "But--" More sputtering.

He chuckled.

I didn't know what else to say. Why didn't he say anything back? Did he like me back? Well, I wasn't going to ask him. I crossed my arms.

We drove in silence for many miles.

Finally, he cleared his throat again and said, "I should admit, I like you, too." Of course, he did. I was very likable.

Conversation resumed, and moved on to more neutral topics. Among other things, it turned out Jayden had a regular poker game with his buddies. Now, that sounded interesting...

"Mom! We're here!" I yelled as Jayden, and I walked in the front door. I did not immediately see her in the kitchen or family room--which was odd because it was close to dinnertime. I figured she'd be cooking up a storm in anticipation of my arrival. I didn't smell anything delicious.

"Are you sure it's all right for me to stay here?" Jayden asked, looking around.

I imagined how it must look to him: a small condo with worn but comfortable furnishings, complete with a handmade afghan on the back of the couch and some of my framed childhood artwork on the walls.

"Of course, it's okay. Mom always says my friends are welcome." I stalked around the house. Her fancy new car was outside; where was she? "Mom!"

Her bedroom door opened, and she emerged, belting her robe, her hair in total disarray.

Jayden chuckled. "There she is."

"Mom!" Did she have a man in her room? I was shocked.

"Wow," she said. "You guys made good time from KC. I wasn't expecting you until a little later."

"We'd be happy to get out of your way, Mrs. Hote," Jayden said, smiling.

"Oh, Jayden!" Mom said. "It's so nice to meet Ella's boyfriend for once."

She stepped towards him with her hand out.

That was premature. "He's not my boyfriend," I said.

Jayden smiled like the cat with a whole flock of canaries as he shook Mom's hand.

"Of course not, dear," Mom said, but she said it like she didn't believe me.

"Thanks for letting us stay here," I said, rising above it.

"Don't hurry back," she said, turning and heading back into her bedroom.

I decided it was just as well that she hadn't cooked me a feast. I had some detective work to do--at a restaurant.

"I like her," Jayden said.

"Yeah, I like her, too," I said. "She's a good person."

Jayden just grinned at me. "So, what next?" He pointed at the kitchen. "Are you going to cook for me?"

"Dream on." His humor was pretty contagious. I grinned back.

"I am here doing you a favor."

"I know. I'll buy you dinner." My poor credit card was getting quite a workout these days. "Come on."

When we got to the Freestate Brewery, Crystal was already there waiting at the bar. I'd asked her to meet us in hopes of cheering her up a little. We used to come here all the time together. The high ceiling with ducts and pipes and the assortment of wooden tables and chairs all seemed homey now. It smelled of beer.

She jumped off her stool as soon as she saw us. "You must be Jayden. Wow. It's great to meet Ella's boyfriend for once."

Jayden flashed me his cocky look.

"He's not my boyfriend!"

Crystal scanned him up and down. "Too bad. He's cute."

"I like her, too," Jayden said, smiling.

"Yeah, yeah," I said. "You like everybody." I suppressed my own grin.

We went over to the hostess stand to procure a table.

Crystal sidled up next to me and said quietly, "I'm not sure about being here. What if we run into Zander?"

"Good," I said. "I'm trying to find him." I was truly trying to find my stolen q-computer. "I hope we do run into him."

We followed the hostess to a table. I asked her, "Can I talk to the manager?"

The hostess looked surprised. "Yeah, I guess. I'll go get him."

Crystal and Jayden also looked surprised but sat.

I joined them.

"What's that about, Ella?" Jayden asked.

Crystal and I exchanged a look.

Finally, I said, "There's a guy that worked here that was very interested in my q-computer."

Jayden leaned forward. "You think he might be the one who stole it?"

"Yes." I nodded. "I do. Not that many people even knew about the q-computer."

"Don't forget, you presented it at your defense, and also..." Crystal said.

"What?" I asked her.

"I may have mentioned it online," she said.

"Crystal!" I said.

"What?" she said. "You never said I couldn't." That was true. But I didn't know q-computers were so dangerous. Or so enticing to thieves.

"Please take it down when you get a chance," I said.

A middle-aged man approached our table. "I'm the manager. What seems to be the problem?"

I smiled brightly. "No problem. We're trying to find an employee, Zander...?"

"Zander Smith?" the manager said. "Yeah, good luck. He only worked here for a few days. The police contacted me about him. They said that's not even his real name." The manager looked angry. "You have no idea how much trouble I have with employees here."

"Did he leave a forwarding address or anything?" I asked.

"Nope."

"Did you pay him?" I asked.

"Nope," the manager said. "I cut him a check for the days he worked, but he hasn't picked it up." He crossed his arms. "Good riddance. Did you know he caused a flood in here one night?"

"Gosh, no. I didn't hear that." Gosh? Jayden must be rubbing off on me. "If you hear from him, can you contact me?"

He peered down at me. "Who are you, again?"

"Just a concerned citizen," I said.

"No," he said. "I'm not contacting you. Did you have something relevant to say about the restaurant here?" He waved his arms around.

"Uh, good job?" I said.

He whirled and stalked away.

"Smooth, very smooth, Ella," Jayden said. He chuckled.

Crystal looked upset.

"Are you all right, Crystal?"

"Not really," she said. "I don't understand what happened with Zander. We hit it off so well. I don't get why he disappeared."

I debated telling her I thought I'd seen him following me in KC But didn't that imply he'd been interested in me all along and not Crystal? Oh, no. What if his romance with Crystal had just been a ruse to get my q-computer?

I patted my best friend's hand. "It's a mystery. He'd have to be crazy to disappear on you."

"I agree," Jayden said. "I just met you, and even I can tell that's crazy. You're great."

Our waiter came and took our beer orders. We perused the menus and made some small talk.

The waiter brought our drinks, and we ordered dinner.

"So?" Crystal asked. "Why are you guys here in town?"

I exhaled. "My q-computer was stolen."

Crystal looked confused. "Sorry."

"Well, Professor Smithson reminded me that it's officially university property," I said. "I don't want to get him or me in trouble. So, we came here to build a new one."

"I can't wait to learn how to do it," Jayden said.

I suddenly felt uneasy. Was it a good idea to teach other people how to build what was essentially a luck machine?

"What's that look about, Ella?" Crystal asked.

Darn. She knew me too well. "I think my q-computer might be dangerous. Gladys died."

She paled.

"Avery, our receptionist, is in the hospital. And there's been a lot of other weird luck stuff going on." I summarized everything that had happened since I got my q-computer to work.

"You said something at the party," Crystal said. "Something about luck being a real thing...."

I remembered that. I also remembered I'd been on the verge of thinking something... My brain tingled.

"Earth to Ella," she said.

"So if luck is real...." I glanced up at them, and they both nodded. "What if there's a finite amount of luck in the universe?"

"What?" Jayden furrowed his brow. "Like it can't be created or destroyed?"

"You guys have lost me," Crystal said.

"What if luck is conserved?" I said. "So, if I have good luck, it means I'm taking someone else's good luck, leaving them with bad luck?" My brain was feeling very zing-y. This hypothesis did sort of fit what had been happening. "So, if someone had a lot of good luck, it would have to be balanced out by someone having an equal amount of bad luck?"

"Huh," Jayden said. "So the universe not only conserves

mass and energy, it also conserves luck?"

"Yes." Zing. Zing. "Maybe it's even related to conservation of energy somehow?"

"Huh," he said. "Interesting."

"You guys got me," Crystal said. "I have no idea what you're talking about."

"Sorry, C." I put my hand over hers on the table. "Shop talk. Let's talk about something else." The conversation moved on to other things.

But I thought I was onto something.

After a tasty dinner, good conversation and some yummy brews, Jayden and I dropped Crystal off at her place on the way back to Mom's. It was pretty late.

"I like her," Jayden said as we were driving away.

"Yeah," I said. "You were right when you said she was great. We've been friends since we were little kids. Thank you for being nice to her."

"I think you cheered her up about this Zander guy."

I sighed. "I hope so."

"You think he took your q-computer?"

"I guess," I said. "But where'd he come from? It was almost like he knew about the q-computer before he met me. Crystal said he acted like a spy, and she wasn't wrong."

"So you think he's a spy?" He seemed to be fighting off a smile. "For who?"

I shrugged. "I don't know. Industrial espionage? What other companies are working on q-computers?"

"Hmm." He looked thoughtful for a moment. "I'll check."

We got to Mom's. The night air was cool, and a breeze ruffled my hair. We walked to the front door under the full moon. The front stoop smelled of dust and dry plants.

As I started to put the key in the lock, Jayden said, "Wait a minute. We have unfinished business."

I looked up. He was standing right next to me.

He leaned down and pressed his lips to mine.

Chapter Nineteen

Jayden and I managed to roll into Professor Smithson's--aka my former--lab bright and early the next morning. The large-ish rectangular room filled with black bolted-down lab tables piled high with equipment looked the same. It was kind of bizarre because it felt like it had been years, or at least months, since I'd been here.

I sipped the giant coffee I'd gotten on the way in. I'd slept on the couch poorly, so I was already awake when the sun came up. The smooch situation was totally unresolved. My mom had interrupted us, then we went to bed (separately), and then we were rushing around trying to get to the lab on time. And, okay, maybe I didn't want to talk about it. I was confused about Jayden. He wasn't my usual type of guy, but we had some kind of crazy chemistry.

"This is my old lab." I waved my hand around, noticing the plywood. They still hadn't fixed the window. I had mixed feelings about coming back here. I'd accomplished a lot, and it had felt like home. But, it also turned out to be the source of a lot of problems.

I was experiencing unusual levels of stress. Avery was probably going to be okay, but Gladys wasn't. What would happen next? What would Zander (probably) do with my q-computer?

"Where the magic happened?" Jayden asked with a grin.

"Okay." I sat down and took a sip of coffee. Then, I yawned.

"I'm sensing you didn't sleep so well last night," he said. "You didn't have to give me your bed."

"Yes, I did," I said. "You're here as a favor, and you're too tall for the couch. Your feet hung off."

He grinned lasciviously. I had a feeling I was in for some sexual innuendo. It could be fun. "You know what they say about feet hanging..." He paused. "Nope. I got nothing."

I chuckled. "That's probably a good thing. I was wondering where you were going to go with it." I took a few more coffee gulps and then carefully put the cup on my former desk in front of the plywood-covered window.

Okay, Ella, time to rally. I grabbed one of my lab notebooks. "We should make a shopping list."

"What happened there?" Jayden asked, pointing at the plywood.

I glanced up. "Oh, yeah. The security guard shot at me."

"What!" He looked alarmed.

"I told you about it," I said, flipping through the book. "He thought I was breaking in or something. Glass flew all over the place." I scowled. "And I broke my phone."

"That doesn't sound good."

"Well, he did miss me." I found the page with the equipment list. "And in all fairness, he wasn't a hundred percent at the time, what with the heart attack."

"What!"

"I took him to the hospital. He's okay now. I think." I looked up from the book. "I should ask Professor Smithson."

"My ears are burning," Professor Smithson said from the open doorway. "You are here early. Good." He walked towards us with his hand outstretched. "You must be Dr. Macuill. Nice to meet you." They shook hands.

"This is my advisor, Professor Smithson," I said. "Nice to see you, sir."

"Nice to meet you, sir," Jayden said.

"I've heard good things about you from Dr. Tuche," Professor Smithson said.

"That's nice to hear," Jayden said.

"Sir, have you heard anything about the security guard who had the heart attack?" I asked.

"As a matter of fact, I did hear he's out of the hospital and doing well at home," he said.

"You don't happen to know anything about Dr. Tuche, do you?" I asked.

"I know many things about Ryder Tuche, but I'm not sure they're appropriate to tell you." Professor Smithson flashed us a big smile. "Can you be more specific?"

Now, I really wanted to know what he knew.

"He's on travel now," Jayden said. "Do you know where he is or when he's coming back?"

"He didn't tell you?"

"No." I shook my head.

Smithson laughed. "Are you sure he's even on a work trip? He likes to go on what he calls 'walkabouts,' where he gets out into nature away from technology. One time I went with him to Colorado, and we went hiking in the mountains and got lost."

"That sounds awful, sir," Jayden said.

"No, it was fun, an adventure." Professor Smithson grinned.

Personally, I didn't think I could handle being away from technology for so long. I hadn't had a phone for several hours last week, and it about killed me.

"So, anyway, I came by to drop this off." Professor Smithson dug in his pocket and came out with a wad of cash. "It's two hundred and fifty dollars from petty cash. I know grad students are poor, and you haven't received your first check from Qubyte yet." He held it out.

I rushed up to take it. "Wow. Thank you, sir. I really appreciate it."

"And consequently, it probably would be better if you don't take the new prototype off university grounds," he added.

That was going to seriously crimp my crime-fighting plans. "Uh, yes, sir." I didn't let myself frown.

"I have to go," he said. "I have a faculty meeting. If I don't see you by the end of the day, please email me a progress report."

"Yes, sir," I said.

Professor Smithson left.

"That was generous of him," Jayden said. "Now, you don't have to pay for the prototype."

"Yes, it was," I said. "Especially since I'm pretty sure there's no petty cash fund." Now, I frowned.

"Why so glum, chum?"

"If we have to leave the new prototype here, how will we

use it to counter or find the stolen q-computer?"

"That is a pickle," he said.

A snort of laughter escaped from me. "A pickle?"

"I was trying to lighten the mood." He grinned.

"Mission accomplished." I grinned back at him.

My brain was zinging along. "I had already resigned myself to the additional expense. What if..."

"Yes?" Jayden asked.

"What if we made two new q-computers? One for Professor Smithson and one for us?"

"Brilliant!"

By late morning, we'd finished our shopping and were back in the lab.

"All right," I said. "Here we go!" I flipped open my lab notebook.

Growl, grumble, Jayden's stomach said. He said, "Sorry."

"Or, maybe we should get lunch first before we get all engrossed in all this?" I asked. Yes, I was stalling. The pressure was on: I needed to successfully build not one, but two, new q-computers in a day or two when it had taken me more than two years the first time.

"I could go for lunch," he said.

"What about Mexican?" I was missing all my favorite places. "What about *El Cerdo* Cafe? It's right downtown." Maybe ordinary life would calm my nerves.

"*Cerdo*?" he asked. "What is that, pig?"

I shrugged. "I don't know what it means other than delicious Mexican food."

"Miss Hote, would you join me for luncheon?" he asked.

"What?" I said. "Like a date?" So he did remember our kiss last night.

"Yes, exactly like a date."

Now my pulse raced for another reason."Why don't we see how it goes?" I smiled to lessen the blow.

El Cerdo was just as I remembered it, unassuming decor but friendly staff. As we entered, I smelled garlic and some other unidentifiable spices.

Jayden said, "Hey, we're just down the street from that

brewpub you like."

"Yep," I said. It felt nice to be home. I felt a little calmer.

Jayden and I eased into a booth. The server, a cute young woman, set down glasses of water and handed us menus. I just put mine down on the table.

"What? Now you're not ordering?" Jayden asked.

"I already know what I'm getting --pork enchiladas."

"That does sound good." He started perusing the menu. "How about this chicken and pork dish with a wine sauce?"

I nodded. "Good choice."

The server gave us some chips and salsa. I dug right in.

"How about the beef and pork chimichanga?"

I nodded. "Good choice."

"How about the pork loin tacos?"

Another chip. I nodded. "Good choice."

He blew out air. "Well, you're no help at all!"

"What can I say?" I said. "They've got a lot of good stuff here."

The server reappeared. "Hi, I'm Harper. Do you know what you want?"

"Yes, I'll have the pork enchiladas, some more chips, and some guacamole."

"And to drink?"

"How about some Boulevard beer? Do you have the unfiltered wheat?"

"Yeah." She scribbled on her pad of paper. She turned to Jayden. "And you?"

"I'll have the chicken and pork in wine," Jayden said.

"Drink?"

"The KC Pils." He smiled. "I'm patriotic."

"Got it. I'll put it in right away." Harper continued writing as she walked away.

"How is the KC Pils patriotic?" I asked.

"I'm from KC. I'm supporting my hometown." He smiled again."Why did you order more chips? We still have chips."

I raised and lowered my eyebrows. "Not for long." I snagged a chip and grinned.

"So you like this part of town, huh?" he asked. "Is it considered downtown Lawrence?"

"It's a fun area. I did come here a lot when I lived here." My brain was tingling. I wasn't the only one who came here a lot. A lot of people my age liked to come here. I wondered if Zander had ever been here? I scrolled through my phone, looking for a picture of him.

After a large number of chips and a small number of minutes, Harper brought our beers and more chips and some guac. She may have looked a little surprised as she took away the empty basket.

"Harper, can I ask you a question?"

"Sure." She seemed a little worried.

I held out my phone. "Have you ever seen this guy?"

She peered at the picture. "Zander? Why?"

Jayden started.

"Yes!" I said. "Who is he? How do you know him?"

"Zander Williams," she said. "He used to work here."

"What else can you tell me?"

She shrugged.

"Okay," I said. "Thanks!"

She departed our table.

I debated grilling the rest of the staff. That hadn't worked out so great last night.

"Wow," Jayden said. "How'd you think of asking her about him?"

"I have to text that cop," I said. "Zander's got a pattern. He's worked for at least two places on this block and uses fake and super-boring last names." I did so.

I leaned back and tried to relax. I drank some beer. I ate some more chips.

"What do you have, a hollow leg?" Jayden asked.

I snickered. "Is that a polite thing to say? Anyway, I'm fortifying myself for the massive amount of work we have to do this afternoon."

"Oh?" Jayden had been about to sip his beer but stopped. "How massive are we talking?"

I engineered a large helping of guacamole onto a chip and munched it. After chewing and swallowing, I said, "Well, the trickiest bit was getting the readout resonator to work right."

"Sounds reasonable." Jayden got his own helping of guac.

"The qubits decayed too rapidly?"

"Yeah." I continued enjoying the beer and chips.

"How did you fix it?"

"For that answer, I'd have to consult my lab notebook."

After our delish and filling lunch, I asked Jayden if we could stop by Hannah's softball game. She was supposed to be pitching today. My nervous state had me wanting to check on everyone. So far, I'd resisted stopping by the hospital and checking on Mom.

When we pulled up at the park, though, Hannah wasn't pitching. I scanned the field. There was no sign of her. I would ask the coach, but she looked busy.

I ended up texting Hannah, 'Surprise! At your game. Don't see you. But, good luck!' Ugh. My nerves ratcheted up again.

Back at the lab, I couldn't avoid working any longer.

I put Jayden to work putting the macroscopic components together under my direction.

I focused on the microfabrication. The main component was a dispersive bifurcating amplifier, consisting of a Josephson junction imbedded in a microwave on-chip resonator. I was going to use a resonator design based on a simple coplanar waveguide.

I started the resonator with a wafer of silicon and deposited a layer of niobium. Then I spun on a layer of photoresist and exposed the resonator gaps where I didn't want the Niobium in the finished sample. Next, the wafer was placed into a reactive ion etcher, where the Niobium under the exposed resist was etched away using plasma.

I felt a hand on my shoulder and jumped. I looked up. It was Jayden. "What?"

"It's 9:00 p.m. Are we doing to eat dinner?" he asked.

Outside it was dark. Someone had turned on all the lab lights.

"Come on," he said. "You should take a break."

I realized I was exhausted. Microfabrication was exhausting because you had to focus so closely on everything. "I'm almost done. It just has to go in the N-methyl pyrrolidone to get rid of the remaining photoresist."

166

"You almost have the wafer of etched resonators done?" he asked with surprise. "Already?"

I smiled. "I spent months learning how to do each step. I'm glad I remembered how to do everything. All my notes helped."

"I think you've accomplished enough today," he said. "What do you want to do for dinner?" I stared at him for a moment. How could he knock off? Didn't he know what was at stake with all this?

But I realized my brain was fried. I said, "Let's order takeout from Limestone."

"What kind of place is that?" he asked.

"Pizza."

"I'm in."

At some point during the day, Hannah had texted me back, 'Hey. Sorry I missed you.'

We picked up a pizza pie and ate it at Mom's house. We were so tired that conversation was minimal. We went to bed (separately) right after dinner.

The next day went pretty much exactly the same, except we didn't take the time to eat so well. The pressure was getting to me.

We duplicated our efforts, creating the components for the second machine. At 7:00 p.m. I sent Jayden home, telling him to chill out and eat some of my mom's cooking (she agreed). I ate dinner out of the vending machine and didn't get home until midnight, but we were ready to assemble.

The next day, we put everything together and ran preliminary tests. Everything was shipshape. I was kind of impressed with myself. I'd stashed the 'extra' machine in my messenger bag along with my laptop.

In late afternoon, we were ready to do a test calculation. For our first quantum calculation, I'd chosen '1 + 1.'

"Really?" Jayden asked. He seemed irritable. We'd both been working hard; I couldn't blame him.

"You want to duplicate what I did before, don't you?" I said.

"I guess so," he said. "Good point. Science is about repeatability."

The controlling computer was on. I turned on the

q-computer. "Now, all we have to do is enter the calculation and start it." I hesitated. How much of what happened was the conservation of luck resulting from a q-computer? I wasn't anxious for another bad-luck cloud.

"Do you want me to do it?" Jayden asked.

"No. I'll do it." I moved my fingers closer to the q-computer but still didn't press 'enter.' "I don't want to put you in danger. Maybe you should move out into the hall."

"I'll do it," Professor Smithson said and started punching the keyboard.

Jayden and I both jerked back. Where had Smithson come from?

"There," Professor Smithson said. "It's running."

Jayden and I held our breath. My eyes traveled to the window that wasn't covered with plywood.

What were we in for next?

Chapter Twenty

Professor Smithson had just used the new q-computer. Jayden and I stared at each other. If my conservation of luck hypothesis was correct, now the two of us would have bad luck. I was not looking forward to testing that hypothesis.

Surreptitiously, I'd taken out the coin. I flipped it. Tails. What did that tell us?

"Two." Professor Smithson was staring at the result of the quantum computation. "Good."

A clap of thunder sounded outside. Jayden and I jumped, and I dropped the coin on the floor. It rolled under one of the lab tables.

"Maybe you should turn off the q-computer," I said.

Professor Smithson gave me a weird look. "Why?" But he reached over and switched it off. Did that mean we were safe again?

"It's just that the calculation is done," I said.

Raindrops hit the windows.

Jayden and I got up and looked outside. Rain. It seemed like totally normal natural rain.

"Do you guys have something against rain?" Professor Smithson said. "I know it hasn't rained much these last few years, but it was in the forecast. Didn't you see the forecast?"

"No," I said. "We've been working long hours." Did that mean the rain was or wasn't because of Smithson's good luck? If so, where was my and Jayden's bad luck? Was it possible this new q-computer didn't work like my old one?

"So." Professor Smithson rubbed his hands together. "Do you want to do a real calculation with the q-computer?"

The rain continued to pound against the windows. Thunder

thundered.

I had to admit I was very curious as well as nervous. Did this new q-computer affect luck or not? If so, was the conservation of luck real? And, of course, I wanted to see what kind of calculations a q-computer could do. Was it better than a traditional computer? "Like what?"

"One of my physics colleagues had an idea," he said. "He wanted us to calculate the mass of a quark."

"Well," I said, "that sounds interesting, but I must admit I don't know how to do that."

"He gave me code," Professor Smithson said. "The code should take a regular computer many, many years. Theoretically, it should go much faster on a q-computer."

"Sounds interesting," Jayden said.

"Yes." Professor Smithson started typing.

I didn't know what to think. Were we on the verge of disaster?

"There," he said. "The program started."

"Whoa," Jayden said. "You just started it? You might have warned us."

A huge burst of lightning flashed outside. I jumped. Gee, that wasn't ominous at all.

"What?" Professor Smithson said. "Warn you?"

I had a sudden urge to do a q-computer calculation of my own. I grabbed my bag and ran for the ladies' room. "Be right back," I called on the way out the door.

In the ladies', I pulled out my new secret q-computer, plugged it into my laptop, turned them on, and input '1 + 1 =?' into the q-computer. I stood right next to it until it spit out '2.' I didn't know if that would counteract any bad luck Smithson gave me, but it couldn't hurt.

I speedwalked back to the lab.

"So, I need to get back to Kansas City," Jayden was saying.

Professor Smithson's phone rang. "Just a sec." He answered.

His q-computer was still crunching along.

Jayden narrowed his eyes at me. "Why did you leave?"

"I went to the ladies' room," I said.

"With your bag?" He knew I had the other q-computer in

there.

I gave him a big smile and said, "It's that time of the month." I knew he wouldn't challenge me on that.

Thunder crashed outside the window, and Jayden flinched. "Let's go back to KC," he said.

"I hear you," I said. "But I want to see how the q-computer does with the new program."

And what if Zander was in KC waiting to pounce on us or something? And, yes, I knew that was illogical. I glanced at my phone. No news from the cops in this situation was bad news.

"That new program could take days or months to run," Jayden said. "Or forever."

"Good point," I said.

Professor Smithson hung up and smiled. "I won a big award. Best Professor of the Year. I didn't even know I'd been nominated."

Jayden looked a little sick. "How big of an award is it?" I'd told Jayden my hypothesis earlier that the bigger the good luck, the bigger the corresponding bad luck backlash.

"Huge!" Professor Smithson said. "They give me a big dinner, and I get a plaque. And a special parking space for a whole year."

Jayden relaxed a little. "So, no cash prize?"

"No." Professor Smithson's smile decreased a bit. "Dinner. Plaque. Parking spot. That's a lot."

"That is a lot," I said. "Congratulations, sir. That's awesome. And you deserve it." Our eyes met. He seemed happy and grateful. For a second, I wished he truly was my grandfather.

"So, are we going, then?" Jayden asked. The moment was over.

I cleared my throat. "Yes."

Professor Smithson asked me, "Did you drop something?"

"What?" I asked.

"Earlier, I thought you dropped something," he said.

"Coin," Jayden said.

"Oh, right." I crawled under the lab table. We needed it for the experiment. We wouldn't be following the scientific method if we changed the equipment around in the middle of the experiment.

Then I heard a crash, a loud bang, and wind and rain whipped into the lab. I jerked.

"Oh, no! Are you all right?" Professor Smithson said.

Jayden was standing near the broken window, rain and wind blowing on him. The plywood had crashed onto the desk, narrowly missing him. He stared at the hole, mouth gaping.

"Jayden?" Professor Smithson said. "Oh, dear. I need to call maintenance again."

I scrambled up and ran over to Jayden. He looked wet, but I didn't see any blood or anything. "Jayden? Are you okay?"

He shook off his stupor. "Yes. But I'm going back to KC Now. Are you coming, Ella?"

"Yes." I grabbed the rest of my stuff and started walking for the door.

Professor Smithson smiled. "It was so nice having you around again, Ella, I forgot it was only temporary."

I stepped up to him, holding out my hand. We shook. "Thanks for everything, sir."

"Stay in touch, young lady," he said and then smiled at Jayden. "And it was nice meeting you, Jayden."

"You too, sir," Jayden said.

"You'll be sure to contact us and let us know what happens?" I asked.

"Of course," Professor Smithson said. "Have a safe trip back." Rain was still coming into the lab near the window. "Maybe you should wait until the rain lets up?"

"No!" Jayden said.

I smiled at Professor Smithson again. "Bye." I didn't want to put him in any more danger than I already had.

We speedwalked to the parking lot.

"How come you were under the table instead of standing next to me when that plywood crashed into the room?" Jayden asked.

Good luck? I glanced over at him and walked faster.

In the parking lot, Jayden stepped in a huge puddle of water, soaking his foot. "Oof." He grimaced.

He unlocked the car, and we rushed inside.

"How come I stepped in a puddle, and you didn't?" he asked as he started the car and pulled out.

I shrugged. I was pretty sure he'd figured out what I'd done in the ladies' room, but we were going to be stuck in a car together for the next hour, so why exacerbate the situation?

Conversation was at a minimum as we sped east along Highway 70.

And then I heard a siren coming up behind us.

Jayden glanced in the rear-view mirror and then smacked the steering wheel with the palms of his hands. "Damn it!"

He pulled the car over.

Suffice it to say, we got a speeding ticket, a two hundred dollar speeding ticket. I didn't say a word during the whole debacle.

When Jayden finally put the car in gear and pulled back onto the highway, he said, "You're the one who should pay this."

I debated saying, 'You were the one who was speeding,' but decided against it. "I'll pay it." I shrank back in the seat a bit more. "I don't have the money right now, but as soon as I get it..."

Jayden sighed.

We didn't say anything else until he dropped me off at the B & B. "Thanks a lot for the ride, Jayden," I said. "And for all your help with the q-computer."

"Yeah," he said.

"I will pay the speeding ticket. I promise."

He threw me a glance.

"Am I still invited to poker night?" I smiled. It had come up that he was playing tonight.

"I guess," he said. "I'll text you."

In late afternoon, Mrs. Flores woke me. "Oh, I'm sorry, dear," she said. "Are you still napping? I need help with the towels."

My sleep schedule was all messed up from working almost three days nonstop. And I was a bundle of nerves. What was Zander up to?

"Mrs. F., I can handle some towels." That was about all my groggy brain could handle at this point. I schlepped fresh towels from the laundry room to all the bathrooms.

Afterward, I checked my messages. Jayden had left a text saying he was taking the rest of the day off and to meet me at his place at seven.

Professor Smithson had left a voice mail.

"The program finished already, Ella!" he said. "This is great! I'm going to write an awesome paper. Will you be a co-author? Call me back when you get this."

I was surprised the calculation had happened so fast. Maybe it wasn't as complicated as I'd initially thought?

I called him back. I got voicemail. "Hi, Professor Smithson. This is Ella. Good news about the calculation. I guess I can be a co-author. Thanks for the opportunity. Bye for now."

I texted the cop handling my q-computer case, asking if there was any new info.

On my way to Jayden's apartment, I stopped by Qubyte, Inc. to lock up my new q-computer. Clearly, keeping a q-computer in my room at the B & B didn't work.

In the lab, I locked the q-computer in a cabinet and then locked the lab door behind me. Since you also needed a keycard to get into the building, hopefully, that would keep it secure.

Jayden's roommate Mike answered the door. "Ella!" He smiled widely. "What a surprise!" He still reminded me of a giant leprechaun.

"Surprise?" I said. "I thought I was invited."

He got out of the way, waving me inside. "Sarcasm. I'm not surprised at all. I had a feeling about you two." He closed the door behind me. The apartment was similar to Wei's, but the tech was more expensive. Their flatscreen TV was the biggest I'd ever seen in a private home. I successfully didn't gawk.

"Can it, Mike," Jayden said. Then he smiled at me. "Hi, Ella. Glad you could make it." He smiled. It wasn't a huge smile, but it was a smile.

Yay. He wasn't mad at me about his bad luck. I felt my face light up in return.

Someone cleared his or her throat. "Hey, I'm here too."

"Right," Jayden said. "Sorry. Ella, this is my buddy DeShawn. DeShawn, this is Ella." Jayden's friends were clearly richer than my friends. They all wore fancy designer jeans, super-expensive tennis shoes and hip t-shirts. I wasn't going to feel bad about taking their money.

"Nice to meet you," I said.

"Likewise," he said.

"Can I get anyone a beer?" Mike asked.

We all agreed, and Mike went to the refrigerator. DeShawn followed him.

I sidled up to Jayden. "Professor Smithson said the calculation already finished," I said softly.

Jayden's eyebrows went up. "Already?"

I nodded. "It seems unusually fast, doesn't it?"

He nodded.

"What are you guys talking about over there?" Mike asked.

"Nothing," Jayden said loudly. We followed the guys into the kitchen.

Mike passed beers around. We sat down at the round kitchen table. Mike picked up the deck and shuffled it. "We'll draw to see who deals first. Ace high. Spades high. For each hand, the dealer picks the game and the stakes."

Mike picked himself a two of clubs.

"Nice." Jayden chuckled. He picked a seven of hearts. "Aw."

DeShawn picked a ten of diamonds. "So far, so good."

I drew out a card and looked at it. "Ace of spades." No one here knew I was a great card player. My nerves finally started to calm. Cards, I could do.

"Doh!" DeShawn said.

Mike frowned.

Jayden said, "Nice."

Someone knocked on the front door.

Mike jumped up.

"Were we expecting someone else?" Jayden asked.

"You're the one who broke the men-only barrier," Mike said, opening the door.

A beautiful woman stood on the other side. "Hi, Mike." She immediately looked at Jayden. "Hi, Jayden. Thanks for inviting me, guys."

Jayden glanced at me and then at the woman.

Mike said, "Everyone, this is Ashley. Ashley, this is everyone."

Ah ha. Jayden'd said he was sort of dating an Ashley. This must be her. He didn't mention how hot she was. I wouldn't mind taking her money, either.

She strode inside. "Oh, I know everyone. Jayden's introduced me around before. Hi, DeShawn."

DeShawn seemed a little dazed. "Hi."

"Except her." She leaned over towards me, holding out her hand. "Hi, I'm Ashley."

I shook her hand. "Ella. Nice to meet you."

"Beer, Ashley?" Mike asked.

"Sure." She nodded and took Mike's seat next to Jayden. She rubbed Jayden's arm. "Hi, there."

Jayden looked embarrassed. "Hi."

Mike got her a beer and then sat down. "Okay, Ella's got the first deal."

"Oh?" Ashley asked.

"You missed the draw," Mike said.

"You snooze, you lose, girl," DeShawn said.

"Okay, okay," she said, smiling. "My bad." She practically simpered, and the guys were eating it up. I didn't like her.

Mike passed me the cards.

"Five card stud," I said. "Dollar ante. Max bet twenty bucks."

DeShawn whistled.

"Jacks or better to open." I started dealing.

I won the hand with a flush, diamonds, netting thirty-four dollars. "Nice. Thanks." I didn't let myself smile, but I was definitely feeling lucky.

DeShawn whistled again.

Mike looked annoyed. Jayden looked worried. Ashley stared at me, eyes narrowed. "Who invited her?"

"Jayden," I said. Geez, this woman was irritating.

DeShawn dealt next, five-card stud. I won that hand, too, with a straight, netting twenty-five dollars.

"I don't get it," Ashley said. "Why is she so good?"

I was usually good, but I wasn't usually this good. My new q-computer must be giving me good luck.

"Are you cheating, little Miss Ella?" Mike said.

Jayden said, "Let's have a chat. Outside."

"Fine." I followed Jayden outside. "What?"

"I know you did something with your q-computer today," he said.

"You better not be implying I'm cheating," I said. It wasn't cheating because I'd built the q-computer using my hard-earned skills.

He just stared at me.

"If I win two hundred dollars, I'm planning on giving it to you for the ticket."

"Let's go back inside," he said quickly.

That's what I thought. "Yes," I said. "Let's."

I won the next seven hands. I was up almost three hundred dollars. I'd always been good, but truth be told, this was a new level.

"Whoo." DeShawn pushed away from the table and stood up. "Too rich for my blood."

Mike said, "I didn't know little Ella here was a card sharp."

"Is it card sharp or card shark?" Ashley asked. "She seems like a shark to me."

I looked to Jayden. Surely, he'd defend me.

Nope. Not a word. He'd been surprisingly quiet all night.

"Don't call me 'little Ella,'" I finally said. "And I'm not a sharp or a shark."

"Sit down, DeShawn," Mike said. "Surely, Ella will give you a chance to win back your money."

I shrugged. "Sure. You can have a chance. You've had a chance all along." Not a good chance, but a chance.

DeShawn sat down, and we started playing again.

Chapter Twenty-One

I won four hundred and fifty dollars by the end of the night. What were the odds of that? Apparently, about one hundred percent with my nifty new q-computer. And it wasn't cheating because I, myself, built the q-computer.

Okay, I admit, I did have a nagging feeling that somebody here might get some bad luck. But, I had about four hundred and fifty reasons to ignore that feeling. Besides, nothing had happened yet.

We were all sitting around the table. I was still counting my money--but not in a gloaty way. They were glaring at me.

"Do you want to see if the game's still on?" DeShawn said.

"Sure." Mike shrugged and flipped on the giant flat-screen TV.

"I want to talk to you," Jayden said, throwing daggers with his eyes.

"Whatever." I was fully prepared to give him the two hundred bucks.

Mike's phone chirped. He read it and glanced at Jayden. "Huh."

"What?" Jayden asked him.

"Landlord says your check bounced," he said. "I'm supposed to evict you."

Jayden jumped up, knocking over his chair. "Bounced! There's no way! I had plenty of money in that account." He started typing stuff on his phone.

I started sidling towards the door. I didn't want to interact with Jayden when he was in such a bad mood.

Ashley was standing near the door. "Well, I gotta go. Thanks." She quickly opened the door and left. I wished I was her.

I took another step closer to the door.

Jayden gave me a look that said, 'Don't even think about leaving.' He started talking on his phone. "Representative. Representative. Representative!"

"Wow, look at this," DeShawn said, pointing at the screen.

I joined him in front of the TV. Apparently, there had been some kind of riot at one of the casinos in town.

The newscaster said, "To repeat. Rioting broke out at the Odyssey casino earlier tonight. Reports say one man won one hundred thousand dollars, and then several thousand people started losing. Continuously. No one won anything. They just lost. Repeatedly. The losers started attacking employees and smashing machines." In the background, there was an image of a rowdy crowd and a bunch of cop cars with flashing lights.

"Freaky," DeShawn said, standing right in front of the screen.

"Yeah, weird," Mike said, moving closer as well.

It was weird and freaky.

Jayden hung up his phone. His face was red. He said, "Could you please join me outside, Ella?"

The two of us stepped outside the front door.

"Is everything okay?" I asked.

"No!" he said. "My bank account is all screwed up."

"I'm sorry to hear that." I handed him two hundred dollars. "This should cheer you up a little."

"Thanks." He frowned. "I lost a hundred and fifty bucks tonight. Did you use your q-computer to change your luck?"

I handed him a hundred and fifty bucks more. I figured there was more where that came from.

"Thanks," he said grudgingly.

I smiled. "Are you feeling any better?"

"A little." He almost smiled back.

"That was pretty freaky about the Odyssey." I had a strong feeling I knew where my missing q-computer was--at least tonight.

"What about the Odyssey?" he said. "I didn't see it."

"It seemed like luck might have been acting oddly there, is all."

"You didn't go to the Odyssey tonight, did you?" he asked.

"Me? When did I have a chance to go there?"

"Before you came over."

"No," I said. "I did not go over to the Odyssey tonight." Why not? I wanted to go to a casino. I wanted to go to multiple casinos.

"Do you want to go over there now and check it out?" I asked. "I bet Zander, or whoever stole my q-computer, is over there."

"You didn't answer my question," he said. "Did you use your q-computer today?"

"Well, yeah," I said. "I was worried about Professor Smithson giving me bad luck."

He glared at me, and I had no problem deciphering, 'What about my bad luck?'

I thought about protesting that nothing had been proven but decided against it. Stuff had pretty much been proved at this point. "Sorry." I smiled, trying to look sexy and charming. "Any chance you want to go over to the Odyssey with me and see what's happening?"

"I think you just want to gamble more."

"No." Yes. "Well, maybe a little." A lot. I was having a lucky streak, after all. I should take advantage of it. The corresponding bad luck damage had already been done, right?

"And you want a ride," he said.

"You are such great company, too," I said. "Super-fun."

He was silent for a few moments. "Okay. I'll drive you to the Odyssey if you do something for me."

I cocked my head. Was he about to ask for one or more sex acts? If so, what would I say? Hmm... I was surprised to realize I might be into it even though Jayden wasn't my type at all. Way too boring/nice/nerdy.

"Let me use your q-computer."

"Aw." I was a little disappointed. "Say what now?"

"Let me use your q-computer to change my luck."

"We don't know for sure that will work." Clearly, we both thought it would work.

He frowned.

"But, sure. Okay. It's at the lab. Let's go."

Back at the lab, I used my keycard, lab key, and cabinet key and freed my q-computer from its confinement. I pulled it out and handed it to Jayden. "Is there any chance you can wait, like, ten minutes before you use it?"

"What?" He narrowed his eyes. "Are you going to try to get out of its range?"

I shrugged. "Think of it as an experiment."

He sighed. "All right."

I didn't waste any time and turned and ran out of the lab, down the hall, through the lobby, out the doors, and down the block. At the end of the block, I had to stop because I couldn't breathe. I should really start working out or something. I leaned down, putting my hands on my knees and gasping in air. Eventually, my breathing slowed, and I checked my phone. Fifteen minutes had elapsed.

I started speedwalking back, wondering how long the luck effects lasted.

To be on the safe side, we'd repeat the procedure, but this time, I'd use my q-computer, and Jayden would vamoose. That way, I couldn't lose; neither one of us could lose.

Afterward, I was very careful to lock my q-computer back up.

At the Odyssey, the cops were gone, and the crowds outside had dispersed. I hoped it was open.

"Why are we here again?" Jayden asked as we got out of the car. "Surely, the quantum thief is long gone."

I said, "I want to look around. He might still be here." Probably not. "I'm going to look around. You could also try a little gambling to test out our luck hypothesis some more. If you win a bunch and others lose a bunch, management will probably blame it on whatever happened earlier."

He smiled as we approached the front doors, proving everyone liked winning. "You're kind of sneaky, Ella. I like it."

I smiled back. I was surprised he liked sneakiness. He gave the impression that he was a straight arrow.

"We should play pennies," he said. "We don't want a strong bad luck backlash." He held one of the doors open for me.

"Thanks. Good point." There was no way I was going to play pennies when I couldn't lose. "Uh, for the other people's safety, let's play on opposite sides of the casino." Also, so he couldn't see me winning big. It was dark in here, but it wasn't that dark.

"Good point," he said. "We don't want to endanger people."

The ghostly scent of long-ago cigarettes pervaded the place. There weren't many customers inside. I guessed riots weren't good for business.

"Right." My stomach started jumping around as I recalled a certain woman named Gladys. But that was a fluke, right? She'd been sick. Tonight I wouldn't gamble next to any sickly people.

Inside, there seemed to be an inordinate number of security guards. I smiled and nodded at them. Look at me--I'm a friendly, totally regular customer. There was also an inordinate lack of other gamblers.

Jayden's phone rang. He listened and then hung up right away. "Huh."

"What?"

"That was Mike," he said. "The landlord had a change of heart. He's not evicting me." He paused. "Sometimes, I sort of love your q-computer."

That made two of us. I did not remind him that he might not have had trouble with his landlord if it hadn't been for my q-computer.

"All right." He rubbed his hands together. "What's the plan? How long are we staying? A half-hour? It's pretty late."

"No!" I said. I had to do some gambling after I looked around for Zander.

He raised his eyebrows in surprise.

"Sorry. I took a nap. I'm not tired. Are you?"

"I took a nap, too," he said.

"So, I just meant I need to look around for Zander and that could take a super-long time," I said. "Hey, if you see a guy on crutches, text me." I wasn't worried about taking on a shady guy that was already injured. I figured my chances of sweet-talking him into giving me back my q-computer were better if it was just the two of us.

"Uh, as for how long" I said, "how about I text you when I'm ready to go and we can meet outside, near the car."

"Why outside?" he asked.

"It's just easier." Easier for him to miss my purse and pockets bulging with cash out in the dark parking lot. "Why don't you play here, near the door?"

He shrugged. "Okay. Whatever."

The hundred bucks in my pocket was burning to get out. I speedwalked off before he'd even stopped talking.

First things first: I did need to look for Zander. I decided to speedwalk around the whole perimeter of the casino. That was where people keeping a low profile would be. The offices and such were also along the edge. I took off, keeping an eagle eye out for guys on crutches or covered in hot tats.

I didn't find Zander, but about halfway through my circuit I did find the casino business offices. Headshots of employees hung on the wall.

I stopped short when I saw a picture of that Hernandez guy and right next to him, a picture labeled 'Owner,' of my dad.

"Oh, my God!" I could not believe my dad owned this place. I'd thought he was poor. How could he screw Mom over so bad when he was rich? My whole body shook. I took out my phone to text Mom but I couldn't seem to hit the right keys.

"Are you all right, miss?" the security guard standing right next to me said.

I jumped in surprise. Where the hell'd he come from?

I made myself smile. "I'm fine." I'd have to deal with this later. "I was, uh, just looking for my friend, John. He was supposed to meet me here and I can't find him."

"You can use the PA system to ask him to meet you somewhere," the guard said. He was very helpful. Darn it.

"No," I said. "I'd rather not. He has a ton of tattoos and he's on crutches. You haven't seen anyone like that tonight have you?"

He was quiet for a few moments, considering. "Nope. No tattoos. No crutches. And I've been keeping a very close eye on everything tonight."

That didn't sound good for me. "Oh? Why is that?" I asked innocently.

"Earlier today before I got here, there was a fracas," he said. "So, you don't need any help?"

"Can you tell me where the highest progressive machines are?" I smiled sweetly. There was more than one way to get years of child support for Mom.

"Yes," he said. "Actually, they're right near here." He pointed at the machines near the offices.

Of course. Darn security would be tightest here. "Gosh." Jayden must be rubbing off on me. "Thanks for all your help."

He nodded. "You're welcome." His radio squawked. He took it off his belt. "Allen here. What's wrong now?" He walked away.

I could continue to look for Zander even though the guard didn't think he was here. Or, I could play my hundred bucks and try to win a shitload off dear old deadbeat Dad.

I walked towards the progressive machine.

Chapter Twenty-Two

In the Odyssey casino, I sat down, took a twenty out of my wallet and slid it into the progressive machine. I craned my neck, looking up at the jackpot. It said: $186,000. Cool. I wanted $186,000. I could totally use $186,000. Even after giving Mom a bunch of money, there'd be a bunch left.

I touched the screen and studied the game rules to see what I needed to do to be eligible to win the jackpot. It looked like I had to play all lines with max bets. That would be like sixteen bucks. Oh well. They said it took money to make money. I exited the rules screen.

I glanced around me. No sickly little old ladies. Check. In fact, I couldn't see anyone. It was a little eerie, like a ghost town, being practically the only customer. The casino floor was huge, filled with large metallic slot machines. The lights on the machines and displays flashed every color of the rainbow.

Was it because it was so late? Or because of the riot earlier?

I selected the max bet option. I held my finger over the play button for a few moments. My pulse started racing. This could be it. I could win a giant amount of money and solve all my problems.

I should win a bunch of money if my hypothesis about my q-computer was right.

I held my finger over the button. My pulse zinged.

I carefully pushed play.

My heart hammered as I watched the computerized screen with the simulated wheels spinning. Win, win, win.

Then the screen stilled, filled with 'jackpot.'

All kinds of bells went off. The light on top of the machine started flashing. The numbers on the bottom of the screen started going up and up and up.

Wow. It worked. I was surprised to realize I hadn't been a hundred percent sure it would. I stood up and threw my fists in the air. "Yes! Woo! Yes!"

And the numbers continued to go up.

"Woo! Yes! Go Ella! Go Ella! Go Ella!" I glanced around. It was a little anticlimactic to win big and have no one see. "Yay, me." My voice petered out. What was I doing? Talking to myself?

Okay, worker. Come on over any time now and give me a big old check. A giant check.

I looked around some more. No workers in sight.

I took a few steps towards the offices, ready to run back to my machine as soon as a worker showed up. Nobody was in the business office near me. I went back to my machine and sat down again. It was the wee hours of the morning, of course there weren't a bunch of staff working. I watched the numbers continue to rise and listened to the bells.

Those bells were annoying. I scanned the area around me. Where was everyone? I didn't want to leave my machine. How would they know I was the winner if I left it?

I sat there a few more minutes. Waiting. Nothing new happened.

After a while, I eyed my phone. I didn't want Jayden to lecture me about cheating--somehow he seemed like the kind of guy who was into lecturing--but this was getting ridiculous. Maybe Jayden could find a worker for me and bring them over? If he objected, I could always slip him a few hundred bucks. I punched Jayden's number into my phone.

He didn't answer. It went to voice mail.

That was a little odd.

I sat there a few more minutes, listening to those damn annoying bells.

Finally I stood up on my chair and yelled, "Jayden! Where are you?"

No one answered.

"Anyone! Is anyone here?"

No one answered.

I started getting a very bad feeling. $186,000 was one hell

of a lot of good luck. Had my good luck killed someone? Multiple someones? Jayden?

How big could a bad luck backlash be?

I got up and dashed into the business office, took a blank sheet of paper from the printer, wrote 'Ella Hote won this' on it and dashed back to my machine. I carefully placed the piece of paper on the machine.

I left my purse on the chair and turned and ran to where I thought Jayden was, on the opposite end of the casino, near the front door.

I saw Jayden, slumped over in a stool in front of a penny machine.

I ran up to him. "Jayden?"

He didn't answer. "Jayden!"

I felt for a pulse. He had a strong pulse. Hurray.

I thought about slapping him awake, but instead, I kissed him. That was nicer, right? And I was all about the nice.

His lips were warm. His eyes opened but he continued kissing me for a few moments.

I backed up. "Are you okay?"

"Uh." His fingers brushed his lips. "After that kiss, I'm not sure what I am. What brought that on?"

Why did I do that? I shrugged.

He narrowed his eyes. "Wait. Why wouldn't I be okay? Did you do something?"

I shrugged and felt myself squint. "Maybe?" I needed to get back to my machine. "I need to get back to my machine. Can you find a worker and bring them over." I pointed. "I'm on the opposite end of the casino." I turned and ran off.

"What did you do?" he called after me. But he got up off his chair.

Back at my machine, the piece of paper had fallen on the floor, but my purse was still there. There was still no sign of any workers.

The bells were still annoying.

My phone rang. It was Jayden.

"You better get over here, to the cashiers' cage, near the front."

"Why?"

But he hung up.

I ran back over to the front of the casino.

Jayden waved me over to the cashiers' cage. He pointed inside. "They look dead."

Oh, no. I saw people lying on the floor not moving. My heart plummeted. I was a horrible, horrible person.

"I can't get inside," he said.

"Well, call 911 already," I said. I glanced away and thought I saw a foot sticking out from behind the next row of machines. I ran over there.

Sure enough, it was the security guard I talked to earlier. He was lying on the ground, not moving.

I knelt next to him. "Sir? Are you all right?" He didn't answer. "Sir?"

I checked for a pulse.

He did have a pulse. Thank God.

"Sir?"

He didn't answer. I stared at him. I could slap him. I could kiss him--it worked on Jayden. I shook him. "Sir?"

I wracked my brain, trying to recall what Mom would do. Yell and squeeze his shoulder. "Sir!" I squeezed. No response to either. So, he was unresponsive.

Did he need CPR?

I stared at his chest. It rose and fell regularly. Good.

What else? Skin. The color was good. I felt his forehead and cheeks. They seemed warm. What did that mean?

"Ella?" I heard Jayden call out. "Where'd you go?"

I leaned out from behind the machines. "I'm over here. A security guard is lying here."

Jayden stepped over. "Oh, no. Another body?"

I jerked. "What do you mean, 'body'?"

He gestured back at the cashiers' cage. "There are two people in there. I can't tell if they're dead or alive."

That was not good.

"Did you call an ambulance?" I asked.

He nodded.

I stared at the guard. What was wrong with him?

Maybe I should kiss him. What the hell? I leaned over and planted one on his lips. He didn't react. Darn. I straightened.

"What was that?" Jayden sputtered.

"It worked on you," I said.

"But..." He trailed off.

We needed more than one ambulance. I pulled my phone out of my pocket and dialed 911.

"911. What is the nature of your emergency?"

"I have an unresponsive male at the Odyssey casino."

"We already received your call."

"No," I said. "There are at least three people affected."

The 911 operator exhaled loudly. "How many people?"

"Three," I said. "At least."

"And what's wrong?"

"I don't know," I said. "They're not moving. They're not responding."

"We'll dispatch another... Just a moment." She put me on hold for a few moments. When she came back on line she said, "Are you at the casino?"

"Yes."

"How do you feel?" she asked.

"I feel fine," I said. "Why?"

She didn't answer right away.

"Why?" I asked again. "What's going on?"

"There appears to be an environmental contaminant," she said. "We've had several reports in the area. Normally, I'd tell you to go outside, but people outside and in surrounding buildings have been affected. Shit." She exhaled again. "I don't know what to tell you."

Shit was right.

I knew what the environmental contaminant was: me. Or, more specifically, my big win.

"Shit!" I said. My mind was racing.

"What's wrong?" the operator asked. "Are you all right?"

"Yeah. Sorry," I said. "I'm just worried about these people."

"Me, too," she said softly.

"You're sending ambulances, right?"

"Yes," she said.

I hung up. I had to at least try to get rid of the environmental contaminant.

"What's going on?" Jayden asked.

"I'm going to go try to undo my win," I said. "Wait for the ambulances." I didn't wait for his response.

I ran back to my machine.

The annoying bell was still going off. The light on top was still flashing.

"Here goes nothing." I gathered my fortitude and pressed the 'Repeat the bet' button.

The bell stopped ringing and the machine's screen said 'Game over.'

But the number in the credits section on the screen said '185984.'

"Wow."

I stared at that number for what seemed like forever.

What else could I do to negate my win?

No amount of money was worth becoming a mass murderer.

I needed to do something.

I could unplug it. I got down on the floor and peered behind the machine. I reached my arm in the small space. It just fit.

I pulled the plug.

Chapter Twenty-Three

The machine quieted at once.

I grabbed my purse and ran back to Jayden at the front of the casino. As I approached the entrance I heard sirens.

Jayden asked, "What did you do?"

"I unplugged my winning machine," I said. "We'll see if it helps." I thought I'd undone my win.

Two hazmat-clad people, each carrying a plastic case, came in the front doors. It was disquieting to see them all suited up. Could there be something hazardous here?

One of the people said, "How do you feel?"

"We feel fine," I said. "We're the ones that called you guys."

The second person said, "Where are the injured?"

Four more hazmat-suited people, all with cases, entered. They looked sort of like astronauts. It was a little surreal.

"Take them to the cage, Jayden," I said.

He nodded. "This way." The five of them rushed away.

"We haven't searched the whole building," I said. "But there's a security guard over here." Maybe he was better now? I hoped he was better now. But as I approached, I could see he was still lying on the floor. Why? What was wrong with him?

In the back of my mind, I'd thought maybe they'd all recover immediately if I undid my win. Had I undone my win? If so, it didn't seem to be helping.

They leaned over him, taking vitals. One of them stuck their face right in his face. "Sir? Can you hear me?"

The second one said, "His vitals are good. I don't know why he's not responsive."

The first one said, "Go get the gurney. I'll start an IV."

The second one rushed off.

The first one inserted an IV and held up the bag of fluid.

"Do you want me to hold up the IV bag?" I asked.

Through the clear plastic facemask, he looked surprised. "Sure," he said. I was startled at how young he looked; he was my age.

I knelt down next to them, took the bag and held it up in the air.

"Are you sure you feel all right?" the EMT (I was guessing he was an EMT) asked.

"Yeah." I stared at the guard's face. His color looked better and he seemed to be breathing more regularly.

"What happened here?" the EMT asked.

"I'm not sure," I said. This was technically true.

The guard's eyelids fluttered and then he opened his eyes. "Where am I? What's happening?"

Oh, thank God! What a relief! Hopefully everyone else would wake up now, too.

The EMT leaned over him. "You're at the Odyssey casino, sir. Can you tell me your name?"

"Tom," he said. "I'm Tom Allen." He glanced around. "Why am I on the floor?" He looked at me. "You!" He strained upwards like he was going to try to get up.

"Please lay back, sir." Then, the EMT stared over at me.

"Me?" I said and laughed like it was crazy that someone would say 'you.'"

"I dreamt a beautiful woman kissed me," Tom said. "You." He pointed at me. "I dreamt you kissed me."

The EMT stared at me some more. With him in the hazmat suit, it was disquieting.

"Huh. How unusual," I said. Not really, considering I did kiss him. Had he been conscious then? He didn't seem like it. "Of course, we did meet earlier, in front of the portrait of the, ah, owner."

Tom leaned back. "Oh, right."

The second EMT rushed up to us, rolling a gurney. The two of them got Tom onto the gurney. One of them took the IV bag from me.

"Well, good luck to you, Tom!" I said as they started rolling him away.

Tom said, "I feel okay. Is this really necessary?"

They stopped for a moment.

The EMT said, "Yes, Tom. It's necessary."

I took a step away and then took another step away.

The first EMT said to me, "What do you think you're doing?"

"Going home?" I said.

"Nope. Nuh-uh," he said. "You're coming with us."

"Is this about the kissing?" I asked. "Because he dreamt that." Not really. But I was sure my kissing didn't do anything to him. A hundred percent sure. Ninety-nine percent sure.

"No," he said. "It's not about the kissing. You're coming with us. You're under quarantine."

Well, crap. That sounded awful. "No, thanks. I'm fine," I said. "There's no need to quarantine me."

"It's not a request," the EMT said, his voice hardening like steel.

I thought about running away for the briefest of seconds, but was interrupted by Jayden saying, "Can you believe they're quarantining us, Ella?" He'd come up behind us and I hadn't even noticed.

"How are the people from the cashiers' cage doing?" I asked.

"They had a little trouble getting to them," he said. "But once they started IVs they seemed to perk right up."

Hmm. So whatever happened to them it was cured by an IV? Weird. Absentmindedly, I put a dollar in the slot machine closest to me and pressed the 'Play' button.

"Seriously? Are you playing the slots now?" Jayden asked. "You have a problem."

"I'm not playing and I don't have a problem." But my eyes were glued to the screen. Now it said, 'Game over.' Damn.

My EMT said, "Are you two coming?"

"Of course we're coming with you," Jayden said. "Right, Ella?" He nudged my shoulder with his shoulder. "We cooperate with authorities."

Damn. I knew he was too straight-laced. Why couldn't I be hanging out with a criminal? "Of course," I said.

Outside the front doors, two ambulances were already pulling away, sirens blaring. Some cop cars pulled up, lights flashing. The cops didn't get out of their cars, though. They all sat inside watching us. Again, eerie.

The night air was coolish and refreshing. It seemed totally normal. It was jarring to feel the wind on my face amidst all the chaos of suited figures, flashing lights, and sirens.

Jayden and I followed EMT one and two as they pushed Tom out to their ambulance. They loaded him into the back. The one I'd been talking to got in next to Tom. "Go ahead, you two," he said. "He pointed at the closest cop car."

The cop in the driver's seat got out and opened the back seat.

I wanted to protest that we hadn't done anything, that we didn't deserve to be in the back of a police car, but I bit my tongue.

I guess Jayden and I stood there too long because the cop said, "Get in. We're just taking you to the hospital."

Jayden and I got in.

The EMT closed the ambulance doors and ran to the front seat. Within moments they put on the siren and zoomed away.

Soon we were driving away with our own siren.

"How do you feel?" the cop in the passenger seat, a woman, asked Jayden. It was hard to hear her over the siren.

"I feel fine," Jayden said.

"What?" the cop asked.

"I feel fine, too," I said.

"What?" she asked.

"I feel fine," I said more loudly. "How long is this going to take?" I didn't feel fine. I felt guilty. Was Tom okay? He seemed okay. What about the others?

"What's happening at the casino?" Jayden asked.

"This whole area is cordoned off," the female cop said.

"Shit," Jayden said, shaking his head.

At least he didn't blame me.

"Yeah," the driver said. "No one in or out. We think the whole area is contaminated somehow."

I hoped that wasn't true, or if it was true, the contamination-- $186,000?--had dissipated.

I leaned back and tried to relax. No go. I didn't like riding in the back of a patrol car. It made me feel like some kind of criminal. And I wasn't a criminal. There were no laws about quantum computers. I hadn't broken any laws.

So why did I feel so bad?

Soon we pulled up at the emergency room. The female cop let us out of the car.

Phew. It felt like being freed from prison.

A couple other hazmat-suited people approached me and Jayden. "Please come with us." They led us inside and through empty hospital corridors. I knew it was very late at night, but it was eerie to see it so empty. Apparently eerie was the word of the day, or night. We ended up at a big empty room filled with cots. Was it a cafeteria? "Please wait here."

"Why are we the only people here?" Jayden asked.

"You're the only people in the affected area still standing," one of the men said.

My spirits sank through the floor. "Oh no," I said. "How are the others?"

"We don't have that information," one of the men said.

"How many people are we talking about?" I asked, dreading the answer.

The other man said, "Someone will be by to take samples from you." They both pointed inside.

Jayden and I entered.

They closed and sealed the doors behind us.

I suppressed the urge to say something like 'Our first night together.'

Jayden sighed as he sat down on one of the cots. He didn't say anything like 'This is a fine mess you've gotten us into,' which I sincerely appreciated.

I sat down on the cot next to his. I debated what to say. Jokes weren't appropriate and 'Sorry' didn't cover it.

He put his head in his hands and yawned.

I yawned, too. Why was yawning contagious? Finally, I said, "I'm sorry." There was nothing else I could say.

He sighed again. "It's not your fault. We both agreed to do an experiment."

It was my fault. He really was a very nice guy, damn it. "Thank you for saying that."

195

He yawned again.

"You should try to get some rest," I said.

He glanced at his phone. "It's almost three a. m. I didn't know it was so late. You should get some rest, too."

"I'll get some rest if you get some rest," I said. I felt too guilty to rest but he should.

"Okay." He lay back on the cot. "But just for a minute..." His voice trailed off.

"Sleep tight, Jayden," I whispered and then lay back on my cot, knowing there was no way I'd be able to sleep.

Chapter Twenty-Four

The next thing I knew, I was lying on a cot in a big room and the sun was streaming in through the windows. Tom the guard lay on the cot next to me, snoring like a band saw. Every cot was full and there were, like, three dozen cots. On the bright side, everyone looked okay, healthy. Thank God.

I smelled hospital mixed with the faint scent of coffee.

"Morning." Jayden sat on the cot next to me. "You snore." He grinned at me.

I couldn't help grinning back. "Morning. But you're wrong, I don't snore." At least I'd never been told that before. And I'd spent the night with quite a few people. "Maybe you're confusing me with Tom, there." Tom definitely snored. I pointed at Tom.

Tom twitched.

"No." Jayden grinned some more. It was kind of annoying. "It wasn't Tom. It was you."

Tom stopped snoring and opened his eyes. "Where am I?"

Jayden spread his arms wide. "Welcome to quarantine."

Tom frowned and sat up. Then he caught my eye and said, "You!"

Oh, no. Here we go again.

"I dreamt you kissed me," Tom said. I did kiss him.

Jayden chuckled. "I had the very same dream." Oh, right, I kissed Jayden last night, too.

"You're welcome," I said. They were lucky to get kissed by me. They should appreciate it.

"What?" Tom and Jayden said at the same time.

"You're both welcome," I said.

"Is that a good idea?" Tom asked. "Going around kissing people during a quarantine?"

"Well, it wasn't a quarantine at the time," I said.

"Are you the reason it's a quarantine?" Tom asked with furrowed brow.

I was. But it wasn't in the way he thought--not from kissing. I felt the corners of my mouth turn down.

"Ella kissing you didn't have anything to do with the quarantine," Jayden said.

A little girl, wearing pink princess pajamas, spoke behind me. "Who's Ella and why's she kissing people?" She held a granola bar or something very like it. It looked good.

Jayden laughed.

"She's no one," I said.

"But he said--" the little girl said.

I interrupted. "You all are very cheerful for people in quarantine."

That sobered them all right up.

"Is there any food?" I scanned the room. People were waking up. "Coffee?" I would definitely kiss someone if it got me a cup of coffee.

The little girl pointed towards the counters near the door. "Yes. There's food over there. Men in weird big suits brought it in." She took a big bite of her bar.

"Are you with your mom or someone, little girl?" Jayden asked her.

Mom. Did my mom know about the quarantine? Was she worried about me? What about Mrs. Flores? I pulled out my phone. I had about thirty missed messages and texts.

"Yeah, you shouldn't just be wandering around by yourself," Tom said.

The girl giggled and ran off.

I started scrolling through my messages.

Mrs. Flores left me a bunch of messages asking where I was. I quickly texted her back that I was working and would be back at the B & B when I could.

Mom left me a message 'checking in,' followed by more and more messages asking why I hadn't texted her back. I called her.

She answered right away. "Ella?"

"Yep. How's it going?"

"Why didn't you text me back?" she said. "You always text

me back."

"Not that time my phone fell in my soda," I said.

"Did your phone fall in your soda?"

"No. Sorry." What to say? I scanned the room. The others were waking up. Should I say I was greedy and tried to win a bunch of money off dad but instead ended up putting forty-ish people in the hospital? "Uh. I was working late. My phone died and I didn't have the charger."

"Oh," she said. "Of course you were working late. I should have thought of that."

"So, how's everything with you?" I asked.

"I'm fine," she said. "Hannah's foster mom Amelia called over here at the house looking for you though. You should call her."

I couldn't recall Hannah's foster mom ever calling our house. "Okay. That doesn't sound good. What did she say?"

"I wasn't here," Mom said. "She just left a message for you to call her back."

"I better call her, then," I said. "I'll check in later, okay?"

"Sounds good," she said. "Bye."

"Here," a male voice, Jayden's voice, said from up near my shoulder.

I turned and smelled coffee. Hurray.

Jayden handed me a big paper cup of coffee and a granola bar. "I snagged you a bar, too."

Wow. He was nice. "Thanks!" I took a sip. Not bad.

He sat on his cot. "How did your mom take the quarantine news?"

I must have given him a telling expression because he said, "You didn't tell your mom the quarantine news."

"No," I said. "Why worry her?" I leaned towards him. "Plus, we both know there's nothing to it."

Behind me the little girl said, "How do you know there's nothing to it?"

I startled and twisted around. Somebody should put a bell on her.

"Where's your Mom?" Jayden stood and led her away.

I texted Hannah, 'I hope everything's okay.'

She didn't text me back. But that didn't mean anything. I

looked at the time. She could still be asleep. Or she could be at school. I couldn't remember when high school started. The students weren't supposed to use their phones at school.

I called Hannah's foster mom but it went straight to voicemail. Huh. I didn't know her well enough to know if that was normal or not.

I sipped my coffee.

I ate my granola bar.

I watched the crowd. They all looked fine. Apparently, cancelling out my big win cancelled out their bad luck-- eventually. I dodged a bullet there.

I sighed. I couldn't do that again, play a progressive machine with my good luck amplified. It was just too dangerous.

I checked the news but there was nothing about the quarantine. Maybe it was too soon? There was a boring story about the riot at the Odyssey yesterday--which considering it was a riot, was a good trick. How do you make a riot boring? Somehow, they managed it. Hundreds of people somehow compared notes at the casino and realized none of them were winning anything. Not one penny. Supposedly, rioting ensued. The news had a picture of a burned-out car in the parking lot. I hadn't seen any sign of it when I was there.

The morning dragged on.

I played virtual poker on my phone, but somehow without any real money in the game it was boring.

The morning dragged on.

"What'cha doing?" the ubiquitous bell-needing little girl asked.

"Where did you come from?" Jayden asked."I thought I took you back to your mom." He'd been lying on his cot.

"Playing a game," I said to the girl.

"I want to play a game!" she said.

I was dying of boredom. "What game did you have in mind?" I asked.

She shrugged. "I dunno." She was pretty cute in her little princess outfit. What games did I know that she could understand? Poker was probably too complicated.

"I do know a game we could play," I said. "Craps."

The girl giggled. "That's a funny name."

"Ella," Jayden said in a lecturery tone. "No."

"Relax, Jayden," I said.

"I want to play craps!" the girl said.

The problem was we didn't have any dice. I pondered. "You don't have any dice, do you?" I asked Jayden.

He said, "Nope." Well, it was a long shot. I wished I had my dice with me. But there was another possibility...

Eureka. "Do you have a piece of paper?" I asked.

He pointed at the counters over by the door. "There's some over there."

The little girl hovered near my cot, no doubt excited to play a game.

I stood. "You look like a princess," I said.

"Gosh." Jayden grinned and said, "Thanks.".

He was pretty funny. "Obviously, I wasn't talking to you, Jayden." I pointed at the girl. "You look like a pretty princess."

She simpered and said, "I know."

I started walking over to the counter and she followed. "What's your name?"

"I'm Abbie."

"What a pretty name," I said. "I'm Ella." Sure enough over by the doors were some office supplies next to the continental breakfast. "I'm going to make some dice."

"How do you do that?" Abbie asked.

"Well, we're going to cut up two sheets of paper into six squares each. And then we'll write the numbers one, two, three, all the way up to six, on them."

"I know my numbers!" Abbie said. "Can I help?"

"Yes, you can," I said. "I'll do the cutting and you can write the numbers."

"Yes!" she said, acting like this was the best idea since the beginning of ...ideas.

Once we had our two sets of dice, I stood. "We need more players." We walked back towards the other people. "Do you have any money, Abbie?"

"Yes," she said.

Abbie and I rounded up the other four kids and I taught them the rudiments of craps. "So, to summarize, we 'roll' a die by picking one of the pieces of paper without looking at it."

"I think my phone has this game," a very freckly eleven-ish-year-old said. He was staring down at his phone, flicking through screens. "You wanna 'roll' numbers that have already been rolled, right?" He glanced up from his phone.

"Yes." I smiled. Taking these kids' money would be like, well, taking money from babies. "All you need is some money to bet with."

Abbie pulled a dollar out of her pocket. "I have a dollar."

"Excellent," I said. "Everybody get out their money."

From right behind me, Jayden said, "Ella," in a very growly voice.

I startled. I hadn't known he was there. I pointed at the kids. "Practice 'rolling the dice.'" We'd put the two stacks of paper in two different plastic bowls.

I turned around, smiling. "Yes, can I help you with something?"

"You can't seriously be considering playing craps with a bunch of kids!" he whispered with vehemence. Mister goody-two-shoes strikes again.

"It's a couple dollars," I said. I pointed around the room. "You don't see any parents objecting do you? I'm doing a service, basically baby-sitting all the kids." I felt a little pang. I'd had a lot of fun spending time with Hannah when she was a kid. I was a little concerned she hadn't gotten back to me yet. I hoped she was all right.

He looked like he hadn't considered that I might be helping the parents.

"You're welcome to help me if you want," I said. "You can keep an eagle-eye on me to make sure I don't corrupt any minors." A small grin may have slipped out on my part.

He looked confused. Finally, he said, "Okay. I can help." He held up his forefinger. "But they're betting with paperclips. No money."

I shrugged. "Fine."

I turned back to the kids. "Hey, everyone, I'd like you to meet my lovely assistant Jayden."

"Lovely assistant?" he said. Oops. That may have been a bit of a Freudian slip.

I nodded, smiling. "He's going to help us play craps."

Jayden got a box of paperclips from the office supplies, and we all got to playing. Gradually, we accrued an audience of bored adults.

I wouldn't say any actual gambling occurred, but the kids did laugh a lot and practiced their numbers.

My phone rang. It was Hannah. Hurray.

I poked Jayden. "I have to take this call. Can you take over here?"

I stepped away before even hearing his answer. "Hannah? Are you all right?"

"No," she said. "Yes. I don't know." She sounded like she'd been crying or was about to start.

"Just slow down and tell me what's going on." I walked over to the window. We were on the ground floor. The sun was shining, a breeze was blowing right on the other side of the glass. It looked like a totally normal day out there. It was a little jarring since it was not a normal day in here.

In the background, the crowd around the craps game cheered loudly.

"I ran away," Hannah said. "Can you come?"

I eyed the window. Maybe I could come. I wanted to come. "Where are you?"

"I'm at that coffee shop you like."

"Here in KC?"

"Yeah." She sniffled.

"Yes. I'll come." I looked around the room. "I'll be there as soon as I can." No one was paying any attention to me. I opened the window and climbed out.

Chapter Twenty-Five

I caught a ride over to KC Cafe via an app. The driver had no idea that I'd escaped from quarantine--which was a very good thing. People tended to get worked up at words like 'quarantine.'

Jayden called when I was in the car, but I didn't answer.

When I arrived at the cafe, Hannah was sitting at the tall counter against the front window. It still smelled like cinnamon inside.

She jumped up when she saw me come in.

I ran over and wrapped her in my arms. "What is it? What's wrong?"

She started sobbing. My heart was breaking because her heart was clearly breaking. I had to blink back tears. I needed to be strong for her.

"I'm here for you Hannah," I said. "But I can't help you if you don't tell me what's wrong."

She lifted her head. "I'm pregnant!"

"Oh," I said. "Is that all?" Phew. I felt relieved.

"Is that all!" she shrieked. "It's a lot."

I patted her back. "You're right. It's a lot. But it's not like you're dying."

She stepped back from me. "I might as well be."

"Oh, come on, Hannah," I said. "Dying?"

She wiped her face with her sleeve. "My foster mom Amelia said I was out if I got pregnant."

"Ouch." Hannah had been with Amelia the longest of any of her foster families.

"She said I shouldn't have sex."

While sensible, I wasn't sure that was practical advice for a seventeen-year-old. "Why didn't you use protection?" I asked softly. I'd had the protection talk with her. More than once.

"We did!"

"Ouch." Now that was unlucky. My breath caught in my throat. Could all my messing around with luck have hurt Hannah? I tried to get a grip. One step at a time, Ella.

At least she'd stopped crying.

"Sit down," I said. "Let me buy you a beverage."

"Okay." She sat. "I want a green tea."

"Sounds good," I said. "Two green teas coming up."

At the counter, the employee said, "Hey, you're the craps lady."

I had a moment of disorientation. "What?" I'd just been playing craps at the hospital but how could she know that?

"You taught us how to play craps. Are you here for another game?"

Oh, right. We'd played craps here at the coffee shop, too. Could Crystal be right about my so-called problem? Nah. "No," I said to the employee. "Not today. Please give me two green teas."

A little while later I handed Hannah a tea and sat next to her at the front counter. I patted her hand. "I promise you I'll help you through this, whatever happens."

She took a sip of tea.

"So, first things first," I said. "How do you know you're pregnant?"

"I haven't had my period in, like, three months," she whispered, glancing around the shop. There weren't any other customers.

No wonder the employees wanted to play games.

"Three months? That seems like a long time." It also was long before I got my q-computer to work. Phew. I unclenched parts of my body that I hadn't even known I could clench.

I glanced at her stomach. Did pregnant women show at three months? I didn't detect any bulge.

"Yeah," she whispered. "I'm kind of irregular. So the first month, I wasn't too worried. But now..."

"Yes, three months is a long time." I took a sip of tea. "But you didn't take a home test or anything?"

"No," she said. "I didn't want Amelia to see it."

"All right. I think we need to go to Planned Parenthood. Now." I got up off the stool. "I know where one is."

"But I don't think my insurance will cover it."

"It doesn't matter," I said. "I have my credit card."

The Planned Parenthood clinic was in a small strip mall near the coffee shop. Inside, it reminded me more of a low-end tanning salon than a doctor's office. They had a giant sign above the check-in desk that said, 'Prenatal Care. Postnatal Care. Family Planning.'

While Hannah was in with the doctor, I called Amelia again. It went to voicemail and I left a message. "I'm with Hannah. She's okay. This is Ella."

I called my mom.

She answered right away. "Did you find Hannah?"

"Yeah," I said. "More like she found me."

"Is she all right?"

"Yes." I paused, not sure what to say. I didn't want to break Hannah's confidence, but Mom was generally very helpful. Finally, I said, "We're at Planned Parenthood."

I heard Mom draw in a long breath. She didn't say anything.

"Mom?"

"I take it you don't want me to tell that to Amelia if I talk to her?"

"No. Just tell her she's okay."

"Okay," she said. "Gotta go. I'm at work." She hung up.

I got bored sitting in the Planned Parenthood waiting room. The 'Safe Sex' posters and 'Protect Yourself from STDs' posters all seemed pretty dated. The plastic chairs were not super-comfortable.

Jayden called again. I answered out of boredom. "Where the hell are you, Ella!"

"Uh." He sounded mad. "You sound mad."

"Yeah! There's a little thing called a quarantine that I'm stuck in! And you're supposed to be stuck here, too! And, oh yeah, it's all your fault!" Yep. He was mad.

"Gah," I said. "Reak. Up. Sor." I hung up.

He immediately called back. "How could you hang up on me, Ella? The police--"

Just then the doctor, a middle-aged Caucasian woman, came out from the back. "Who's here for Hannah Kirkpatrick?"

"Sorry, Jayden." I hung up again.

I stood. "Me."

The doctor approached me. "You can't be her mom."

"I'm, ah, her Big Sister," I said.

"You look nothing like her."

"Not her bio-sister, her Big Sister," I said. "From Big Brothers, Big Sisters. Hannah's a foster kid."

"Oh, dear." The doc rubbed her face.

"She's okay, isn't she?" I asked. "She's just pregnant, right?"

"Legally, I'm not allowed to discuss her condition with you."

My phone rang again. I glanced at it. Not Jayden. Amelia. "Oh. This is Hannah's foster mom, Amelia. I need to take this."

"Ella?" Amelia asked. "You found her?"

"Yes." I studied the doctor. She looked grim. "She's basically okay, I think. But maybe you should talk to the doctor." I handed the doctor the phone. She walked down the back hall, talking.

Darn. I couldn't hear what she was saying.

I was getting a very bad feeling. I was getting a not-pregnant feeling. But if Hannah wasn't pregnant, what was wrong?

Finally, the doc came back and gave me back my phone. "Both Hannah and Amelia said I can tell you what's up. Come on back to the exam room."

We walked down the hall together, stopping outside one of the small examination rooms. My heart was pounding.

The doctor knocked on the door. "Hannah?"

We heard a muffled, "Come in," from inside.

We went in.

Hannah was sitting in a chair, dressed, looking scared. "What's going on? Why so many tests? You said you didn't think I was pregnant after all?"

"I just talked to your foster mom and told her what's going on," the doctor said. "I'm afraid I have bad news."

I stepped over to Hannah and grabbed her hand. "Whatever it is, we can take it," I said. "Hannah's tough."

Hannah glanced at me and then looked back at the doctor, nodding.

"I'm sorry to say, it looks like you have cancer, Hannah," the doctor said.

Now this did not compute. My chest felt like it was being crushed.

"Wh-what?" she asked. "I don't understand."

"We looked inside you with our equipment, right? I said the scans looked unusual. And then I took some samples and tested them." She paused for a breath. "You tested positive for the BRCA gene. I think you have cancer. I made you an appointment right away with an oncologist. Amelia's meeting you over at KC Medical Center."

No. This was impossible. Hannah was just a kid. She couldn't have cancer.

"What?" Hannah asked. She looked like she might fall down any second.

I put my arm around her shoulder.

The doc said, "Do you two understand what I'm saying? Cancer. You need to go meet your foster mom at the Med Center immediately."

"Come on, Hannah," I said. "I'll take to you meet your mom."

She looked up at me. "Cancer?"

I needed to be strong for her. "I'm sorry, sweetie," I said. "It's not fair. But I'm here for you. And Amelia's gonna be here for you, too."

The doc shook her head. "Even with the gene, it's very unlucky to get cancer so young."

Unlucky? My heart started pounding again.

At KC Medical Center (where I'd started the day), Amelia was waiting for us near the front doors. Wow. She must have broken the land-speed record to get here from Lawrence.

She ran to her daughter. "Hannah!"

"Mom!"

They embraced and both started crying. I felt myself tear up again.

I cooled my heels next to them in the lobby, trying to look unobtrusive.

Eventually, they separated and I approached. "So, do you know where this oncologist is?"

"Yes," Amelia said, glancing at her phone. "Dr. Murray gave me all the info." She turned towards the elevator. "This way."

Suddenly a big crowd of familiar people exited a hallway and entered the lobby. They were saying things like, "Good," "Finally," and "I can't wait to get home."

A little girl said, "Look! It's the kissing girl who ran away!" It was pretty princess Abbie from earlier.

Hannah and Amelia looked at me with 'Huh?' in their eyes.

"Text me the doctor info," I said quickly. "I'll catch up with you."

They nodded and got in the elevator.

Jayden was with Abbie and her mother. Of course. He said, "Ella? Is that you? Where have you been?"

"Around." I shuffled my feet a little. "I've been here the whole time." Sort of. Okay, not.

He said, "The police want to talk to you."

Chapter Twenty-Six

The police wanted to talk to me. Ugh. I debated running away, but considering they were, well, the police, I figured they'd track me down eventually.

Jayden had given me the contact info before he left with the others.

Reluctantly, I called the officer. I looked out over the lobby. Would this bland room be one of the last things I saw as a free woman? I sniffed. Would these medicinal smells be the last things I smelled?

The phone rang.

"Ms. Hote?" the cop answered.

"Yes," I said, dreading the worst. Did they put people in prison for sneaking out of a quarantine? For how long? Was he about to appear and slap the cuffs on me?

"We got news about your stolen computer thing," he said. "Just a sec..."

"Oh?" They weren't calling me because I slipped out of quarantine. Yay!

He paused, then said, "We believe your computer was stolen by a man named Zander Magillicutty."

I knew it had been Zander! And now, I also knew why Zander'd used such bland pseudonyms.

"You're not going to believe it, but this Zander guy may have been involved in the shenanigans at the Odyssey casino yesterday. He's an employee, or, I guess, now, a former employee."

I'd believe it, I'd totally believe it, but I tried to sound surprised. "Oh?"

"Yes. Security footage shows him taking the computer

prototype onto the casino floor and doing something with it right before the craziness began."

"Oh?"

"Does that computer of yours have any special properties that would cause it to affect the electronics in the casino?" This was a surprisingly astute question on his part.

"Uh. Not that I know of." Technically, I didn't know one hundred percent for sure. I may have been ninety-nine percent sure...

He sighed. "Yeah. It was a long shot." Not so long.

"But, wait," I said. "Does that mean you've recovered my computer? And this Zander guy is in custody?" Yay!

"No," he said. "I'm sorry to say he slipped through our fingers. He's one lucky son of a gun." Damn. Zander clearly knew about the q-computer's power and how to use it.

"You don't say," I said.

There was a moment of silence.

"So?" I asked. "Anything else?" Was this where he lowered the boom about skipping out of quarantine? Were some cuffs in my future?

"Nope," he said. "We'll keep in touch." He hung up.

I stared at my phone in surprise. That was it? No trouble with the police? No mayhem? No mishaps? In the lobby of the hospital, people continued walking by, on their way to or from doctor's appointments.

Hannah. I rushed to the elevators.

My heart descended at the same rate the rest of me ascended in the elevator. The Zander debacle made me forget Hannah's problem for a few moments, but now it came rushing back.

On the floor with the oncologist, everything was even more muted than downstairs. The walls and carpeting were a vague beige color. The lighting was muted. Some kind of musak was playing in the background, muted.

I approached a big check-in desk where a nurse in light blue scrubs sat . Behind her the muted Royals game was on the large flat screen.

Can I help you?" she asked softly.

"I'm looking for Hannah--"

She interrupted. "Yes. They said you could go on back. They're meeting with Dr. Nguyen." She pointed down the hall.

I walked down the hall, with my heart dragging behind me on the bland carpet. I stopped outside the office labeled 'Dr. Nguyen.'

"Yes?" The middle-aged Asian woman sitting behind the stylish wooden desk asked through the open office door. She had on a pristine white lab coat. Two familiar-looking women sat facing her in equally-stylish wooden chairs on the other side of the desk.

Hannah and Amelia swiveled around.

"Ella!" Hannah said.

"Please join us," Amelia said. The wrinkles around her mouth looked deeper than ever.

"Hi, I'm Dr. Nguyen. You must be Ella." She pointed at the one remaining empty chair in front of the desk. "I was just saying a strong support system increases the odds of a long and happy life." At least she didn't say 'the odds of survival.'

I sat. "I'm ready to support Hannah with whatever she needs."

My phone trilled. I glanced at it. There was a new text from Jayden. 'Tuche's back. Get to Qubyte ASAP.' I had a second of relief as I realized Tuche wasn't dead or something.

"What?" Hannah looked at the phone in my hand.

I turned it off and put it back in my pocket. "It's nothing. Please continue, doctor."

"We ran some tests and I'm afraid the news isn't good. Ovarian cancer. It is very unusual for a young woman Hannah's age to get this diagnosis," she said, consulting the screen on her desk. Judging by the doc's Southern twang she was from Tennessee or thereabouts. Somehow it made all this seem even more surreal. "Often there's a genetic component in these cases. Have any of your relatives had any trouble?"

Amelia grimaced. "Hannah's an orphan. We don't have any information about her family."

"Just my luck," Hannah muttered.

"Don't give up hope. We're developing new treatments every day," the doctor continued. "We can target your treatment to your specific DNA..."

After almost a solid hour of medical jargon, my head was swimming and Dr. Nguyen let us go.

The three of us waited for the elevator.

"Wow," I said. "That was a lot of information."

Amelia clutched a pile of papers to her chest. "Yeah." She was supposed to study the info and agree to a course of treatment for Hannah.

Hannah herself looked dazed.

"We're going back to Lawrence," Amelia said. "Can you join us?"

I'd pulled out my phone. Jayden had left a bunch more texts. "I actually have to go into work. There seems to be some kind of emergency."

"Please?" Hannah said.

"I can't get fired, sweetie," I said. "How about this. I'll call my mom and ask her to meet with you to help you go over the materials. And we can all meet up or vid-chat later?"

They looked uncertain.

"You know she worked in the oncology department for years," I said. "She's got a lot of expertise. I don't understand any of this stuff, myself." Except to know it's all bad.

"Okay," Hannah finally said.

"Yeah. That sounds helpful," Amelia said. "Really helpful."

At Qubyte, Inc. Avery was not sitting out front at the reception desk. My nerves started ratcheting up again. Why wasn't she out of the hospital yet? Had something else happened to her?

I ran back to the quantum computing lab.

But there Avery sat in the lab with some other people. "Oh, thank goodness!" I ran up to her and hugged her. "I'm so glad to see you. When did you get out of the hospital? Are you all right?"

She seemed surprised at all the attention, immediately trying to extricate herself. "Thanks, Ella." Oh, right. We hadn't known each other very long.

I stepped away from her. "I'm just glad you're doing better." I resisted the urge to force her to tell me exactly how she was doing. Had she made a full recovery?

Jayden and a couple of gray-haired Caucasian men I didn't recognize also sat there with Dr. Tuche. In-person, if anything, Dr. Tuche looked even more distinguished with his neat white beard and full head of white hair. Somehow the lab looked different with the big boss inside it, more official and important.

They were all staring at me.

Jayden stood. "Ella! There you are." He approached me, saying quietly, "What took you so long? Dr. Tuche's been wondering where you were." He still looked disheveled. Sleeping on a cot at the hospital did not agree with him.

Had that only been last night? It seemed like a century ago.

I glanced around the room. I wasn't comfortable telling a bunch of strangers Hannah's medical condition.

I took a step towards Tuche. "Dr. Tuche, sir." I held out my hand. "It's a pleasure to meet you in person."

He stood up and shook my hand slowly. "Likewise. I think."

I tried to smile at him.

I don't know how successful I was, because he said, "Avery, gentlemen, why don't you give us the room?"

Avery looked surprised. The two strange men looked surprised. Jayden looked really surprised. The four of them stood up. The two strangers headed towards the door.

"Catch you later," one of them said.

The other said, "Yeah."

Avery slowly followed them out the door and exited after throwing us one last glance.

Jayden just sort of stood there. "Me, too?"

"Jayden can stay," I said.

Dr. Tuche shrugged. "Okay." He sat back down. "Why haven't you been at work, Ella?"

"I had a family emergency," I said.

Jayden looked surprised. He sat back down as well.

I remained standing.

"I'm gonna need more," Dr. Tuche said.

I sighed. "My little sister was diagnosed with ovarian cancer, just now. We were meeting with the oncologist."

Jayden looked stunned. "Hannah?" I'd told him all about her, how she was a great athlete and sweet, and basically all around awesome.

"Yeah." My eyes felt heavy with tears suddenly.

"Oh, no," Jayden said.

"That is very bad news." Dr. Tuche studied me carefully, like he was trying to discern if I was lying or not. I must have passed the test because he said, "I'm sorry. That's awful." He paused. "I really need to talk to you, but it sounds like you should go be with your family. They need you more."

"We have plans for later." I sat down. "What's up?"

He stared at me for a few moments. Finally, he said, "I'm concerned Ella. There was a quarantine? That you snuck out of? Jayden's been telling me strange things. And my colleague, your Professor Smithson, even asked me unusual questions--which I can't help thinking is your influence."

Did that mean Professor Smithson believed me that q-computers might affect luck? That would be a speck of good news amongst all this gloom. I didn't like disagreeing with him.

Dr. Tuche had kept talking. I'd missed some of what he'd said. "So, in conclusion, I'm sorry."

I must have missed an important bit. "What?"

"Sir," Jayden said. "This doesn't seem fair. You can't do that to her. Ella's in the middle of a very difficult time."

"Wait," I said. "What's happening?" What was he doing to me? "I don't understand."

Dr. Tuche said, "As I said, I'm suspending you, Ella."

What? My brain was having trouble processing.

My phone pinged. Professor Smithson had texted 'Are you all right?'

My brain jump-started and I was angry. How dare he suspend me? I didn't do anything wrong.

But I knew I couldn't lose my temper. "Dr. Tuche, of course I'll abide by your wishes," I said. "But can you tell me what I need to do to get off suspension?"

He looked flabbergasted. "Huh..." Obviously, he hadn't thought that far ahead.

"Please let me know, sir," I said. "I'm happy to do whatever tasks or research you need to prove myself." An idea had occurred to me. And it was not a nice idea.

"Hmm." Dr. Tuche didn't seem to know what to make of me at this point. Did he just expect me to crawl away with my tail between my legs? That wasn't me.

"I'll just get my personal property together, then," I said. "Jayden, didn't you say you had a short appointment right about now?"

Jayden stared at me with a stupid look on his face.

"Out of the lab," I said. "Now."

Jayden turned to look at Dr. Tuche, who frowned at him. Then, he looked back at me. "Yes," Jayden said unconvincingly. "I have an important appointment. Not here." He was talking a little robotically.

"I'm disappointed with you, Jayden," Dr. Tuche said. "You really shouldn't be leaving willy-nilly in the middle of the work day."

Jayden departed. I could tell he had no idea what I was about to do.

I suppressed a crazy giggle at the 'willy-nilly' as I went over to the cabinet and unlocked it. Yes, I was more than a little on edge with everything that had been going on.

"That young man also needs more supervision," Dr. Tuche said quietly, shaking his head. He turned to me. "Now what are you doing, young lady? You can't take Qubyte Inc. property with you."

"I understand, sir," I said. "This is my thesis project. I'd shown it to Jayden."

"Oh?" He looked interested in spite of himself. Good, I'd hooked him.

Before my conscience could get the better of me, I turned on my q-computer and did a calculation, with him standing right next to me. "You can see, it works well, sir." I immediately started packing it back up.

"Wait," he said. "That was too quick. I didn't see what happened."

Then, I flipped the coin. Heads. "I hypothesize I can get a bunch of heads in a row." I also hypothesized his bad luck backlash was equal and opposite to my good luck. Therefore, as long as I wasn't too lucky, he wouldn't be too unlucky.

"Several heads in a row?" he said. "I don't believe it. Are you saying you can do it because of your quantum computer?"

"Yes, sir." I flipped the coin. Heads. Flip. Heads. Flip. Heads.

Flip. Heads.

"What's happening?" he asked, face slack. "Is it a trick coin?"

"No. It's not a trick coin." I held it out. "You can try it."

He took it from me and promptly dropped it on the floor.

I started walking towards the door. "I am a team player, sir. If you say I'm suspended, I'm suspended."

We'd see how Tuche liked being under a bad luck cloud. 'Strange stuff,' my ass.

Chapter Twenty-Seven

When I went back to the B & B, Mrs. Flores seemed surprised to see me. "Are you all right, dear? You're not sick, are you?" she asked, bless her heart.

Sick. Like Hannah. My anger at Tuche was overcome by my sorrow for Hannah. "My sister Hannah is sick," I said.

Mrs. Flores covered her mouth with her hand. "Oh, no. Nothing serious, I hope."

I looked into her eyes and nodded slowly. "I'm sorry to say it is."

"Oh, no. That lovely girl I met? That's horrible. If there's anything I can do, please let me know."

What a good woman. I spontaneously hugged her. "Thanks. I appreciate that."

After a few moments we let go of each other.

"So, why are you home in the middle of the day?" she asked.

"I'm, uh, having an issue at work," I said. An almost-getting-fired issue.

She gave me a questioning look.

"It's a long story, I'd rather not get into it." It was too depressing. I didn't know what I'd do if I lost my job.

"Okay, dear," she said. "I'm not glad your sister's sick, but I'm glad you're here now. I have to go get my driver's license renewed. Today's the deadline. I must admit..." She laughed nervously. "I must admit, I've been procrastinating. I've been dreading the test." She looked up at me. "So, can you cover the B & B for me this afternoon? It would really help me out."

Since Mom was helping Hannah and Amelia, I'd been thinking I would go back over to the casino and see if I could find anything out about Zander Magillicutty. "Okay. But I have a quick errand first."

She smiled. "Thanks. I'll tell my friend Mabel she's off the hook. Her hip has been bothering her, anyway." She picked up her phone.

I zoomed up the stairs to my room, did a little calculation with my q-computer to enhance my luck and hid it in my underwear drawer under a bunch of feminine products. Ha. That was the last place a guy like Zander would look.

The Odyssey looked surprisingly normal when I arrived. Same plain walls, multicolored carpet, and pinging machines with people putting money in. You'd think after all the excitement of the last day or so, something would look different. But, nope. I casually strolled back to the business office area. I stopped in the hall in front of Dad's photo on the wall. The last thing I wanted was to run into him. I scanned the office through the windows into the hall. No sign of Dad. Good.

But, no sign of Zander either. Bad. There were plenty of signs of office workers, dressed in office clothes, however, sitting at desks looking at computer screens. Only four desks didn't have employees sitting at them.

What now?

If I was a stolen q-computer, where would I be?

If I was a stolen q-computer, I'd be long gone. On the run somewhere with Zander.

But I couldn't search random somewheres, I could only search where I was. I shrugged. One of these desks might be his, and there might be some kind of clue about where he'd gone. Of course, the cops probably already searched, but I might be luckier than them.

I squared my shoulders and took a confident step into one of the areas with an empty desk.

"Whoa, there, little lady," a man said. "Where do you think you're going?"

I swiveled, my heart thundering in my chest.

"Oh, it's the kisser." Tom the security guard flushed. "What are you doing here? You're not looking for me, are you?"

"Uh..." My eye caught the picture of Dad. "Hi, Tom. I'm, uh, looking for my dad."

"Who's your dad?"

I pointed at the portrait on the wall.

"Wow. Mr. Hernandez is your dad?" He squinted. "You never said anything. He never said anything. And you seem a little old..."

"Not Hernandez. John Hote's my dad." Apparently Dad had never bragged about me at work. I couldn't say I was surprised.

He froze for a second. Then he said, "Mr. Hote's the owner."

I nodded in a serious owner-like manner, I hoped. "I know."

He took a step back, holding up his hands, palms out. "I didn't know. Sorry for bothering you, ma'am." He stepped away backwards, facing me.

Wow. This was the first time my dad actually helped me. I turned and walked into the office like I deserved to be there.

Everyone turned to look at me.

"Has anyone seen Zander today?" I asked.

"No." "Nope." I was met by a lot of shaking heads. At least they knew a Zander.

"Anyone know where he is?"

"Nope." More shaking heads.

"Where's Zander's desk?" I asked forcefully.

They pointed at one of the empty desks.

One woman in a suit stood and walked into the hall to talk to Tom who was still loitering outside.

I stalked over to the desk in question and sat down in the chair. The top was clean. The computer was off. I touched the space bar to wake it up in case it was sleeping. The login screen appeared on the monitor. I had no idea what his password was. But I was looking for a q-computer. I pulled out all the drawers of the desk. They were empty except for some office supplies.

I leaned back in the chair.

A young woman approached me. "Do you know where Zander is?" She was pretty with an upturned freckle-covered nose and seemed very young. "I'm worried about him."

"Why worried?"

"Well, you know he sprained his leg. He was supposed to be working on a special project for Mr. Hote, but something happened."

220

"Mr. Hote?" So my dad was the mastermind of all this? My heart started thundering again. I should have figured Zander was too stupid to be a mastermind. "Do you know anything about the project?"

She pressed her lips together and shook her head back and forth slowly.

"Is this his desk?"

"Yeah."

I pushed the chair back so I could see underneath it. Nothing. There was nothing here.

"Is there anywhere else he kept his stuff?"

She pointed at the corner of the room. "He had to keep his crutches over there." Sure enough, two crutches leaned in the corner. So, Zander didn't have a sprained ankle any more? Considering how troublesome he'd been hobbling around on crutches, that probably wasn't a good thing.

I stood and walked over, with pretty-nose following after me. Crutches. Check. I didn't see anything else.

One of the guys in the office threw a balled up piece of paper at the trash can in the corner. He missed. The paper hit the can and rolled next to my foot. I leaned down to throw it away. Was the can raised up from the tile floor? It appeared to be floating. Weird. I dropped the paper wad in the can and lifted it up.

Underneath was my beautiful, gorgeous, stolen q-computer. I felt my face break out in a huge smile. I grabbed it, put the can back and stood.

"What the hell do you think you're doing?" It was Zander's voice. I twirled. It was the rest of Zander and he was glaring at me. What was he doing here? Weren't the cops after him? "Give that back!"

"No," I said quietly. People in the office were starting to stare at us. "You know it's mine."

"Thief!" he said too loudly.

"Let's take this in the hall." Before he, or anyone else, could do anything, I sprinted out of the office.

He ran after me. So, leg definitely feeling better, check.

In the hall, he grabbed for the q-computer. "Give it back!"

I dodged him. "No!"

He grabbed for it again and got a hold of one edge, but I didn't let go.

"Let go," he said. "You're going to break it." That was an interesting idea...

He grunted and pulled and slowly it slipped from my grasp.

"Shit," I said as he stood there holding my q-computer. We stared at each other for a moment, both breathing heavy. I clenched my fists.

Cradling my q-computer in his arms, he smirked.

I lost it. I threw a right hook right at his nose. It threw him off balance and he took one of his hands from the q-computer and touched his bleeding nose. "You bitch!"

"Me, a bitch? You're the bitch!" I punched him again, in the eye. He dropped the q-computer.

I scooped it up off the floor. I knew I might not have it for long though.

The floor near us in the business area was tile. I held the q-computer over my head and smashed it down on the tile. It flew into a dozen pieces. I stamped on the biggest ones, crushing them. Ha. Zander didn't deserve my q-computer.

"Ella?" I turned. It was my dad. He was standing there with Tom and the suited woman. "Tom said you were looking for me? What the hell is going on here?"

Suddenly, I felt queasy. How much of that had Dad seen? So much for first or second impressions. Wait. What was I worried about? He was the bad guy here.

Zander, looking the worse for wear, said, "She attacked me and stole casino equipment from me. Arrest her!" He shrieked on that last bit. Blood streamed from his nose and trickled from a cut above his eye.

"Is that true, Ella?" Dad asked. Even though I didn't know him, the disappointment in his eyes was crushing.

It took a few moments to get my dry mouth to work. "He, uh, deserved it," I said. "I was just defending myself and my property. And anyway, he's the criminal. The police are looking for him."

All the office workers were pressed up against the windows or in the doorway.

The girl I'd talked to earlier stepped up to us. "She brutally assaulted Zander. He didn't do anything to her. She's crazy." She ended by pointing her shaking finger at me.

"I press charges!" Zander screamed. "She's a thief and an assaulter! Arrest her!"

Dad looked from me to Zander and back again. Finally he said, "Tom, call the police."

All the way to the police station I felt nauseated and my pulse raced like I was running a marathon. I couldn't believe that was my first real interaction with my dad. I couldn't believe he'd had me arrested. I couldn't believe any of this.

Was Dad a bad guy? Was he some kind of mastermind?

I didn't feel any better at the station as they took my picture and pressed my fingers to a fingerprint-taking machine. I didn't feel any better as they took my stuff or as they made me enter a jail cell. The cell smelled of sweat, pee, and despair.

There were three other women in there. The old woman was drunk, lying on a bench, reeking of booze and snoring like a band saw. The eighteen-ish girl sitting on the bench ignored me.

The middle-aged white woman taking up the final space on the bench glared at me. "What's your story?"

I stood near the bars, facing the interior of the cell. "What's it to you?"

She narrowed her eyes.

I turned around and faced out of the cell.

There was nothing to look at out there. The hall was empty. My pulse gradually quieted, but I still felt sick. The minutes dragged on.

I thought I got a phone call?

I started to turn around to ask middle-aged-woman but she was standing right next to me. She punched me in the stomach.

Surprise! Initially, I was just shocked.

I involuntarily leaned over. But then, after a couple of seconds, pain blossomed in my gut. I couldn't breathe. I tried gasping for air.

She sauntered back over to the bench and sat, grinning a little.

My nerves and the punch combined to bring up my stomach contents. I went to the metal toilet in time, puking in the tiny bowl. After I puked my guts out, flushed, and then rinsed my mouth out in the tiny metal sink, I turned and glared at the woman.

She smiled back at me, pleased with herself.

I knew it would be stupid to get into a brawl with her, but, damn, it was tempting...

We stared at each other for a while. We stared at each other for a while longer.

After a while, honestly, I was getting bored.

She must have been, too, because she looked away.

I stood there near the sink for what seemed like a long time. Finally, I said, "Don't we get a phone call?"

She sort of laughed and said, "What's it to you?"

Okay, this was all probably karmic payback for punching Zander or something. But enough's enough, isn't it? "Seriously? Don't we get a call?"

"Why don't you ask for one?" she said sweetly.

Well, I knew that sweetness was suspicious, but... I stepped up to the bars. "Phone call! I want my phone call!"

A cop eventually appeared with a large taser. "Shut the fuck up, or you'll be sorry."

I jerked back from the bars.

After I didn't know how long (because I didn't have my phone), I gradually sank to the floor and sat there near the bars. I must have fallen asleep.

"Do you want a phone call or not?" A female officer glared at me.

"Uh, yes, ma'am." I got to my feet. Jesus, my neck hurt. "What time is it?"

"Three o'clock."

"In the morning?"

"Duh." She shook her head, walked me down the hall, and pointed at an old landline.

Well, shit. I didn't know any phone numbers. They were all on my phone. And who the hell could help me this time of night? I couldn't bother poor Hannah or her mom. I shouldn't bother Mom; she was an hour away and didn't need this problem. Obviously, I couldn't call my dad.

I stood there for a few moments.

There was a small piece of paper taped to the wall. I peered at it. 'Bail Bonds! Good rates! Good service!'

What the hell. I called the number.

"Bail Bonds. What can I do for you?" a tired-sounding man said.

"Uh, I'm in jail."

"Really, honey? Shocker. Who are you?"

"Ella Hote. Can you get me out or what?"

"What'd they charge you with?"

I tried to recall everything they'd told me when I got here. It had seemed unreal then and it seemed unreal now. "Assault. Breaking and entering."

He whistled. "Is that it?"

"Destruction of property."

"Well, shit, girl," he said. "You've been busy. I can't come until they open at nine a.m. You should get arraigned tomorrow morning. It'll cost you."

"Morning?" I may have sounded a little whiny.

"Welcome to the criminal justice system." He gave me a little more info, and we hung up.

The matron led me back to my cell. Ugh, 'my cell.'

There was still no room on the bench. I sat down on the floor in the corner and leaned back. My stomach still ached.

I tried to tell myself it was worth it. I'd gotten my q-computer back from a criminal. He could have hurt people with it.

I started to feel guilty about how I'd hurt people with my q-computer, but I squashed those feelings deep, deep down.

I didn't think being arrested would help my job prospects any. Dr. Tuche had already been mad at me. I was probably fired. Being fired would make it tough to find another job.

I knew Mom would be extremely disappointed in me.

My friends probably would be, too.

Hannah would be very disappointed if I didn't contact her like I'd promised I would. I hated breaking promises to her. This was the first time I'd broken a promise to anyone. And breaking a promise to a girl with cancer was l-o-w. I felt l-o-w.

And how would I tell Hannah I got arrested? Oh, no, Amelia might not even let me see her anymore.

I tried to calm my racing mind.

All that calming accomplished was I remembered I was supposed to help Mrs. Flores. I let her down, too.

I let everyone down.
Shit. I'd really screwed up this time.
My eyes filled.
I wasn't going to cry.
No way.
But I wouldn't bet money on it.

Chapter Twenty-Eight

The minutes in jail crept by.

I must have fallen asleep again at some point because the next thing I knew, the sun shone brightly through the window high on the wall. And I was the only one left in the cell.

The female cop from last night walked up and unlocked the cell. "If it isn't sleeping beauty. You got your arraignment." She opened the door. "Come on."

I ended up in a noisy courtroom chock-full of people, standing, or sitting in rows of chairs. A middle-aged gray-whiskered man in a rumpled suit rushed up to me and said, "Ella Hote?"

"Yeah," I said. "Who are you?"

He didn't answer, instead holding out a clipboard. "Sign here." Seriously? Paper?

I couldn't make heads or tails of what its legalese meant. "What is it?"

"Just sign it. There's no time to explain. It's how I get paid. Do you want my help or not?"

Since he was the only one here for me, and I was guessing my odds of getting out of here would plummet without him, I signed.

A bailiff or something read my name. The clipboard guy stepped towards the bench and said some stuff.

The judge said stuff and pounded her gavel. I didn't understand any of it.

The bailiff said someone else's name.

The clipboard guy came back to me, tearing off a piece of paper and handing it to me. I still couldn't believe they used dead trees in court. "Here. You plead not guilty. The court will be in touch with your trial date."

I took the piece of paper as if in a daze. "I have a trial date?"

"No," he said. "Weren't you listening?" He turned away. "The court will be in touch. Jesus, newbies." He darted over to another woman in the crowd with his clipboard.

Another officer led me back to the front of the jail, where I collected my personal belongings.

Of course, Mrs. Flores had left about ten voice mails. I didn't have the heart to listen to them.

Outside, it was as hot as ever, which was a good trick since it was only about 10 a.m.

I checked the bus schedule on my phone and tracked down the nearest stop.

At the B & B, Mrs. Flores was not happy. Of course, I would have bet large amounts of money that would be the case. And I couldn't blame her. "Where have you been, Ella?" she asked. "I missed my test." She took a step toward me. "And then, I got very worried. You didn't come home. You didn't call or anything." She looked so concerned my heart about broke from guilt. I'd let her down.

"I'm sorry, Mrs. Flores." I gulped. "I know I let you down. If you want to fire me, I understand."

"What happened?" she asked. "I called your mom, and she didn't know anything. I called the police, and they said you had to be missing for twenty-four hours before they could do anything."

"I'm sorry." I didn't want to tell her I had spent the night in jail. Odds were she'd fire me if she found that out.

She tilted her head. "You're not going to tell me?"

"I'd rather not, ma'am."

She stared at me for a few moments. "Your mom told me more about your little sister Hannah. Such a sad situation. I may have thought of something that might help a little."

She pawed through the papers on the front desk. "One of our guests had a couple of tickets for the Royals game tonight that he couldn't use. I think it's sold out. Oh, here they are." She held them up. "Do you think you and your sister could use them? You said she played softball, right? It might cheer her up."

I accepted them with gratitude. "Thank you! That's a

wonderful idea. It'll definitely cheer her up. I don't think she's ever been to a pro game."

"It's lucky I had them," she said. "I'm glad I could help."

I texted Hannah immediately to invite her. She was thrilled to accept.

I had the beginnings of an amazing idea of how I might, just might be able to help Hannah. Royals stadium held almost 40,000 fans...

I'd called Jayden and asked him to fire up the q-computer at Qubyte. He'd taken some convincing but eventually agreed. So, I was very nervous as Hannah, and I arrived at the game. Was I really thinking about doing this? Was I really thinking about trying to use luck to help her?

Odds were I'd get hurt, but at this point, what did I have to lose?

Hannah was positively bubbling when we walked into the K. "Wow! Look how big it is!" she said. "Ooh! Look at that neat fountain! Wow! Look at all the people! Look at the grass; it's so green. Is it real? What are all those W's on the wall for?"

I laughed, delighted to see her so happy. It was even a beautiful evening, not too hot.

She couldn't seem to stop smiling. "What?" she asked, looking at me.

"Don't you ever take a breath?" It was wonderful to see her forgetting her troubles for the moment. I couldn't stop smiling either.

She breathed in and out loudly. "There. Satisfied? So, where are our seats? Are we gonna get hot dogs?"

I shifted my big bag, trying to get a better look at the seat numbers. "Of course, we're getting hot dogs."

"Can I get a beer?" she asked.

I wavered for a second. She was underage, but what if she didn't make it to legal drinking age? I shook my head. I wasn't going to think so negatively. "No. Of course you can't get a beer. You're underage."

The sound system played rousing sports music. The stadium was mostly full, everyone already in their seats, talking and enjoying their refreshments.

We continued our seat quest. "I think they're down there." I shifted my bag again so I could point.

"Why'd you bring your computer?" she asked.

Because I was going to save her life. Maybe. I didn't want to get her hopes up, in case it didn't work. "I'd like you to, ah, help me with an experiment."

"Seriously? You're working? Now? We're at a frikking Royals game."

I found the row with our seats. Most of the other fans were already there.

"Ooh, the game's supposed to start in a few minutes," she said. "Let's hurry and sit down."

Standing at the end of the row, I pointed and said, "Sorry, we're in there." The people in our row stood to make room for us. So, they were nice people. Damn.

As we made our way down the row, I kept my eye out for kids. I didn't want any kids sitting near us. I wasn't sure what I'd do if there were kids nearby but I'd do something.

But I didn't see any kids in our section. Phew.

Hannah and I sat.

"Wow," Hannah said. "These are great seats. Lucky us."

They were great seats. "Yeah, lucky us." We were behind home plate, only a few rows back.

"Hey, is that one seat down there red?" she asked. "Why is that? All the other seats are blue, aren't they?"

I shook my head, smiling again at her enthusiasm. "I don't know. All I know is this stadium is historical. It's from the 1970s or something."

"Wow," Hannah said. "That's ancient."

"I know why it's red," the man sitting on the other side of her said.

She eagerly turned to him. "Why?"

I tuned them out and took my q-computer out.

"What's that you got there?" the man sitting on the other side of me asked.

I didn't want to get drawn into conversation with anyone. Truth be told, I didn't want them to become real people to me. Was this guy next to me a parent? I squelched that thought. I was getting to be a good squelcher.

I glanced around, looking for kids again. None in the immediate vicinity. Good.

"What's that?" the man asked again.

"I think the game's about to start." I pointed down at the field.

He eagerly turned to the field, where players were running around, doing something.

Hannah continued to chat with the guy next to her.

Did I dare do this?

I watched Hannah. She smiled and laughed, her face flushed. She deserved a chance to go to other baseball games. She deserved to go to prom and graduate high school. She deserved the opportunity to go to college and get married and have kids. She deserved a life, or at least a better chance for a life.

I looked around. We were essentially surrounded with 40,000 people. They were probably mostly good people. They didn't deserve to get cancer or anything dire like that.

If my conservation of luck hypothesis was correct, Hannah would just need a little good luck from each of them to get better.

Of course, I didn't have any hard data to back up my hypothesis. But I felt in my gut that it was true.

They made announcements.

Everyone except me stood up.

Pulse thundering, I turned on the q-computer.

The strains of the National Anthem started. A breeze blew, bringing the scents of beer, popcorn and anticipation.

"Oh, say, can you see, by the dawn's early light..."

Hannah poked me. "Stand up, Ella."

I stood but couldn't muster up the ability to sing. My heart hammered my chest. Was I going to do it?

The music crescendoed. *"O'er the land of the free and the home of the brave!"*

I felt myself tear up a little. We were all united, 40,000 brave people.

Everyone sat and I joined them. I believed people were innately good. I believed folks would give a little good luck, would take a little bad luck to save a girl's life. We could unite and save Hannah. I blinked back tears.

I leaned over towards Hannah and handed her my q-computer. "Here." I had to clear my throat. "Take this."

"What? Now?" she asked, staring at the field. "It's the first pitch."

"Please," I said. Apparently, I was going to do it. "It's important."

She raised her eyebrows but took the computer.

"I need you to enter exactly what I say," I said. "Are you ready?"

"Why can't we watch the game?"

"We will in a second. Are you ready?"

"All right."

The baseball fans in the neighboring seats were giving us dirty looks. "Enter one plus one equals, and then hit return."

"Is that it?"

"Yes. Do it. Now. Please."

"All right." She typed it in with one finger. "There." She looked up at me.

My head was shoved back, followed quickly by a horrible pain in the middle of my forehead. The pain was too much...

I came to, head pounding, with a stranger in a uniform staring into my face. "Miss? Can you hear me?" He shined a small light into my eyes. I appeared to still be in the stadium in my seat.

"Who're you?" I asked. "Where's Hannah?"

I was surrounded by people staring at me.

Hannah shoved her face in front of mine. "I'm here. Oh, good. You're okay."

My forehead was killing me and I felt like I was going to vomit.

"Can you tell me your name, miss?"

"She's Ella Hote," Hannah said.

The EMT turned to her. "Please back up a bit, miss. I need her to tell me her name." He turned back to me.

I said, "Ella Hote."

"We're going to put you on this stretcher now," he said.

"I don't want to leave," I said. "This is Hannah's first game."

He seemed to ignore me. He and his partner got me on a

stretcher and started wheeling me away. All the jostling was not helping my head.

Everyone in the stadium cheered for some reason. The announcer said something about the game.

Hannah followed after us.

"Hannah, go back to your seat. I don't want you to miss the game."

"Yeah, right," she said. "And, don't worry, I've got all your stuff."

I looked at one of the EMTs. "I really don't want to leave."

"Fine," he said. "We'll take you to the first aid station and assess you there."

"But no promises," the other one said.

I finally lay back and relaxed a little. "What happened? Why does my head hurt so much?"

"You got hit by a ball!" Hannah said. "Right smack in the head.

"Unlucky," the EMT said.

It was hard to think around the throbbing. But, maybe, just maybe, it meant my plan worked?

Chapter Twenty-Nine

In the first aid station at the baseball stadium, I could periodically hear the roar of the fans. It was dark in the small room and it smelled like old popcorn, sticky soda and stale beer.

My head hurt. A lot.

"Why don't you turn on a light or something?" I asked the EMT sitting with Hannah and I. He was reading something on his tablet.

"The power's hinky." He shook his head and his close-cropped brown hair didn't move.

"It was crazy!" Hannah said, face flushed. "The ball headed right for your forehead. Smack! And everyone around us, like the whole section, was so surprised they all dropped their drinks and hot dogs and everything. Food and beer and soda was flying all over." She wiped a wet spot on her shoulder.

"Huh." It sounded like a lot of bad luck all around. Could Hannah have gotten some good luck? Was she cured? "How do you feel, Hannah?"

"Me? Fine. Why? I didn't get hit by the ball and only minorly by a beer. The question is: how do you feel?"

Fine didn't tell me anything. She felt fine before.

"A little better than I did," I said. "The pain meds must be kicking in."

"You should see the huge bump you have in the middle of your forehead." She grinned. "You look sort of like a unicorn."

"Heh, heh." I knew she was trying to cheer me up.

The EMT's radio squawked. "Jorje, come in."

The EMT picked up his radio and pressed a button. "This is Jorje. What?"

"Get out here! The whole stadium is puking! The beer must

have something in it!"

"On my way," he stood. "Are you ladies okay for the moment?"

"Yeah," I said weakly.

"Get out there, dude!" Hannah said. "They need you."

He didn't have to be told twice. He ran out with his bag of gear.

"Everyone's puking?" Hannah said. "That sounds horrible. I'm glad we're not out there."

The crowd roared and it sounded like a 'Boo.' So not everyone was puking.

She twisted around to face the door. "I wonder what's happening with the game?"

"Go check."

"No. I couldn't leave you."

"Please. I'm fine. I'm just gonna lie here and rest."

"Well..."

"I insist." I felt bad about ruining her first pro baseball experience.

"I guess it couldn't hurt to take a peek." She stood. "But if I see any puke I'm coming right back!" She walked to the doorway. "I'll be back soon."

Before I knew it, the game was over and Hannah was standing over me in the first aid station.

"I've never seen anything like it," she said. "So many errors! Every single score was the result of a mishap."

How could the game be over already? Had I fallen asleep? Did that mean I didn't have a concussion? You weren't supposed to sleep if you had a concussion, right?

I gingerly sat up. My head didn't hurt quite as much--which meant I didn't feel like I was about to die. "Where's the EMT?"

"He never came back. There was a massive case of food poisoning, er, I guess it was actually in the beer. Beer poisoning? I'm glad I didn't drink any. I think they called in a bunch more EMTs. They were actually giving out free bottles of water!" She stopped and wrinkled her nose. "There's a lot of puke out there."

If the game was over, we should leave. Could I drive? I swung my legs over the side of the cot. So far, so good.

235

She reached for my arm. "Should you be doing that?"

I stood. "Well, I'm not staying here all night." Dizzy, I swayed.

"Careful!"

I took a step towards the door. "I guess you better drive."

"All right," she said. "Where are we going?" She grabbed my big bag with one hand, and my arm with the other.

"Let's go to my mom's," I said. "She's a nurse."

She made a laughing noise. "Really? Your mom's a nurse? I know she's a nurse." Then, she scrunched up her nose and moved her face near my face. "Are you sure you're okay?"

"Close enough." I nodded. Ooh. Dizzy.

But the next time I was conscious I was not at Mom's house. I lay in a small high bed with pastel-colored blankets to match the pastel-colored walls. I appeared to be in the hospital. I looked around the bland room. The sun shone brightly, throwing stripes of light on the walls. There was another patient sleeping on another bed across the room.

My head still hurt.

Where was Hannah? Where was my mom?

I debated yelling for a nurse.

But a dark-haired man napped in the chair between the beds, his face resting in his hand. Was he here for me or the other patient?

I craned myself up on my elbow. It was Jayden. What was he doing here? "Jayden?"

He stirred. "What?" Looking at me, he sat up. "Oh, thank God. Ella, you're awake."

"What are you doing here?" Where was Hannah? Where was my mom? "Not that I'm not glad to see you."

"I'm here to see you."

"For that matter what am I doing here?"

"I guess there was an accident at the Royals game? You got hit in the head by a ball. A lot of other weird stuff happened at the game, too. It was on the news."

Gulp. "No one else got hurt did they?"

"Beer poisoning," he said. "I didn't even know that was a thing."

"Me neither. Did they all recover?"

"Yeah. So..." I knew he was going to ask what I'd done at the game, why I'd asked him to turn on his q-computer.

I ignored it. "Where's my mom? Where's Hannah?"

"Your mom had to go to work. Hannah had an appointment with her oncologist." He looked grim. "She's charming, by the way." He shook his head. "It's horrible to see such a young person so sick."

"When did you meet Hannah?"

"A little while ago." He pulled his chair closer to my bed. "I was actually here to visit Dr. Tuche. I ran into Hannah and Amelia in the elevator."

My heart sunk. I was afraid to ask. "Dr. Tuche? Please tell me he's okay."

Jayden nodded. "They're releasing him later today." He paused. "He twisted both his knees in some kind of freak accident." He paused again. "Supposedly."

"Both legs! That sounds horrible." My heart was still in the basement. "It was my q-computer, right?" I regretted impulsively firing up my q-computer in front of him just to prove a point.

Jayden nodded. "I think so."

"Does Dr. Tuche know it?"

"I'm not sure. He's definitely suspicious." He glanced at his phone. "He insisted on talking to me. Actually, I told him to meet me here about now."

Damn q-computer. "Is my bag here?" I glanced around the room and didn't see any of my stuff.

Jayden shrugged. "I don't know."

I was going to smash that damn thing. "Can you look around for it?"

He stood up. "Okay. Why?"

I didn't answer that. "Do you know why my mom's not here?" I asked in a little voice. I knew it was immature, but I missed her.

He walked towards the drawers. "As I understand it, she wouldn't leave your side for the first couple days or so. But her boss finally said she had to come in or she was fired."

"Couple days?" Damn. "How long have I been here?"

An elderly nurse with short white hair and hot pink scrubs

wheeled Dr. Tuche into my room.

Both his legs were wrapped, sticking straight out. He wore some kind of track suit with the legs cut off. He badly needed a shave and his hair was in disarray.

"Jayden!" Dr. Tuche said. "And Ella! You're conscious? Good."

The nurse parked the wheelchair near my bed. "Can you take it from here, sir?" she asked Jayden.

Jayden walked back to his chair and sat down. "Yes."

The nurse walked out.

Dr. Tuche stared from me to Jayden and then back at me.

We didn't say anything. The silence grew oppressive.

Finally, Dr. Tuche said, "Well? Don't you have something to tell me?"

"What would that be, sir?" Jayden asked.

Dr. Tuche gestured at his legs. "Do you know anything about this?"

"Uh..." Jayden said.

Dr. Tuche faced me. "Ella? What do you have to say for yourself?"

"I'm sorry you got hurt?" I said.

He stared at us some more.

I couldn't tell if he knew anything or not. If he didn't, my confession would just make things worse. But, he did seem suspicious. "I apologize," I finally said.

"For what exactly?" he asked.

"We..." I glanced at Jayden. "Er, I mean, I, suspected my quantum computer might affect luck. But no one seemed to believe me."

Jayden stayed silent.

"So, it could be that when I used my q-computer right near you I stole your good luck." I could feel my eyebrows moving up my forehead and my nose wrinkling. "So, you had a kind of luck deficit?" I quit talking.

"That's it?" Dr. Tuche asked. "Are you asking me or telling me? You gave me a luck deficit?" He faced Jayden. "What do you have to say about all this?"

Jayden said, "Ella does have a hypothesis called conservation of luck."

Ella has it? Implying he didn't share my hypothesis?

"Seriously?" Dr. Tuche asked.

Hannah ran into the room with Amelia trailing her. Amelia looked shell-shocked. Oh, no.

But Hannah looked happy, excited.

"You'll never guess!" Hannah said, eyes flashing and cheeks flushed. "The doctor says I'm all better! Complete remission. My cancer totally went away!"

Chapter Thirty

It worked! My plan worked. Hannah was cured. My eyes filled with tears as my heart filled with joy. She deserved it. "Oh, I'm so glad, Hannah. That's wonderful." It made everything that had happened worth it.

"Yeah!" Jayden said. "Congratulations!"

"It's a miracle," Amelia said.

Dr. Tuche's head turned this way and that, like he didn't know where to look. "What's happening here?"

"I had cancer but I got cured by a miracle, or something!" Hannah bounced up and down. Her smile diminished slightly. "Who are you again?"

"This is Dr. Tuche, my boss," Jayden piped up. His boss? Not my boss? Oh, right, I was suspended.

"Uh, nice to meet you, sir. I'm Hannah."

"What happened to you?" Amelia asked, pointing at his legs.

Dr. Tuche frowned and said, "I don't want to talk about it."

It felt weird to be lying flat on my back with so many people standing around me. I tried to sit up. I started getting really dizzy. The room spun around and around.

Hannah ran to my side. "Ella? What's wr--"

Everything went black.

When I came to, it was dark outside, but several people still crowded around my bed in the lighted hospital room.

"Thank God, Ella!" Hannah said.

Something was lying on my legs. I glanced down. It was my q-computer. My hand was near the keyboard. Oh no. Did that mean it had been used? By me? Did I steal someone's luck? "Hannah, are you all right?" My voice came out as a croak.

In the background, I heard Jayden say, "I think it worked, Professor Smithson."

Hannah leaned down and put her ear near my mouth. "How do you feel?"

I tried to talk again. "Hannah, are you all right?"

She opened her eyes wide. "Am I all right? I'm fine. Are you all right?" She straightened up.

I could see a bunch of nurses and doctors, and in the back Amelia, Jayden, Crystal and my mom.

Mom approached the bed. "Oh, thank God." She leaned down and kissed my forehead. Why did everyone keep saying that?

Crystal handed me a glass of water with a straw.

I drank greedily. "What's going on? Why are you all here?"

Mom said, "Bottom line: you almost died. Your friend, Jayden," she twisted around to smile at him. He smiled back. "Your friend Jayden said your special computer would save you and it did."

An older woman in a long white coat stepped forward. "Yeah, I don't understand it, but we, uh, thought we lost you, but then we didn't. Welcome back."

"Yeah," Jayden called out. "Welcome back!"

Everyone cheered.

It was touching to see so many people care about me. I was a little surprised, truth be told. My eyes filled. "Thanks, everyone. And thanks, Jayden, for what you did."

The doctors and nurses, with the exception of the older woman, started filing out of the room, talking amongst themselves. I heard snippets of "If I hadn't seen it, I wouldn't have believed it," and "Amazing," and "Wow."

The doctor in charge (I surmised) said, "When things settle down we're going to have a conversation about what happened here."

"Yes, ma'am," Jayden said.

I nodded.

She left with one last backward glance at us.

"Did someone call Mrs. Flores and tell her what's going on?" I didn't want her to think I'd just blown her off. Or that I was dead.

"I'm on it," Jayden said, pulling out his cell.

Mom, Amelia, Hannah, and Crystal crowded around the bed.

"Crystal." I reached for her hand, and squeezed it.

She smiled at me, looking a little teary-eyed herself.

"Did you fix me?" Hannah asked.

"Yeah," Amelia said. "This is all very unusual." She pointed at the q-computer.

"What's going on?" Mom asked.

"Yeah," Crystal said.

Jayden met my eyes and smiled. "It's Ella's invention. Tell them, Ella."

I laughed a little. "I've already told you. It's my master's research, my quantum computer."

They still looked confused.

"Quantum mechanics works with probabilities," I said.

Jayden was nodding.

"And what's luck but something improbable happening? So, this little baby," I caressed it, "this little baby makes improbable things happen. But..." I held up a finger. "We think..." I glanced at Jayden.

"Yep," he said.

"We think, probabilities, or luck, are conserved," I said. "So, if a very improbable good thing happens it's balanced out by one or more improbable bad things happening."

"Really?" Hannah wrinkled her nose. "So, if that's true, all that bad weird stuff that happened at the baseball game cured my cancer?"

Amelia stepped forward. "Thank you. Thank you, Ella."

"You're welcome." I yawned.

"Oh, we should let you get some rest," Crystal said.

"No..." I yawned even wider. "Well, maybe."

"We'll go then," Hannah said. "I'll see you tomorrow, Ella. I'm glad you're okay."

"Yes. Good bye." Amelia put her arm around Hannah's shoulders and they started walking out.

"Bye!" I called after them.

"Me, too," Crystal said. "See you tomorrow."

"Okay," I said. "Thanks for coming."

Mom hovered over the bed. She and I looked at Jayden.

"I want to ask her something," he said.

"Okay," Mom said. "See you tomorrow." She departed, leaving the two of us alone (except for the soundly sleeping woman in the other bed).

"Did I hear you talking to Professor Smithson earlier?" I asked. "I didn't see him. Was he here?"

"Yes," Jayden said. "He was operating his q-computer back in Lawrence. I was on the phone with him."

"Lawrence seems pretty far away," I said. "Do you think it helped?"

"It couldn't hurt," he said. "And before you ask, I double-checked before we hung up. He's okay."

"Good." I didn't want anything to happen to him. "I owe him a thank you as well."

"Anyway..." Jayden said.

I yawned again as I looked at him. "What do you want to ask me?"

"How did you know you could cure Hannah's cancer?"

"I didn't know for sure," I said, eyelids dragging down. They must have given me some crazy-good drugs. "I just had a feeling. There was no way to know until I did it. So, I did."

"I'm so amazed and impressed," he said. "You're amazing and impressive."

Got that right... I was starting to drift off.

"So, when are you going to let me take you out on a date?"

I was instantly awake as if I'd been hit by lightning. "What?"

"Ella, please go on a date with me." He leaned over the bed a little with an earnest expression. My eyes were drawn to his amazing eyes.

"Uh..." I was terrified, like I'd never been terrified before. "I don't, uh, think that's a very good idea."

He leaned back. "What?"

"No, thanks."

"But we have too much chemistry," he said. "I've never had so much chemistry with someone."

"You're a good person, Jayden." Frankly, he was too good for me. "But I'm not right for you."

"Are you sure?"

"Yes."

He stood there for several moments, looking like a kicked puppy. My heart would be breaking--if I had a heart, which I clearly didn't.

Finally, he turned and left.

After being so exhausted, it took me a surprisingly long time to get to sleep.

Chapter Thirty-One

Mom and Crystal came and picked me up the next day. Everyone there at the hospital seemed a little uncomfortable with me. They didn't seem to know what to make of the miracle lady-- and I guessed I couldn't blame them. I was quite dizzy or woozy during the entire journey home.

Anyway, Mom and Crystal soon had me settled in my old bedroom. They told me something about how they'd be taking care of me and watching my medication and other stuff, but I was still kind of out of it.

The next thing I knew it was dark and Mom was sitting on my bed. "I brought you soup," she said. "You need to try to eat something."

I didn't feel like eating. I felt like going back to sleep. "Why?"

"Your body needs fuel."

I took the bowl of soup and shoveled some into my mouth. She still looked upset. "Relax, Mom. I'm on the mend." Then, I had a scary thought. "I am, aren't I?"

"Yes." She patted my shoulder.

"What's wrong?" I asked.

"I can't believe your father basically had you arrested. I am so mad at him..." Her voice started increasing in volume. "I could kill him. When I think of my poor baby spending the night in jail I could kill him." She stared at me. "Too bad he wasn't sitting next to Hannah when you cured her with your q-computer." I heard the implied 'I could kill him.' again. I'd never seen her so negative. She was usually loving and nurturing.

Whatever energy I'd mustered to eat the soup was flagging. "Can you take this?" I handed her the bowl. Was the room spinning?

I started drifting off but before I did, I heard her say, "I think I'm going to invite him over."

The next time I woke up, I felt much more like myself. I didn't know if I'd healed or they'd decreased my meds dose or what. I was alone in my bedroom. The drapes were closed, but the sun still streamed into the room. "Hello?" No one answered.

I had to pee, so I levered myself out of bed and very carefully made my way to the bathroom. I got woozy. I headed back to bed.

Crystal burst in the front door. "What are you doing out of bed?"

I inclined my head towards the bathroom. Mistake. Dizzy.

"Oh, right," she said. "Sorry I'm a little late. Professor Smithson cornered me on campus and wanted to know how you were doing."

I carefully put one foot in front of the other, on my way back to my bedroom.

"Let me help you." She rushed up and put my arm across her shoulder and we stepped back to my room together.

Once I was back in bed, she said, "Professor Smithson wants to come over. What should I tell him?"

I wasn't going to win any beauty contests at the moment, but he wouldn't care. "I guess it's okay."

"Okay," she said. "I'll text him." She texted and I relaxed. "There," she said. "That's done. Now, how are you?"

"Better." Especially when I wasn't moving.

"I have good news," she said with a huge smile.

"I like good news," I said.

"The police took Zander into custody for stealing your q-computer and for causing the riot at the Odyssey and some other stuff. There's tons of evidence, witnesses and security footage." Her smile grew. "He's in deep shit. I heard they're even denying him bail." Crystal was another kind, nurturing woman. I'd never seen her gleeful about someone else's misfortune before.

"I'm glad he's getting the justice he deserves," I said, reaching for her hand. "But I'm sorry he hurt you. I'm sorry for whatever part I played in that."

She pulled her hand away. "He didn't hurt me." Her eyes

looked full. "He's just an asshole."

"Well, I agree with you there. Huge. Asshole."

We smiled at each other for a few moments.

"So, how's Jayden taking all this?" she asked.

I shrugged. "Jayden? How would I know?"

She frowned at me. "What do you mean, how would you know? Aren't you guys, you know, together?"

"No." I felt my forehead crinkle. "Why would you say that?"

"The two of us had a heart-to-heart while we were waiting by your bedside in the hospital, hoping and praying you'd recover." She took a breath. "He told me he was going to ask you out. What happened? Did he lose his nerve?"

"No."

She jumped up. "What did you do, Ella!" What was she getting so worked up about?

"Me? I didn't do anything. Jayden and I aren't right for each other."

"Honestly!" she said. "How can you be so smart about some things and so stupid about other things!"

"I have a master's degree, I don't think I'm stupid about any things."

"*Aaargh*!" she said.

Someone knocked on the front door.

"I'm going to get that." She held up her forefinger. "But this conversation isn't over."

In a few moments, Professor Smithson sauntered into my bedroom, looking as dapper as ever. The smiled leaked off his face when he saw me lying in bed. I must not have looked my usual awesome.

"Hi, there, Ella." He spackled the smile back on. "It's nice to see you. You look like you're on the mend."

"Nice to see you too, sir." It was nice. I suddenly longed for him to be my grandfather. He was so kind and solid and reliable. "Thanks for coming."

Crystal dragged a chair up near the bed. "You can sit here, sir."

He sat in the chair. She resumed her spot on the edge of the bed.

"Are you on the mend?" he asked.

"I think so." I glanced at Crystal and she nodded.

"Good." He leaned back in his chair. "So, that was pretty strange, all that that happened at Royals stadium. Did you really cure Hannah's cancer?"

"Thanks for your help." Jayden said he helped, didn't he? "It looks like we cured her." Thank God. That was a good thing that happened because of all of this. No matter what else happened, that made it all worth it.

"I'm sorry I didn't believe you about quantum computers affecting luck." He glanced down for a moment and then back up at me. "It's so weird. How did you figure it out?"

"Data." I grinned. "Like you taught me."

He grinned back. It was the first genuine positive expression I'd seen from him today. "What do you think we should do with all this?" he asked.

He was one of the world experts in quantum computing. "You're asking me?"

Professor Smithson smiled a little. "Of course. You made this important discovery."

I almost felt like I was being transformed in the warmth of that smile. "Thanks for your confidence in me, sir. I'm not sure what we should do. It seems pretty dangerous."

He nodded. "Sometimes being cautious and uncertain is the wisest response."

"It's definitely very dangerous," Crystal said. "But it also has the potential to do great things. I mean, curing cancer, people would do anything to do that."

She was right. But that also sounded dangerous. Desperate people could do anything. I should know. Hadn't I risked everything, put many people in danger to save Hannah?

"I'll ponder it," he said. "You ponder it, as well, Ella." He faced Crystal. "You, too, Crystal."

"Yes, sir," I said.

"Sounds good," she said.

He stood. "Well, I'll let you get more rest, then. Take care." He took a step towards the door.

"Uh, sir, have you heard anything about my job at Qubyte from Dr. Tuche?" Was I still suspended? I did indirectly hurt both of my boss's legs. Odds were I was fired--with extreme prejudice.

I'd be lucky if he didn't press charges.

"It's too soon to tell," he said. "Ryder is still pretty worked up. I think we should let him cool off a little."

That made sense. "Bye, sir."

"Bye, Ella." He left.

Crystal said, "I should make you something to eat and then you should rest more."

"Sounds good." She went off to the kitchen.

On the bedside table, I spied my phone. I picked it up. I knew something that would make me feel better. Winning a little money...

Around dinnertime, Crystal came back in my room. "Your mom thought you might want to take a shower."

"I like showers." I might even physically be up for it. "Care to assist me?"

She smiled. "That's why I'm here."

On our way to the bathroom, she whispered, "Your mom's up to something. I'm not sure what."

"What do you mean?" I whispered back.

"I don't know. She's acting odd." That was mysterious.

After I'd taken a shower (bliss!) and Crystal and Mom and me had eaten dinner around the actual kitchen table in the actual kitchen, someone knocked on the front door. We were still sitting at the table.

"I probably shouldn't get up." I was still feeling intermittently woozy.

"I wonder who that is?" Crystal said as she got up.

Mom didn't say anything. So, yes, a little odd. Check.

Crystal went over to the front door and opened it. A middle-aged man stood there. "Hello? Can I help you?" she asked.

It was Dad.

Chapter Thirty-Two

My deadbeat dad, who had me arrested (!) stood at my front door. What did he want?

Mom had a very strange expression on her face.

Crystal had a confused expression on her face. "Are you in the right place?" she asked. "This is the Hote residence." She didn't have any idea who he was, and why would she? He'd never been here.

"I'm John Hote," he said. "I was invited."

"Hote?" Crystal's head whipped around to examine me and Mom.

I sort of nodded. What was going on here?

Mom said, "Come on in, John. Join us." She pointed at the table.

John (I couldn't think of him as Dad) walked in on eggshells. As I watched him check out my lifelong home, I imagined how it must look to him: shabby worn furniture and carpet, my childish artwork on the walls. Who cared what he thought? We may have been poor, but we were good people.

At least Mom was, and I tried to be.

"To what do I owe the honor of this invitation?" he asked.

I was basically still staring at him. How did he have the nerve to show his face here?

Crystal said, "Hi, Mr. Hote. I'm Crystal Miller. I'm Ella's best friend. How do you know the Hotes?" She started closing the front door.

"I'm Ella's Dad," he said.

Crystal stumbled.

John walked gingerly over to our well-used table and sat in the fourth chair.

Crystal soon joined us. She examined me and Mom, in turn.

Me and Mom didn't say anything. I was still in shock he'd shown up. I didn't know what Mom's excuse was.

"Well, I'll say it," Crystal said. "How could you have Ella arrested? She had to spend the night in jail. On the floor! And a mean woman punched her!"

Mom faced me. "You didn't tell me that." In her expression, I read, 'I could kill him.' I started to get very uneasy. What was she up to?

John held his hands up, palms out. "I sincerely apologize about that. I didn't know what was going on. Zander said..."

"Zander!" Crystal shouted.

I finally found my voice. "What's your relationship to Zander?"

"Yeah, what were the two of you up to?" Crystal asked.

Mom stood and walked to the back of the house. She didn't say anything.

"I just asked him to keep an eye on you, Ella," John said.

"Gee, that's not creepy at all," I muttered. It was very much creepy.

Mom came walking back into the kitchen with my messenger bag. What was she up to?

"I swear I didn't tell him to steal anything from you," he said. "I would never do anything to hurt you."

Mom sat down with the bag. She snorted. "That's rich." She leaned over the table towards him and sneered. "You've done nothing but hurt Ella." She was in a mood I'd never seen before.

John held up his hands again. "I just wanted to know about Ella. I feel bad about not being involved in her life. I still don't understand what happened at the Odyssey. Why did he win so much money? Why did everyone get so upset..."

"You know he lied to me," Crystal said. "A lot. He took advantage of me. He broke my ..." She didn't finish but I knew she meant he broke her heart.

"I'm sorry," he said. "I'm sorry. I'm sorry. I had no idea he would take those actions."

Mom opened my messenger bag and got out my laptop and the q-computer.

"Mom?" I said in a stern voice. "What are you doing?"

She pushed them across the table at me. "Use it."

"Wait," he said. "What's going on?"

Crystal said, "Use it."

They were seriously advocating hurting him via my q-computer. Hurting people was not why I'd made the q-computer, or gotten my master's degree, or my bachelor's degree, or gone to school, or sang in the church choir, or played a little poker. Hurting people was not why I'd done anything in my life. I wasn't perfect but I'd never deliberately tried to hurt someone.

I'd hurt people--that was hard to admit--but it had been accidental.

I tried to help people. That's was Mom had taught me. And, Crystal'd taught me that, too.

"Ella. Jail. Your. Fault." Mom bit off each word like it was poison.

"I just wanted to get to know Ella, I promise." John seemed clued into the fact that he was in some kind of danger. "I wanted to apologize. I wanted, I want, to make amends to Ella and to you too, Evelyn."

"Amends?" Crystal seemed mesmerized by the word.

"Yes. I've been going to Gambler's Anonymous," he said. "I got my one year chip recently."

Mom stopped looking quite so fierce. "Is that true?"

This all sounded ridiculous to me. I may have snorted a little.

John put his hands below the table. "Wow. This is hard... I recognize I hurt you, Evelyn. Badly. For many, many years. I was a bad husband to you. And when Ella was born I was a worse parent. I know I can never make up for all the pain I caused you, but I am sincerely sorry, from the bottom of my heart."

No one was buying this crap, were they? But Mom and Crystal both had tears in their eyes. "Spare me."

John turned to me. "And Ella, I'm am so, so sorry. My heart breaks when I think of what I put you through. I know I can never make it up to you, missing your childhood, missing your whole life up until now. Missing you." His eyes filled. "I hope you know even though I wasn't with you, I love you with all my heart and I am very, very proud of you."

Yeah, right. But why were my eyes hot with tears?

I blinked rapidly. "Whatever," I said. "How does any of that crap match you arresting me? I was arraigned. I'm going on trial. That is all your fault!"

"I swear, that was all a misunderstanding. I dropped all the charges. You're not in trouble. The authorities have totally cleared your record." He looked worried. "They should have contacted you. I thought that was why you invited me over."

"Did they contact you?" Mom asked.

"I've been out of it," I said. "I've only used my phone once since the accident and I didn't check any of my messages."

"If you're cleared, that's awesome!" Crystal said.

Mom pulled the q-computer back near her.

I slowly started to get up. "I better go check."

Crystal jumped up. "I'll get your phone. Where is it?"

"Right near the bed."

She ran off and then ran back, handing me the phone.

I scrolled through and there was a voicemail from the Kansas City Municipal Court. It said, "Ella Hote, all charges against you have been dropped."

"Yay!" I said. "I'm not in trouble anymore!"

"What a relief," Mom whispered.

"Yay!" Crystal jumped up and down a little.

"Why did you invite me here?" John asked.

Mom picked up the q-computer and put it back in the messenger bag.

"I know there's nothing that could truly make up for what I've put you through, but if I can do anything, please let me know," John said after we didn't answer him.

"You can tell Ella about Gambler's Anonymous," Crystal said.

Mom raised her eyebrows. "Why would he do that?"

"Don't bother," I said. "I couldn't care less."

John stared at me. Finally, he said, "Gambler's Anonymous has questions they ask folks. Has gambling ever made your home life unhappy?"

Mom snorted. "I'll say."

John continued. "Did you ever lose time from work or school due to gambling?" Stupid. That happened to everyone.

"Huh," Crystal said, staring at me and nodding.

"Do you often gamble until your last dollar is gone?" Also stupid. Plenty of people lost money gambling.

"Ella," Crystal said.

"What?" Mom asked.

"Did gambling ever cause you to have trouble sleeping?" No. Never happened.

"I sleep like a baby," I said.

"Ella," Crystal said. "I think you have a problem."

"What?" Mom asked.

"They do say there can be a genetic component to addictive personality types," John said.

"We've had just about enough of you!" I said. "Get out of here, you deadbeat!"

He held his hands out in front of him again. "The last thing I wanted was to upset you. I'll go." He walked to the front door and exited.

"I don't understand what's happening here," Mom said, looking from me to Crystal and back again.

"I think Ella has a problem," Crystal said.

I took a deep breath, trying to calm down. Crystal meant well. I shouldn't bite her head off. "All due respect, Crystal, but you don't know what you're talking about."

"I think I do," she said.

"Maybe we should talk about this," Mom said.

Deep breath. "I'm going back to bed."

"I'll help," Crystal said.

"Don't bother." I hobbled back to the bedroom.

Crystal was crazy, totally crazy.

So why was I so uncomfortable?

Chapter Thirty-Three

Professor Smithson called the next day and asked me to come into the university to his lab, if I was up to it. He said he'd invite Dr. Tuche and try to put in a good word for me.

I couldn't resist that offer so I got up, took a shower, got dressed, and took a taxi (Mom loaned me the money) into school.

As I walked across campus among the students, I felt more like myself than I had in quite a while. Had it really only been a few weeks since all this started?

In Professor Smithson's lab I was glad to see Dr. Tuche, even if he barely fit between lab tables with his injured legs. On the other hand, I was nervous to possibly see Jayden.

And they still hadn't fixed the broken window, if you can believe it.

"Jayden?" I said. "I didn't know you'd be here."

"How did you think Tuche would get here?" he said, totally matter-of-fact. "It's not like he can drive in his condition." Good point. I peered at him. Was he glad to see me? Mad? I couldn't tell. He seemed a little robotic.

"So, thanks, everyone, for coming," Professor Smithson said.

Dr. Tuche pointed at the plywood. "What happened there?"

"Somebody shot at me," I said.

Dr. Tuche jerked but since Jayden and Professor Smithson didn't react (already being familiar with the story), he didn't pursue it.

"Yes, thanks, everyone," I said. I knew Lawrence wasn't exactly convenient for Jayden and Dr. Tuche. "I appreciate it."

"Well, clearly, we have something important to discuss,"

Dr. Tuche said, indicating his cast-clad legs. "I wouldn't have believed it, but it seems that Ella's q-computer affects luck. Data doesn't lie."

Jayden frowned. Did that mean he thought people lied? Did he think I lied?

"I concur," Professor Smithson said. "Ella's q-computer affects luck. The question is: do all q-computers affect luck or only Ella's?"

I had no idea. I shrugged.

Jayden said, "I've been doing experiments, coin tosses, over the last couple days with the Qubyte's q-computer and data shows it does not seem to affect luck." He glanced at me. "It did seem to strengthen the luck effect when it was on with one of Ella's q-computers. We have data to prove it." Yay, data.

"One of?" Professor Smithson asked. "How many q-computers does Ella have?"

Shoot.

"Ella, why don't you take that question?" Jayden said in a strict tone. He was acting like he didn't like me at all. Damn.

"I built a q-computer for my master's degree," I said. "And it was stolen by a guy named Zander." Who was spying on me for my dad--but I didn't say that. "That computer was destroyed." By me--but I didn't say that.

Jayden narrowed his eyes. "How?" he asked. "When?"

I ignored his questions. "And, of course, Professor Smithson, you have my q-computer. I guess you used it when I was in the hospital?"

He nodded.

"Thanks, by the way."

"Ella," strict Jayden said.

"And I may have built another one, as well," I said.

"That explains it, then," Professor Smithson said. "That's the one you used to fix your little sister?"

"That's the one you had in the Qubyte lab?" Dr. Tuche said.

"Yes," I said, answering both questions.

The three men stared at me. If their stares held disapproval, that was their problem. Not my problem. Nope, not my problem at all. So why did I feel so bad?

"The question is: where do we go from here?" Professor

Smithson asked.

"Yes, that is the question," Dr. Tuche said.

The four of us looked at each other for a few moments.

"As I see it, there are really only two choices," I said. "We can destroy the two remaining q-computers I built." And, presumably, I would be out of the q-computer business. "Or, we can try to study them. Maybe even write some papers on them." Presumably, in this case, I'd be working on q-computers.

Finally, Jayden said, "Cat. Bag. Out."

Professor Smithson looked at him.

Dr. Tuche said, "Good point, Jayden."

"And it's hard to ignore the curing cancer thing," Professor Smithson said.

I held my breath. I liked the employed option better.

"Yes," Dr. Tuche said. "That is hard to ignore."

Jayden shrugged. "We could even do a crowdsourcing thing: get enough people together, and you can cure your loved one of cancer."

"Wow," Dr. Tuche said. "That's really out-of-the-box thinking, Jayden. But it sounds unethical."

"I'm not saying we would charge money for it," Jayden said. "People would just need to find a bunch of other people to volunteer to take a little bad luck--the more people the better."

Professor Smithson exhaled. "Very far out of the box." He turned to me. "What do you think, Ella?"

"Jayden's points are all excellent." I smiled at him. He didn't react. "But I'm the new kid on the block here. I'll abide by what you think we should do."

"I think we have to continue to investigate this phenomenon," Dr. Tuche said. "When can you come back to work, Ella?"

"So, I'm allowed to come back to work?" I asked carefully.

"What now?" Professor Smithson looked from me to Dr. Tuche and back again.

"Of course," Dr. Tuche said, not explaining to Smithson he'd suspended me. If he was willing to push that all under the rug, I could do so as well. Look at me, pushing. Push, push.

"In that case," I said. "I can be back at work tomorrow." I wasn't a hundred percent healthy yet, but I could do a good impression of it. So, yay, work.

"All right, then," Dr. Tuche smiled weakly at me and then turned to Jayden. "Let's go. I'm tired."

"Yes, sir." Jayden stood and walked to Tuche's wheelchair.

Professor Smithson and I said goodbye to Tuche and Jayden and vice versa.

Once they'd departed, Professor Smithson said, "Is there something wrong between you and that young man?"

"Nope," I said. "I don't know what you're getting at."

He scowled at me like he didn't believe me, but said only, "I could lecture you on all the things you've done wrong, and probably mistakes I don't know about, but you've been injured pretty badly and I don't believe in kicking people when they're down. Plus, someone who cures kids of cancer can't be all bad. Despite everything, I'm proud of you, Ella."

My eyes felt heavy with tears.

"So, can we pretend I lectured you and you've learned your lessons?" he asked.

I couldn't speak without clearing my throat. "Uh, yes, sir. Lecture received."

I added in a quiet voice, "Thank you, sir."

I had an afternoon of freedom in my hometown and I knew just what I wanted to do... I arrived at Wei and Malik's apartment and pounded on the door.

Malik opened the door and smiled. "Ella! Wow! We heard you were injured. I'm glad to see you're okay." I wasn't totally recovered, but he didn't need to know that.

Wei pulled the door open wider. "Actually, we heard you were dead. And that you cured a girl's cancer."

Yeah, I rocked. But I smiled modestly. "As you can see, not dead."

"What are you doing here?" Malik asked.

"I was hoping we could get the band back together one last time and play some poker." I'd done a little q-calculation earlier and was feeling very lucky.

Wei rubbed his hands together. "It's a little early in the day, but I wouldn't mind winning money off of you." He waved me inside.

"I'll call the guys." Malik pulled out his cell.

Wei grabbed his box of poker chips from the shelf and stalked into the kitchen, placing the chips on the table. He sat and started taking out chips.

In the meantime, Malik was talking to one of our buddies.

"So, how much would you like to wager?" Wei said. "A hundred, two hundred, three hundred?" He grinned greedily. "I heard you got a big new job." He heard a lot of things, evidently. He held out his empty hand.

I pointed at his hand. "What's that?"

"Show me the money," he said.

"I don't have any money actually on me," I said.

"Okay. Go on over to the ATM," he said. "We'll wait."

I knew for a fact the ATM wouldn't help. I didn't have any money in the bank to take out. "You can float me some credit. I'm good for it."

He held up his hands. "Whoa! No credit. Cash only. You know that."

"Oh, come on," I said. "You guys have known me for years. I'm good for it." Plus, I was sure I was going to win, so it didn't matter if I didn't have any cash.

Malik was off the phone and walked into the kitchen, hearing us talking. "I can drive you to the ATM if you want."

"No," I said. "It doesn't matter if I have cash. It's a sure thing I'll win."

"I appreciate your confidence," Malik said. "But there's no such thing as a sure thing."

"Yes, there is," I said.

"I don't care if you're the Good Witch of the North," Wei said. "No credit."

I sidled up next to Malik. "Can you loan me a little scratch?" I asked quietly.

He stared at me. "Why? You have a new job. Don't you have money?"

"No!" I said. "I don't have any stupid money! What's it to you? Just give me a loan. I'm good for it."

He stepped away, staring at me. "No money and you're still trying to gamble?"

They didn't understand. "I know I'll win!"

Malik shook his head. "I think you have a problem, Ella. You have a gambling problem."

Wei had stood up. "Obviously, you have a problem. You better leave." He pointed at the door.

I stamped my foot. "Why does everyone keep saying that!"

Chapter Thirty-Four

It wasn't often I had actual free time and I needed to make the most of it. I called Crystal. "Hey, girl. How's it going?"

"Fine," she said slowly. "So, I take it you're not mad at me anymore for my gambler's anonymous comment?"

I was kind of mad, but I knew she thought she was doing the right thing. "Of course, I'm not mad at you. I couldn't stay mad at you. You're my best friend."

"Thanks," she said. "You're my best friend, too. So, are you feeling better? You sound like you're feeling better."

She hadn't heard my good news. "I'm going back to work at Qubyte tomorrow!"

"Wow. That's great! I'm happy for you," she said. Hey, that was so intense with your dad, huh? You know your relationship with your dad has a profound effect on the other relationships in your life--especially with guys."

I wasn't sure I believed that.

She continued. "Are you going to forgive him?"

My good mood was evaporating. "I guess it was good that he apologized. I never thought I'd see that happen. But...I don't think I can ever forgive him. I mean, a person only gets one dad, right? He wasn't there for me. He dropped the ball."

"He had a good excuse," she said. "Well, not a good excuse, a problem. Ugh. I don't know how to describe it."

I felt my lips transform into a sneer.

She kept flailing. "He has a serious problem."

She was much kinder than me. "You are a good person, Crystal," I said. "Do you want to hang out?"

"Yes," she said. "I'll drive. If you go somewhere with me, I'll even treat you to a free dinner, with beer."

I snickered. "Low blow. You know I like beer and I don't have any money. Yeah, okay."

She picked me up outside Malik's apartment and we drove off.

As we approached the hospital, I was a bit mystified. "Why are we going to the hospital? Do you need to stop by work?"

"Nope," she said with a mysterious smile.

"What's up?"

"Think of it as an adventure..."

I was intrigued.

The two of us were soon walking into a bland meeting room in the basement of the hospital. An older woman in hot pink scrubs rushed up to us, "Welcome, welcome, everyone's welcome. Help yourself to coffee." She pointed at a rickety folding table set up with an old-school coffee urn and a pile of sad-looking donuts.

I did enjoy donuts. I got some snacks. Crystal employed her willpower and avoided the donuts. We took our seats. "What is this?" I asked her as others sat down in the rows of seats.

"Shh," she said. "Just listen."

Pink-scrubs lady stood behind the podium and said, "Today Justin wanted to say a few words." She nodded at a super-hot guy.

Super-hot Justin stood up and walked behind the podium. "Hi, my name is Justin."

"Hi, Justin," everyone in the audience said.

"What do you think that tat is on his neck?" I whispered to Crystal. "Mickey Mouse? That's kind of weird."

She said only, "Shh!"

I turned my attention back to super-hot guy.

He proceeded to tell a pathetic story about how he gambled away his rent money, his tuition money, his food money and now he was living on the street, blah, blah, blah. I couldn't believe it-- he seemed so hot and so normal.

After talking, he came and sat next to me. He smiled at me (of course). But we couldn't talk because other people stood up and told other pathetic stories.

Pink-scrubs finally stood up at the end. "I see some new people. Would one of you like to stand up and tell us your story?"

Crystal poked me. "Ella."

Super-hot guy smiled again and said, "Ella huh? I'd like to hear your story."

I liked that smile. I wouldn't mind seeing it some more. I wouldn't mind seeing even more of him.

"What the hell." I stood up and walked to the front. "Hi, my name is Ella."

"Hi, Ella."

I stood there. The people sitting in the rows of chairs all stared at me, expectantly, clearly wanting me to tell them another pathetic story. I didn't have a pathetic story. I wasn't pathetic.

Crystal called out, "What did you try to do today?"

"I was just at my friend's apartment," I said. "We were going to play poker."

"Why didn't you?" someone else called out.

"I don't happen to have any cash and they wouldn't let me play on credit. How rude is that?"

Some of the people in the audience actually booed.

"What?" I asked.

"Why don't you have any money?" Crystal called out.

I felt myself sneering again. She was getting on my nerves. "I may have lost money gambling, in the past, but this is different. I'm sure I would have won today."

More people booed. Were they allowed to do that? I thought they were supposed to be supportive?

"Seriously," I said. "I would win." They didn't understand.

"Boo!"

Pink-scrubs got up. "We'll have none of that. This is a safe place. Ella should feel safe to tell her story without judgment. We're all here to support each other."

I threw up my hands. "I'm out." I went back to my seat.

Pink-scrubs said a few more things and the meeting adjourned.

Hot Justin leaned over. "Hey there, Ella." He smiled.

"Hey there, Justin." I smiled back.

He handed me a pamphlet. At the top it said. 'How do you know if you have a gambling problem?'

Sneer.

"Read it," he said. And then he got up and left.

Pink-scrubs came over to us. "The first step is admitting you have a problem."

"I don't have a problem," I said. "I don't know why people keep saying that."

Crystal met the eyes of pink-scrubs.

Pink-scrubs said, "If other people think you have a problem, people that love you..."

Crystal nodded.

"You have a problem."

Was that a little frisson of fear I felt?

"If you're afraid, that probably means I'm right," Crystal said. "If you're afraid of something, it probably means it's important."

Damn. She knew me too well. "When did you get so wise?"

I sulked in the car on the way to Freestate. I couldn't believe Crystal had ambushed me like that. But I refrained from yelling at her. I did know she meant well.

Once we sat down, Crystal handed me the pamphlet that I had deliberately left in the car. "Read it, girl. I mean it. I love you and I mean it."

"Fine." Instead of crumpling it and throwing it on the floor, I carefully put it in my purse.

We had a nice dinner, laughing and talking about old times, enjoying the gourmet beer and burgers. Yay, Crystal. She was a treasure in my life.

If she thought I had a problem, I needed to seriously consider it. I would read that pamphlet. I would consider going to one of those meetings again.

When she dropped me off at Mom's I said, "I know we don't agree on everything, but I also know you're one of the best parts of my life, maybe the best part. Thanks for being such a good friend, Crystal. I treasure you."

A tear rolled down her cheek. "Thank you for being such a good friend, Ella. I treasure you, too," she said, her voice husky.

Chapter Thirty-Five

The next morning, I took the bus directly to Qubyte (Mom loaned me the money). I felt something unclench as I walked into the lobby and saw Avery sitting at her desk.

"Avery! It's so wonderful to see you," I said. "How are you feeling?"

"I'm okay," she said. "How are you? I heard you got hurt."

"I'm okay." I pretty much felt back to normal. "I'm glad you're okay."

"I also heard you cured a girl's cancer," she said.

I didn't know the rumor mill was so efficient. "It does look like it." I felt a hand on my back. Was it Jayden? I whirled around to see the Hot Optometrist.

"What's that, Ella?" Dr. Sanchez said, flashing his enticing smile. "You did cure cancer?"

Avery nodded. "That's what she said. Dr. Tuche said she did, but, wow."

"Yeah, wow," Dr. Sanchez said. "That's impressive."

I wondered what Jayden thought of me curing cancer.

"Ella?" Dr. Sanchez asked.

"Sorry, did you say something?" I asked.

"I asked if you wanted to go out for a drink some time?" he said.

I glanced back at Avery and her eyes were open wide like she was really impressed.

I was surprised to realize I wasn't quite so impressed myself. Of course, he wanted to buy me drinks, who wouldn't? I smiled slightly and said, "Maybe."

He laughed like he couldn't actually believe I wasn't dying to go for drinks. "What?"

He wasn't all that. "I don't even know your first name," I said.

"Ethan," he said.

"Nice to meet you, Ethan." I turned to go.

"So, drinks?" he asked.

"Let's play it by ear," I said.

He laughed again. "Oh, playing hard to get! I like it. I like a challenge."

My interest in Hot Optometrist was waning. "Whatever."

Was Jayden here yet? I quickly walked through the lobby to the q-computing lab.

Jayden wasn't in yet. Only Dr. Tuche was there, and he did not look comfortable sitting in his wheelchair with his legs sticking out straight.

"Ella!" he said. "Good. I'm eager to start experimenting. We need to get a bunch of data so we can publish a paper."

"Is Jayden around?" I asked.

"No. He said he had to do something on the way into work. Did you bring your q-computer?"

I held up my messenger bag. "Yes, sir."

"This is going to be great." He rubbed his hands together. "We're going to change the world, Ella." He wheeled closer to me and put a hand on my arm. "We're going to try to help people." He seemed to blink tears from his eyes. "We might be able to save a lot of people." I was guessing there was a backstory there.

My eyes grew teary. I'd be honored to save people. I had to do some blinking of my own.

"But, first things first. Let's duplicate the coin tosses you and Jayden did earlier."

Yay. More coin tosses. "Yes, sir." We got to work.

After about an hour of coin tosses and turning computers on and off I was dying of boredom. Focus, Ella. You still have a good job. That's a good thing.

I couldn't help sighing.

"What?" Dr. Tuche asked.

"How about a break?" I asked. "I could go get us coffee from next door?"

"I would love a coffee," he said. "I'll even buy." He dug out his wallet.

"That sounds good," I said. That sounded like the only way I could afford to buy coffee.

He passed me some cash.

"We better turn off all the q-computers first," I said.

"Yeah." He glanced up at my face. "Okay. Good idea."

Over at the coffee shop, I tried calling Mrs. Flores. I needed to apologize for leaving her high and dry and find out if I still had a job. She said she'd give me time but that was a few days ago. I didn't know how she would handle things without me. But it went to voicemail.

I eventually got two coffees and walked back to Qubyte.

Inside the lobby, my phone rang. I tried juggling the coffees and answering my phone. I did manage to answer my phone, but I lost hold of one of the coffees ...just as someone walked by. That someone was Jayden. I spilled hot coffee all over him. He made "Ooh, ooh," noises.

I gulped.

"Ella? Hello?" Mrs. Flores said. "Are you there?"

Jayden stared at me.

"Yes, Mrs. Flores," I said.

I tried waving at Jayden, but the remaining coffee was endangered. He grabbed it.

"Ella?" she asked.

"I'm just checking in," I said. "How are things over there?"

"Things have been going great," she said. "Thanks for sending that nice young man over to help me while you've been gone."

My stomach quivered. I had a feeling I knew who the nice young man was.

Jayden stared at me.

I looked back at him. "Uh, Mrs. Flores, who was that again?"

"Why, your boyfriend, Jayden, of course," she said. "He is so sweet. You got a good one there. He's been a life-saver."

I felt sick. Sick with fear. "I'm, uh, glad everything's going well," I said. "I'll be back tonight, if that's okay?"

"Sounds great," she said. "Oops, a guest. I need to go." We hung up.

"Was that Mrs. Flores?" Jayden smiled. "She's sweet."

I felt terrified. "She said the same about you. Thank you very much for helping her." Crystal's wise words echoed in my mind. "I apologize for spilling hot coffee on you." I needed to woman up.

"Let me guess, you've been using your q-computer?" He grinned.

I grinned back as pterodactyls flew around my stomach. "So, uh, Jayden," I said. "I, uh, owe you an apology about what you said the other day, about you and me."

He raised his eyebrows, as if saying 'elaborate please.'

The pterodactyls turned into tyrannosaurus rexes. "You were right," I said. "There's something between us. We should explore it."

"Golly."

I couldn't help it, a burst of laughter erupted from me.

After a second, he joined in. Once he caught his breath, he said, "I knew you'd come around."

"How?" I said. "I didn't even--"

But he didn't let me finish. He leaned down and pressed his lips to mine.

The universe seemed to stop.

When we separated, I could only whisper, "Golly."

Wise Crystal had been right. I hadn't been in love.

Until now.

Science Fact: Quantum Computing

Quantum computing is a special type of computing that utilizes quantum phenomena to perform operations on data. This is a new and active area of research in the real world, and many experts believe it may revolutionize computing.

To help us understand what's special about quantum computing, let's look first at traditional computing.

Traditional computing is based on binary digital electronics which are made of transistors. The term binary refers to the fact that there are only two possible states: zero or one. Thus in traditional computing, data can only be encoded into binary digits, or bits, which are zero or one. Physically, this means the transistors are either switched off or on.

Quantum computers do not use bits, but rather, quantum bits, also called qbits or qubits. (Incidentally 'bit' is a misnomer here since it is a combination of the words binary and digit.) The important thing about qubits is they can have many more than two states because of quantum mechanical superposition.

Superposition is a fundamental principle of quantum mechanics. It comes from the underlying mathematics of quantum mechanics. This math states every particle is both a particle and a wave and thus can be represented by something called a wavefunction. Wavefunctions are described in terms of probabilities and have unusual properties. For example, because of wavefunctions, particles can be located in an unlimited number of places at the same time.

Probably the most famous example of superposition is the Schrodinger's Cat thought experiment. We put a cat inside a box with a small amount of radioactive substance and poison. It the radioactive substance decays, the poison vial breaks and the cat dies. If not, the cat lives. The point is before we look inside the box, the cat is considered to be in a superposition of an alive and a dead state. Once we look inside, the wavefunction collapses and one reality is instantiated. The cat must be alive or dead. Thus, the act of observation is powerful; observation itself creates the outcome. Note we cannot observe the superposition itself--just the consequences of it.

Therefore, because of superposition, in quantum computers instead of two possible states there are an infinite number of possible states. Thus, quantum computers could work on millions of computations at once.

An operational quantum computer could be used to decrypt many of the current cryptographic systems--including those considered 'uncrackable' by conventional computers. Another application of quantum computers could be quantum database searches--which would be much faster than conventional methods.

For more information and details about his and other topics, check out the Physics Is Fun website: www.physicsisfun.net

Thank you for reading *Conservation of Luck*. I hope you enjoyed it!

- For more info about me or my work, please visit my author's website, http://www.lesleylsmith.com/. Sometimes, I post links for free fiction downloads!
- Please check out the Physics Is Fun website www.physicsisfun.net for lots of information about fun physics topics.
- Reviews help other readers find books. I appreciate any and all reviews.
- A sneak peek at my new book *A Jack by Any Other Name* follows.

−Lesley L. Smith

A Jack By Any Other Name

Chapter One

"Mr. Jones, we need you to kill a man." The stranger glanced around nervously. A crowded restaurant was no place for such talk, even though people often thought it was. The high noise level only gave limited privacy. And, to be fair, although every table was occupied in this dining establishment, the thick carpeting and tablecloths effectively muted the clink of silverware and hum of conversations.

I shook my head. "You are mistaken, sir. I'm not an assassin. Killing is more of a hobby with me." I was a musician, a singer. And I wasn't even on duty right now. I was home on Earth for some much-needed R & R. This guy shouldn't be bothering me while I was on holiday. To give him credit, though, I was an excellent assassin, in addition to being an excellent singer.

"The only thing you should be doing here is eating," I said. "Have you had dinner? Would you like to join my wife and me? We've finished this lovely bottle of wine, but we can order another."

He leaned over the table. "I'm not here to eat." His rumpled twentieth-century-style suit didn't exactly inspire confidence. It was doubtful he had the judgment or the funds to call for a hit.

"Oh, come now," I said. "I insist." He had irked me by interrupting an evening with a delightful damsel--my wife and first officer. He either needed to go away or calm down and eat with us.

Or maybe I'd have to kill him, after all. It does not do to encourage bad manners; one should retaliate urbanely but firmly.

Where was the lovely Gina? She'd gone off to the

washroom a while ago. She should have returned by now. I stood up to get a better look at the rear of the restaurant. Was she on her way back to our table even now? Sadly, there was no sign of my lady.

As I sat down at the romantic table for two, a small dark spot appeared on the stranger's tie and quickly started leaking red fluid. He looked startled and tried to say something, but only blood came out of his mouth. He collapsed on the floor. It all happened quite quickly.

And then I felt something push me into the table. Pain radiated from my back and coursed throughout my body. That was not part of the plan.

I realized that apparently, the rumple-suited stranger wasn't the only one who'd been shot.

What a bother.

"Mr. Jones? Jack?" a woman said.

I opened my eyes. I lay in bed surrounded by white walls, white sheets, beeping equipment and a beautiful woman in a white uniform. "Where am I?" I asked. "What happened?"

"My name is Sophia." She leaned over me a bit, giving me a view of cornflower blue eyes and perfectly even pearly-white teeth. "You're on Earth in a Duplication Center. I'm sorry to say you were murdered." She added gently, "You were shot."

I jerked back, and my body responded sluggishly. "What? Clearly, I'm alive. I'm not murdered. What are you talking about?"

"I don't know many details about the crime." She pushed a blonde curl behind her ear. "I'm a duplication engineer. Your original body was murdered, but we cloned it and downloaded your memories. Unfortunately, the last thirty-two years of your memories were lost, deleted." She shook her head. "It's unusual. It very nearly was a true murder."

Murdered. A new body. I couldn't talk for a moment. Finally, I said, "Thirty-two years of memories? What year is it? How old am I?"

"It's twenty ninety-five."

Twenty ninety-five? Bizarre. I remembered it being twenty-sixty-three.

"You were fifty years old." She had a great bedside manner,

273

very calm, and seemed truly concerned about me. I felt safe. And it didn't hurt that she was one of the best-looking women I'd ever met.

Wait. "Fifty?" I didn't remember being fifty, forty, or thirty, for that matter. And I didn't feel fifty. I held up my arm and looked at it. I flexed. It looked the way it always looked, didn't it? I stared. It did look kind of flabby and pale.

"Your new body is eighteen years old, and you have eighteen years of memories, so you feel eighteen. For all intents and purposes, you're eighteen." She smiled at me. She had a nice smile. Dimples. I had no idea what fifty-year-old me would have thought, but I liked dimples. This woman was very hot--all athletic curves and bouncy blonde curls. This me thought he'd like to get to know her better. A lot better.

"Sophia, huh?"

She nodded.

"*Shall I compare thee to a summer's day? Thou art more lovely and more temperate....*"

She interrupted me with a giggle and then said, "Let's focus on your recovery for now. Can you sit up?"

I tried to sit, but my muscles were still too weak. It was weird to think this was a new body. It seemed like my regular body.

"We'll try again later, Jack," she said.

I searched my memories, but they seemed to be all there, my childhood and teen years. Unfortunately, I even remembered my parents' deaths years ago (cancer and cancer). And I'd never had any siblings. I was alone.

I guessed if I had no recollection of my later life, I wouldn't know it was missing, right? "I don't understand. I know I recorded my memories regularly--at least for the eighteen years I remember. I assume I kept recording. How could someone get to them? And who cloned me?" Cloning was very expensive. "Am I rich?" Please say yes.

"The Terran Cultural Committee paid," she said. "You must be important to them."

Why was I important to the TCC? The TCC traded Terran culture and technologies for alien culture and technologies and also kept an eye on Terran citizens and colonies throughout the galaxy.

If they cloned me, presumably, the fifty-year-old me was important. Would the eighteen-year-old me be? What if I wasn't? Did they ever repossess cloned bodies?

I had another disturbing thought: I'd lived a lifetime and didn't know anything about myself. "Who am I, er, who was I?"

She touched her holo-pad. "The data says Jack Jones was the captain and lead vocalist of the TCC's premiere spaceship, the *Shakespeare*, before his murder." She glanced at me. "You basically flew around the galaxy and sang."

I did love singing and music, so that part sounded good. Exploring the galaxy sounded good, too. Being the captain also sounded good. Huh. Yay, me.

"Did they catch my murderer? Who was it? Why'd they murder me? What happened to him, her or it?"

"I don't have that information. Sorry." She threw me another glance. "It, ah, also says here you have a wife, Gina Gomez, and she's your first officer."

"A wife? I don't remember any wife." Family! Maybe she could tell me what was going on. Maybe she could comfort me in my time of need. "Please call this Gina woman." I hoped she was hot.

Sophia looked at her pad again. "Uh, actually, the TCC says you're not supposed to contact your wife. When you wake up, we're supposed to contact a Noah Anderson from TCC." She scrunched up her nose; it was adorable. "I already called him. Sorry. He's on his way."

I felt an urge to reassure Sophia. I reached for her hand and massaged it gently with my fingers. "It's okay."

She showed me her dimples again. Beautiful.

Whatever happened, I didn't want to forget her. "Hey, I bet memory recording has advanced a lot in the thirty years I've forgotten."

She nodded.

"You don't happen to have any spare gear lying around, do you?"

She bit her lip. "Well..."

I gazed into her eyes; they were beautiful, the color of a Terran sky right before sunset.

"I guess that would be okay. We do have a lot of tech here.

I'll find something for you."

"Thanks." That was one mission accomplished. I wasn't going to lose my memories again if I could help it. I was going to record my memories every day, and hopefully, they wouldn't get lost or deleted this time. Hey, I could do it every morning right after I brushed my teeth.

I settled back in the bed. Maybe this Noah guy would have some answers for me.

In the meantime, maybe I could research my murder and my pre-murder life and the TCC and the *Shakespeare*. "Can I borrow your pad while I wait?"

A seemingly bigger-than-life-sized version of a man stood next to my bed. He looked like a mountain--or a bear, a shaggy gray-haired bear. Did bears get gray fur?

Was this the murderer here to finish the job? I flinched.

"What's wrong?" the man said. "Oh, right, you don't recognize me. I'm Noah." He searched my face.

My face must not have given him the expression he sought.

"Noah Anderson."

I shrugged. "Okay."

"I'm here from TCC."

"Good," I said. "Maybe you can tell me what the hell's going on?"

He sat down surprisingly gingerly on the edge of the bed. It creaked. "You got shot, buddy."

"I know that."

He held up his hands. "Okay, okay. Don't get your panties in a bunch."

Panties? Did men wear panties in this era? Or was this guy an asshole? My fists involuntarily clenched, but I didn't have the muscle tone to keep it up. Shit. I deflated.

"Who are you? Who shot me and why? Did they catch him? Why did TCC bring me back? What happened to my memory recordings?"

He shifted, and the bed rocked. "We're not getting off on the right foot here. I'm Noah. I'm your best friend. I'm sorry you got shot. I'm sorry your recordings were lost. We're still trying to figure out what happened. We don't know who or what shot you.

We don't know if it was some kind of anti-TCC plot or if it was personal, or both. We're investigating."

"Anti-TCC plot? That doesn't make sense. Neither does personal. I thought I was a singer. Who hates singers?"

He leaned towards me and whispered, "The *Shakespeare* doesn't just spread Earth's culture around the galaxy. Really, the TCC is a bunch of spies. And you, of all the spies on a ship chock-full of spies, you were the biggest spy of them all."

Wow. "Really?" A spy? That didn't sound right. I didn't feel spy-y.

"Jack?" Noah asked. "Did you hear me? You were a spy."

"I heard you," I said slowly. "Am I still a spy?"

"That's a good question." He rubbed his chin.

"New topic," I said. "You've had a month to find my killer." I'd read the news reports about my murder. "Did you get him? If not, any leads? And most importantly, am I still in danger?"

"We didn't get him." He shook his head. "We're not even sure the murderer was a 'him.' We haven't made progress on your murder or the mystery man who died after accosting you in the restaurant."

"No progress?" That seemed hard to believe. Was it possible they didn't want to solve my murder? That wasn't right. I shook my head. "Why not? Crimes should be easier to solve on Earth, not harder."

"Our best operative was out of commission, for one thing."

"Meaning what?" I asked.

He gave me an odd look.

Huh. "I'm the best operative?"

"Yeah," he said.

That was at least a little gratifying. On the other hand, how good could I be if I got murdered?

He paused for a moment, looking around the room. "At least you were."

"What am I now?"

"That's the question, isn't it? Since we haven't solved the murder, we don't know if you're still in danger or not. My gut tells me you are. What do you think?"

I surveyed my gut. It did not feel good. "My gut tells me I'm screwed."

"You always did have a good gut." He smiled a grim smile that didn't reach his eyes. Frankly, it was a bit scary. This guy was my best friend? He seemed like he could break somebody in two if they looked at him wrong.

"We'd like you to go back on the *Shakespeare* and try to draw out the killers," he said. "What do you think?"

"What? 'Draw out'?" I'm embarrassed to say my voice squeaked. "You want me to be bait?"

"I keep forgetting you're not the old Jack." Noah grabbed my arm and then dropped it.

It flopped down on the bed.

"But you're definitely not him. You're not in very good shape. Your cloning was kind of a rush job."

Rush job? What did that mean?

He continued. "The *Shakespeare*'s leaving in a couple of weeks."

I tried to control the squeakiness in my voice. "I understand you all have made a large investment in me, and I really want to find my murderer or murderers." I took a deep breath. "I'm willing to go on the ship. But can't I go incognito or something?" I didn't want people shooting at me right off the bat.

He considered. "That's a good idea. But..."

"But what?" Squeak. Damn.

"Your singing voice is pretty distinctive."

I really, really didn't want to be a singing sitting duck. "Uh, what about if I'm Jack's son? I could have inherited his voice, right?"

Noah tilted his head. "Yeah. Not a bad idea, not bad at all. That could work."

Over the next two weeks, I was a good boy and did my physical therapy and voice training. TCC brought in several brutal therapists and kept me busy morning, noon, and night.

I did record my memories every day right around toothbrush time.

In the wee hours, I researched my old life and the *Shakespeare*.

Everything ached, but I was getting my muscle tone back, and I could sing pretty well. The squeakiness went away, at least.

Nurse Sophia, excuse me, dupe engineer Sophia seemed dazzled by my voice. She somehow managed to be hanging around every time I worked with my vocal coach. What was it about women and singers? Whatever it was, I liked it.

Her friendly, delighted smile always brightened my day.

One night near the end of my stay at the dupe facility, she approached me. "You know, you were the most famous singer of your generation. Sentient species all over the galaxy sing your praises." She grinned and looked at me expectantly. "Pun intended."

I grinned back at her. I was tired of being treated like a piece of meat to be therapied into submission. It was nice to be appreciated, and she was awfully hot. I wanted to be treated like an actual person. I wanted Sophia to treat me like a man.

"You like me," I said. "Your beautiful smile was one of the first things I saw when I woke up."

"I thought you were cute." She pointed at me playfully. Another beautiful smile lit her face as she turned away to attend to her other duties.

"Maybe you could show me some of Jack's old performances?" I called after her as she walked away. I'd seen a lot of them already, but I figured it'd be extra fun watching them with her.

The better I felt, the more pissed about my situation I was. You couldn't just kill me and get away with it. The only bright spot was Sophia.

Once I was mostly recovered, in preparation for our new mission, the TCC booked my crew and me at a place in North America called Red Rocks. Our manager claimed I was still too weak to participate in any theater or dancing, so I was to do musical interludes--whatever they were. I insisted my dupe engineer accompany me--for my health, of course.

It turned out the venue was beautiful, a natural amphitheater made of red sandstone. We were to perform out in the open under the stars. I was psyched.

Noah had told me I had singing and spy skills, but I had a strong feeling that enticing women with my voice was my greatest skill. I was about to find out.

Sophia waited with me backstage before the show. I had high hopes for our after-show festivities.

In the meantime, I was going to meet Old-Jack's wife, Gina, in person for the first time, so I was a little nervous. What did you say to a wife you'd never met? She might not even know I'd been cloned. Awkward.

She showed up, very curvaceous, arm in arm, with another crew member, a Carter Nillion, at the last possible moment. Carter was also a good-looking guy, maybe not as good-looking as me, but not bad. They were both very attractive for old people. What were they--forty? The way they hung off each other, I assumed they were together.

"Greetings, Gina, Carter," I said with a flourish. "*The course of true love never did run smooth.*" Getting murdered definitely interfered with love's course.

I'd been in a lot of shows as a teenager and had been known for quoting the bard. When I studied the old version of me, he'd kept it up. Yay, Jack.

This version of me didn't know Gina and Carter, but if I had, I'd be guessing they were nauseated from the expressions on their faces.

"Who are you?" Carter asked.

"Yeah, who the hell are you?" She leaned toward me and glowered.

I stepped back, and Sophia squeezed my hand. I glanced at her, and she showed me those delectable dimples and nodded encouragingly.

Gina was intimidating. I was married to this? "I'm, uh, a new member of the troupe, Jack Jones Junior, at your service." I bowed with a flourish. I was good at flourishes.

Carter's mouth fell open.

Gina's skin seemed to pale under its chocolatey hue. "Jack didn't have a son."

"Yes, he did," I said.

"No," she said. "Who's the mother? No. I would've known."

"Uh, he didn't know about me." I just thought of that. Brilliant. It would explain why I didn't know much about the last thirty years of Old-Jack.

Of course, it probably made me less bait-y. But as far as I was concerned, that was a good thing.

Gina narrowed her eyes at me. "Did Jack tell you about what we did in the mud springs of planet Geryon 876 d?"

I didn't react. I had no idea what they did in the mud springs. I knew what I hoped they'd, we'd, done in the mud springs...

"With those three native girls?" she added.

Maybe Gina wasn't as bad as she seemed. I smiled. "Sounds fun, but sorry. Never met him. But I do look forward to working with you and becoming friends." My smile grew. "And hearing your stories about the mud springs on Geryon 876 d, of course."

It was big of me to befriend my ex-wife, who clearly had hooked up with another guy, but then, I was big. Even murder couldn't keep me down!

Yeah, I was a little amped up about the show.

Gina and Carter exchanged a look.

"We're not working together," Gina said. "I'm the captain. I approve all the crew. I didn't approve you."

"I work for TCC." I waved my arm around backstage. They'd set all this up, after all. "I'm in this show, and I'm in the crew."

"But..." Gina looked around backstage. The crew was treating me like I was supposed to be here. Because I was. I was practically the star of the show. Hadn't they put this whole thing together for me?

Carter finally said, "Nice to meet you, I guess. Your dad was a good man, a good friend." And yet Carter hooked up with his wife so soon? It had only been about a month since I'd been shot. I'd have to keep an eye on this guy.

He poked Gina with his elbow. So far, he wasn't looking too nefarious.

"Yes," Gina said. "Nice to meet you."

"So, gosh, Jack hasn't had a chance to introduce me yet," Sophia said. "I'm Sophia Olsson. It's so nice to meet you."

Gina and Carter introduced themselves to her politely.

"And what's your relationship with Jack Junior here?" Gina asked.

"Nurse?" Carter smirked.

"Oh, we're lovers," Sophia said. We hadn't done it yet,

but that boded even better for our after-show festivities. "He's wonderful." She leaned up and planted a juicy kiss right on my lips.

My eighteen-year-old body responded enthusiastically. The kiss must be a promise of coming attractions. I really liked Sophia. She was my favorite homo sapien. Of course, she was one of the only homo sapiens I knew, but still...

"How old are you, young lady?" Gina asked.

Sophia smiled at her. "Twenty-five."

Carter coughed. "Standard Terran years? Wow. You're practically a baby."

"Thank you," Sophia said, and then, I could swear, she batted her eyelashes.

My former first and second officers didn't look happy. Ha. Yay, Sophia.

One of the stagehands came up to us. "There you are. We need to do sound checks. And Costume has been looking all over for you guys. You two go over there." He pointed Gina and Carter towards Costumes, and they followed his directions.

"You--" he pointed at me "--come onstage."

"Can I come?" Sophia asked.

"Whatever," he said.

As we walked onstage, Sophia said, "I'm proud of you, Jack. Was it difficult seeing Gina with Carter? How long were you together?"

I'd been investigating myself. "Decades." But she didn't want to hear about that. Buck up, Jack. I tried to smile. "Well, *the play's the thing...*"

"Why do you keep talking like that?"

I blew out a breath. "I'm trying to fit in. That's how Old-Jack acted."

She smiled at me. She had an adorable smile. "That sounds like a lot of work. Seems to me that being murdered is a good excuse to let Old-Jack go."

She made a good point, and I was still feeling that kiss. "Your wish is my command. So, Sophia, I appreciate all your help. I appreciate you. What do you say, after the show, you come back to my hotel room?"

"I thought you'd never ask." Hello, dimples. "But forget the hotel. You're coming home to stay with me."

The sound check and the costume fitting passed in a blur.

I felt excited but nervous, too. According to the biography of Jack Jones, he'd, or rather I'd, given hundreds of concerts over the years. So, why was I nervous? Maybe there was something wrong with this body?

If it hadn't been for Sophia at my side, I would have been a wreck. But she kept smiling at me, flashing her dimples, nodding, holding my hand or rubbing my arm.

After what seemed like forever, it was finally time for me to go on.

"I'll just sit here," Sophia said, planting herself delicately on a stool in the wings.

As I walked onstage, I looked out into the crowd, and it was packed, with people--mostly homo sapiens--sitting shoulder to shoulder on the sandstone benches under the stars. Clouds scudded by, alternately hiding and revealing the moon. The breeze was warm and lovely, not unlike Sophia. I glanced at her.

She waved charmingly.

When the music started, the sound was so amazing I turned around to check if an orchestra had snuck in when I wasn't paying attention.

They had.

Where did they come from? There must have been thirty musicians dressed all in black, sitting in folding chairs, reading music from black stands. They sounded wonderful. I loved live music; the human energy was exhilarating.

The lead violin gave me a look like 'quit staring.'

"Ready, Jack?" the guy talking in my earbud asked. "There's sheet music on the stand, there."

I nodded. I needed the music. Supposedly Old-Jack never needed the music.

As I listened to the notes melding together, I lost myself. The only thing that mattered was the melodies, the chords, and the harmonies. The soul-transporting beauty.

My part started in the next measure. I breathed in deeply.